Reflecting Love's Charms

DIANE GREENWOOD MUIR

Cover Design Photography: Maxim M. Muir

ISBN-13: 978-1534865860
ISBN-10: 1534865861

Don't miss the first books in
Diane Greenwood Muir's

Bellingwood Series

All Roads Lead Home – Bellingwood #1
A Big Life in a Small Town – Bellingwood #2
Treasure Uncovered – Bellingwood #3
Secrets and Revelations – Bellingwood #4
Life Between the Lines – Bellingwood #5
Room at the Inn – Bellingwood #5.5
A Season of Change – Bellingwood #6
Tomorrow's Promises – Bellingwood #7
Through the Storm – Bellingwood #8
A Perfect Honeymoon – Bellingwood #8.5
Pages of the Past – Bellingwood #9
The River Rolls On – Bellingwood #10
Look Always Forward – Bellingwood #11
Out of the Shadows – Bellingwood #12
Holidays are for Family – Bellingwood #12.5
Unexpected Riches – Bellingwood #13
Reflecting Love's Charms – Bellingwood #14

A short story based
on the Biblical Book of Ruth (Kindle only)
Abiding Love

CONTENTS

ACKNOWLEDGMENTS

The Bellingwood community continues to grow. One of the best places to meet new people who enjoy all of these wonderful characters is on Facebook. Come spend time with us at facebook.com/pollygiller.

When I think about the number of people who are part of my life and who help me get from book to book, I'm astounded.

My beta readers are more than just readers. They edit, find continuity problems, point out unnecessary words / phrases / thoughts, catch strange grammar and are such a necessary part of my process. These people teach me how much I have yet to learn about the English language and all of its intricacies. Without them, I'd be lost. Thank you to these amazing people: Rebecca Bauman, Tracy Kesterson Simpson, Linda Watson, Alice Stewart, Fran Neff, Max Muir, Edna Fleming, Linda Baker and Nancy Quist. A special thank you to Judy Tew who reads and corrects my final edited copy. She gives me confidence I didn't realize I was missing.

There is no way to say thank you to everyone who encourages me on a daily basis. In small and large ways, I am reminded how important people are to me. From a quick word in a message to a gift showing up in my mailbox, I am touched by the love that each of you share. The world is a wonderful place and I get to see that every day.

CHAPTER ONE

Polly brushed tendrils of hair away from her sweaty face, the gloves she wore making that more difficult than it should be. This was going to require more coffee. Frustrated, she yanked the work glove off her right hand and pushed her hair back, tucking it behind her ear. Rebecca had told her to wear a bandanna, but in Polly's stubbornness, she'd pulled her hair back in an elastic tie. She hated that Rebecca was right.

They'd been tearing up the yard at the Bell House for the last month. It was the only thing she really wanted to have ready for the Sesquicentennial Celebration at the end of July, so she was here every day. Henry had broken up this old cement floor over the weekend and today she was hauling chunks of it to the front. Her back ached, her arms ached, her legs ached. She was hot and sweaty and it wasn't even lunchtime yet.

Polly looked up at the big house, still in awe that it was theirs. It was the last thing she'd ever thought they would do. She and Henry had assumed they would live in Sycamore House forever. But life was all about change and she was as ready for that as anyone.

This house had better be worth it. She was putting more physical labor into its renovation than any of her other projects. When she purchased Sycamore House, she'd been young and naïve, with enough money to do the renovation. Thank goodness, Henry Sturtz had shown up when he did.

Sycamore Inn's restoration had been a joint project and Henry had managed most of it. Both of those renovations had become profit centers and were paying for themselves, but the Bell House was different. They were turning it into their home which meant that in her heart of hearts she wouldn't hire contractors to do work she could do herself.

She did wish that Henry had taught her how to run his skid loader. Polly should have put on her best puppy dog face in order to convince him to let her borrow it. Instead, she was loading chunks of concrete into a wheelbarrow and dumping them in a pile where he could deal with them later. This stunk.

Since she was whining, Polly walked away from the task and back to the breezeway for a break. She looked around, opened the thermos and tipped it into her mouth.

Wandering into the front yard, Polly thought back to the first time she'd been here and scared herself to death. The yard had been a complete wreck; filled with fallen tree branches, tall grass and weeds. The bushes that lined the sidewalk had grown out of control into the yard. Someone had trimmed back the bushes enough on the front side so people weren't attacked by vines when they used the sidewalk, but otherwise it was a mess. Eliseo and Sam Gardner had brought those under control with a chainsaw and hedge clippers.

The front of the house, however, was not under control. Henry had torn down the solarium and front porch. Both were dangerous. Rebecca complained mightily about the loss of the solarium, there was nothing to save. The back porch was in much worse condition and he'd removed it as well. They were trying to decide whether to replace it with a porch or a large deck. The porch would fit the style of the home, but Henry was angling for a more modern deck. She hadn't relented yet.

The front porch had been replaced several times throughout the years and Polly looked forward to its next iteration. She and Henry had already designed it, using columns and a balustrade. He knew she wanted a balcony on the second floor, so he'd incorporated that into the design. Right now, though, the front of the house looked naked and ugly.

Eliseo was bringing the front yard back to life. A beautiful oak and several walnut trees made a mess in the yard, but after all of these years, the oak was immense and gorgeous. One of the walnuts had needed to come down, but the others were still standing tall. There were a variety of trees all over the property, offering shade to most of it. Polly wanted to plant a sycamore or two and maybe a few fruit trees. That would come later.

In one of the photographs Polly had seen of the original Bell House, several outbuildings stood behind what was presently the garage. When the buildings had fallen apart, the structures had been removed, but no one ever bothered with the floors. Once she was finished hauling off all of the concrete from those old floors, Eliseo had plans for another garden.

Polly wasn't thrilled about that. She didn't want to take responsibility for plants and vegetables, but he and Sam insisted, telling her that she needed color in the back yard.

She'd pointed at the arbor walkway on the other side of the house. There was plenty of color in all of that. Eliseo had only smiled and nodded. That worried her. It was going to take a great deal of care to bring it all back to its original beauty. She was just grateful he didn't mind a challenge.

Polly took another long drink of coffee, re-capped the thermos and frowned as she looked at the mess behind the garage. The job wasn't going to finish itself, no matter how hard she wished. She scuffed her foot along the floor of the breezeway, took a deep breath, and went back to work.

An hour later, she dumped a wheelbarrow load and stopped to brush hair out of her face again. Yeah, yeah, yeah. She'd bring a bandanna back this afternoon. Polly pushed the wheelbarrow back and took out her phone.

"I'm hot and cranky," she texted to Henry.

Polly slipped the phone into her back pocket and bent over to pick up another concrete chunk. She chuckled. Henry had broken these up pretty well. They weren't quite as heavy as the hay bales she'd lifted before Eliseo came to work for her, but they were wearing her out. Maybe she should ask to borrow the donkeys and a cart. That would be easier than hauling this stupid wheelbarrow around. When Eliseo and Jason pulled rocks out of the field behind Sycamore House, they used the horses.

She was whining again.

Picking up another chunk, Polly tossed it at the wheelbarrow and threw her hands into the air when she missed. No surprise, there. She had rotten aim, but this was frustrating. Polly stalked over to it, picked up the chunk, and flung it.

Just as it hit the wheelbarrow, the ground shifted. Her brain couldn't work fast enough to figure out what was happening and before she knew it, the earth beneath was falling away from her. Polly scrabbled for purchase, but things were moving too quickly. Dirt, grass, bits of concrete and dust collapsed as she threw her arms out trying to brace herself against whatever was happening.

When she finally stopped moving, Polly looked up through a three-foot hole to the sky. The wheelbarrow was still where she'd left it and she had enough presence of mind to be thankful it hadn't followed her down. No telling what that would have done if it had hit her.

Dust and dirt filled the air, making it difficult to see. Polly took a deep breath, shut her eyes, and flexed her muscles and joints, hoping that she hadn't hurt anything. Something was poking her in the shoulder, but she wasn't ready to turn around and look. She was still taking note of the rest of her body.

First, the feet, ankles, knees and legs. Yes. Everything worked. She could move her hips and waist. Her arms and hands were fine. Carefully, Polly turned her neck. Everything was where it belonged.

She opened her eyes and looked around, hoping she'd given the dust time enough to settle.

The last thing Polly expected to see was a tunnel. She sat upright and then pulled up to her knees, trying to see down the dark hallway in front of her. Sunlight shone in about a foot, so Polly took out her phone, swiped the flashlight on and aimed it into the darkness. She saw nothing but walls, ceiling and floor. Her first instinct was to crawl in, but knew that was probably a bad idea. Henry would be furious. If she had her directions right, it led to the house. That was interesting.

The tunnel itself was about three feet wide and maybe five feet tall. Whoever had done this had put some effort into their work. She'd fallen six or seven feet down into a room and now that she was thinking normally again, she stood and brushed herself off.

Scattered around the perimeter of the room were metal pipes and rods, a huge tarnished vat and wooden shelves that had been pushed up against the walls, but were sagging and rotted.

Polly thought it looked familiar, but she was still in enough shock that she couldn't make sense of what that was. She finally turned to see what had been poking her in the shoulder after she'd fallen.

"Good heavens," she said out loud. "It figures. Who are you and what in the world are you doing in here?"

There were enough bones in the pile to have been a person once upon a time. Using her flashlight, Polly identified the skull and pelvis bone. If it had been upright before she fell in, it wasn't anymore. She didn't want to make any assumption as to which bone had poked her. It was enough that she'd gotten that close. She laughed at the shows she'd seen where some poor hapless soul fell into a pile of bones and came face to face with the skull. Great screaming and flailing about ensued, leaving the person traumatized. Today, she was just glad she hadn't hurt herself.

Polly looked up only to realize she had no good way to get out.

"Please have a signal," she muttered, swiping her phone open again. Then Polly realized she didn't know who to call first. Henry would come right away. He'd know how to shore up the ground so they could get in and out of the room safely. But the rotten side of her wanted to call Aaron first.

Polly snapped a quick picture of the bones and sent it to Aaron, trying to hold back her wicked grin. This time she wasn't calling. He could make all the assumptions he wanted before he made the call himself. He'd do that soon, so instead of calling Henry, she sent him the same picture. It was a race to see who would react first.

"Hello there," she said when her phone rang a split second later.

"Where are you and why are you sending me pictures of bones?" Aaron asked.

"I didn't go far," she said.

"Back to my question. Where are you?"

"I'm clearing out my house and since we're going to live here someday, it's my job to find old bones first."

"You're at the old Springer place?"

"We're calling it the Bell House now," she reminded him.

"I don't have time for this. Is that where you are?"

"Yes. And I'm stuck." A beep alerted her to another call coming in. "Henry's calling. Do I answer it or keep talking to you?" she asked.

"Did you send him the same picture?"

Polly laughed. "Of course."

"He can wait."

"I'll tell him you said so when he yells at me," she said.

"Uh huh. So where did you find your latest?"

"I fell into a hole."

"In the ground?"

Polly tried to come up with a witty retort, but couldn't, so she nodded. "Yeah. Behind the garage. And there's a tunnel that leads to the house."

"You fell into a tunnel?"

"No, I'm in a room. There's a tunnel at one end of the room. Or a walkway or something. But it's dark and I shouldn't go down it." As if he heard her say it, Henry beeped in again.

"No you shouldn't," Aaron said. "That would be foolish. You don't know what's there."

"Exactly. And by the way, I'm fine."

"What?"

"I told you that I fell into a hole. You didn't ask if I was okay."

Aaron took a breath. "I'm sorry. You're right. I didn't. But in my defense, you sent me a picture of a pile of bones. I was a little distracted by that."

"Are you going to come rescue me?"

"Well," he started and then paused.

"Well what? Someone has to help me get out of here," Polly said. "I'm in a hole in the ground."

"Is the ground above you going to be a problem?"

"I assume so. I fell in."

"Call your husband back. Tell him what's going on. And after he gets over being upset, ask him to call me so that we can figure out how to get those bones out of there safely."

"And me," Polly said. "You have to get me out of here safely, too. Right?"

Aaron laughed. "If you've been good. Sending me a picture of a pile of bones before lunchtime on a Monday morning is not how I imagined this day going."

Polly's phone beeped again. "Henry's losing patience. I'll talk to you later. And thanks for all your concern."

Aaron was still chuckling when she switched over to the other call.

"What is that?" Henry demanded.

"Bones. Obviously."

"Where are you and why are you sending pictures of bones?"

"I fell in a hole." Polly pulled the phone away as she chuckled. She was having fun with these guys. It was probably quite unseemly, but if finding dead bodies was her thing, she might as well just deal with it and move on.

When she got back to the phone, Henry was saying something along the lines of "...call for help?"

"I missed that," she said. "We must be breaking up."

"Did you fall in a hole behind the garage?"

"Yeah. It's a room, Henry. And there's a tunnel that looks like it leads back to the house. Do you want me to check it out?"

"No!" he shouted. "Don't you dare."

"If someone doesn't come get me out of this hole, it might be my only escape," Polly said.

"You can't get out?"

She looked around. "No. I can't. There's no way up. I'm going to need a ladder, but I'm worried about the ground above me being dangerous."

"Okay." He went silent and she waited while he thought it through. Even from a distance, she could hear his wheels turning. "Okay. How far down are you?"

"Six or seven feet."

"You fell six or seven feet. Did you hurt anything?"

"There's my good husband. Finally, someone asks me how I'm doing."

"I'm sorry." The sound of chagrin in his voice made her feel guilty.

"Don't worry. I'm fine. I probably bruised my butt, otherwise everything else is in good shape. So are you coming to rescue me?"

"Yeah. I'm coming in from Ames, though. It's going to take time. Maybe Dad and Eliseo can come over."

"I'd trust them," Polly said. "Aaron wants you to call him."

"Why?"

"If they're going to be down here collecting bones, he wants it to be safe. You and he should work this out."

"This is ridiculous. What is that room?"

"Let me send more pictures and I'll call you right back," Polly said.

"Send the pictures and I'll call *you* back. I'm getting hold of Eliseo first," he replied. "I love you and I'm sorry that you're in a hole."

"You should be. But Henry, I'm glad it was me and not you or anyone else."

"That doesn't make me feel much better. Send pictures and I'll call in a few minutes."

Polly took pictures of the other items in the room and sent them to Henry, then wandered over to the tunnel and stepped inside. She would have to crouch to walk through it. Who would have used this? She turned around again and walked the perimeter of the room, then stopped and looked at the wall behind the body. Was that another door?

She pursed her lips and looked down at the bones and back at the wall. If she stepped on something and crushed it, that would be a problem. Her curiosity was just going to have to wait. But if there was another room back there, Eliseo wouldn't want to walk on that part of the yard either. She shuddered at the thought of kids and animals playing back here and falling through the ground. Hopefully these were the only rooms that had been dug out, but now she worried.

"Who are you?" she asked the bones on the floor again. "What were you doing in here? How did you die?"

The phone buzzing in her hand made Polly jump and she swiped it open. "You scared me."

"Sorry. You weren't trying to go down that tunnel, were you?"

She looked back at it guiltily and decided that Henry didn't need to know how close she'd come. "No. I was talking to the bones."

"As long as they didn't talk back. Polly, you're going to be the death of me. How am I ever going to keep you safe?"

"Did you see the pictures?"

"Yeah. That's an old still."

Polly thought for a moment and then realized what he said. "Of course. I've seen pictures of them. That's why I recognized it. Were they making whiskey down here?" she asked.

"Who knows. It will be interesting to find out, though."

"I think there's another room."

He took a quick breath. "Dad and Len are meeting Eliseo there in a few minutes. Dad's got a big ladder."

"Will the ground hold it if we lean against it?"

"Eliseo will make sure you get out safely. Just do what he tells you to do, okay?"

"Did you talk to Aaron?"

"I'm calling him right now. I want you out of there first."

"Darn," Polly said. "No more hauling rock for me."

Henry chuckled. "I think you've done enough of that for now. I don't want you working in the back yard until we make sure the ground is solid."

"I'm fine with that. I was tired of this job anyway. Thanks for taking care of me."

"Why wouldn't I take care of you?"

"It's just so nice to be able to call you and know that someone will rescue me."

"I love you, too," Henry said. "I'm already on my way so don't leave without letting me see that you're in one piece."

CHAPTER TWO

Once she finally got out of the hole, Polly looked down and couldn't believe what she'd managed to do. Eliseo and Bill Sturtz had brought a couple of tall ladders and cut away the remaining ceiling in the room until a ladder safely stood against solid ground.

Polly stood with Henry as the sheriff's department roped off the gaping hole.

"Maybe we should have brought in an archaeologist," Aaron said.

"How in the world do you expect to identify these bones?" Henry asked.

Aaron shook his head. "I have no idea. That's why I called Digger. He's got a better team than I do for something this old."

"How old do you think?" Polly asked.

"We'll have to see what they can tell us about the body, the teeth, the fabric and whatever else is down there," Aaron replied.

She nodded. "This is pretty crazy. I didn't even have to leave my own back yard." Polly's phone rang with a local number. "Just a second," she said and stepped away. "This is Polly Giller."

"Polly? Something's wrong," Rebecca said.

"Rebecca, are you okay? Are you hurt?"

Henry turned around and walked toward her, his brow furrowed.

"It's not me. Stephanie just came in and took Kayla away. They talked in the hall and Kayla was crying. She came back into the room and took her coat and said she had to leave. Polly, she hugged me and said good-bye. What's going on?"

"I don't know," Polly said. "But I'll try to find out. Go back to class and hopefully I'll know more when you come home from school."

"But I can't concentrate. What if something terrible has happened? Can you please come get me?"

Polly looked at Henry. "Not yet, honey. You have to believe that everything is going to be fine. Go on back to class. I'm sure it's nothing."

"It's something." Rebecca's voice broke. "It's something bad."

"Let me hang up and make some calls, honey. I will try to find out what's going on. Okay?"

"Please come get me."

"Rebecca, I'm sorry. Go back to class. I'll contact you later." Polly swiped the call closed, only to have her phone ring again, this time from Jeff.

"Hey, Jeff. What's going on with Stephanie? Rebecca just called me."

"I have no idea," Jeff replied. "She asked if she could take an early lunch, then grabbed all of her things and left. I called her cell phone and she's not answering."

"Henry's here with me," Polly said. "We'll go over to their place and see what we can find out."

"I'll meet you there."

"What's going on?" Henry asked.

She shook her head. "I have no idea. Stephanie left work and picked Kayla up from school. She's not answering Jeff's calls." Polly swiped to call Stephanie's phone as she walked to her truck. "Come with me?" she asked Henry.

He walked to the passenger side of her truck and got in. When Polly got Stephanie's voice mail, she said, "Hey Stephanie. Rebecca and Jeff have both called me. They're worried about you. Tell us what's happening. We can help. Please call me back."

Polly got in her truck and pulled around the sheriff's vehicles and drove toward the highway, then turned left and headed for the trailer park where Stephanie and Kayla lived. The girls were saving money to get into an apartment, but hadn't yet made the move. Stephanie had announced that she'd spent her last winter in the trailer, though. By the time Thanksgiving came, she wanted to live somewhere that she and Kayla could be proud of. They'd done what they could with their little trailer, but it was old and decrepit and not well insulated.

Her car wasn't in front of the trailer, but Polly pulled in, then waited for Henry as they walked up to the front door. Jeff arrived within moments.

"If they aren't here," Jeff said, "I have a key. Stephanie wanted me to be able to get in, if necessary."

Henry knocked, waited a few minutes, then tried the handle. He stepped back so Jeff could unlock the door.

"Stephanie, honey," Jeff said as he crossed the threshold. "Are you..." He stopped talking as they looked around.

The girls had left in a hurry, taking things that were important, but leaving most everything else. The dining room table that Stephanie had rescued and refinished was still there, but photographs they'd had sitting around and hanging on the walls were gone. Polly walked down the hall to Kayla's room and though the bedding was still there, the dresser and closet were emptied of the girl's clothes.

She heard a phone ringing and walked back out to the living room.

Jeff was holding Stephanie's phone. "She left it," he said.

"What in the hell is going on?" Polly asked. "Did something spook her? Why are they running?"

Henry took his phone out. "You need to call Aaron. Something is going on and we aren't equipped to deal with it."

"What am I going to tell Rebecca?" Polly said. She dropped onto the sofa and waved Henry's hand away, taking out her own phone and dialing a familiar number.

"Didn't we just talk to each other?" Aaron asked. "Where did you go?"

"I'm at Stephanie's trailer," Polly said. "She and Kayla left town in a hurry."

"Did something come up?"

"I don't know. They emptied their trailer and she left her phone here."

"She what?"

"Something happened, Aaron. We need you to help us find them."

"I'm busy here. Digger just arrived, but I'll send Stu. You don't see anything there that will give us a hint as to where they've gone?"

"Nothing," Polly said wearily. "Nothing at all." She ran her hand through her hair and when she pulled it away, huffed a small laugh at the amount of dirt and dust she stirred up.

"He's on his way. I'm sorry, Polly."

"Me too. I wish I knew what was going on."

"We'll figure it out."

Polly closed her phone and leaned back. "What could have scared Stephanie so badly? Did she take any strange phone calls at work this morning, Jeff?"

He shrugged. "I don't know. I was on the phone all morning. She was just working in the office."

"Did Rachel talk to her?"

"I don't know. She's keeping an eye on the office for me, but I didn't tell her what was wrong."

"Let me call her." Polly swiped through her contacts and called Rachel.

"Hi Polly. What's going on?" Rachel asked.

"Did Stephanie say anything to you this morning?"

"No, not really. Just the normal stuff. Hello and about how she needed coffee. She and Kayla didn't get back until late last night from some concert down in Des Moines. She felt really guilty about keeping Kayla up late, but they had so much fun, she wouldn't have done anything different. Is she okay?"

"She's gone and we don't know where she went."

"Yeah, but she'll be back, right?"

"It doesn't look like she plans to come back. They packed everything up."

"That doesn't sound right. She was normal this morning. Nothing out of the ordinary."

"Okay, thanks. I'll talk to you later."

Polly dropped the phone in her lap. "Nothing." She pointed to the cell phone in Jeff's hands. "Can you get to last calls on there?"

"I don't know her password."

"Okay. Yeah. I wonder if Rebecca knows what it is," Polly said quietly. "I'm going to have to take her out of school. This will really mess her up. And her birthday is coming up this weekend, too." She leaned forward and propping her arms on her knees, put her head into her hands. "Oh honey, what's going on?"

Henry sat down beside her. "I'll take your truck and pick up Rebecca. If she can help get into Stephanie's phone or if she knows anything else, it's better for her to be with us, don't you think?"

Polly nodded and leaned back to reach into the pocket of her jeans for the keys. "She's going to want to come over here with you. You might as well take her out of school and bring her. She's just like me and needs to see things so she doesn't turn them into a bigger deal than they are. This is already big enough."

"We'll be back," he said.

"Are you okay with work?" Polly asked.

"We're fine. Don't worry."

Jeff walked to the door with Henry and then came back to sit down beside Polly. "Do you think this has to do with her dad?"

"He's in jail. That's why you guys went back to Ohio last year, isn't it?"

"Then that can't be it."

"I hope not. But what else would make them run like this?" Polly asked.

"Maybe Deputy Decker can check into that for us."

"Why wouldn't she tell you or me where she was going?"

He reached over and took Polly's hand. "I have no idea. I keep asking myself that same question. I thought we were family. I'd have done anything for her."

The two of them sat back on the sofa and let the silence of the empty trailer wash over them. Jeff continued to hold Polly's hand and she was thankful for the warmth and support that simple touch offered. They were family and one of their own was gone. She wanted to believe that it would all work out, but right now Polly wasn't sure how. They didn't know where the girls had gone, why they'd left or how to reach them. If Stephanie intentionally left her cell phone, she wasn't planning to contact anyone that way. And besides, if she wanted them to know where she was going, she would have told Jeff. She loved him like a big brother, a father and a best friend, all rolled into one.

Polly gave his hand a gentle squeeze.

They looked up at the sound of feet on the steps, and Rebecca rushed in the front door. She pulled up short, looked around, then ran down the hall to Kayla's bedroom. She slammed the bedroom door before coming back to the living room and without a word, walked past the sofa to the dining room table. Rebecca pulled a chair out and dragged it to the wall between the dining room and kitchen, then stood up on it and rapped the grate on the air vent. It fell off into her hands and she patted around, then snapped the vent back into place and stepped to the floor.

"They're really gone," she said, slumping into the chair.

"What were you looking for?" Henry asked.

"Stephanie and Kayla have been putting money up there since they moved in. Kayla told me it was their running away money." She slowly shook her head. "She bought a throw away cell phone at Walgreens, too. That was also up there. It's gone."

"Why would they need that?" Polly asked.

"I don't know. I just know that there was more than a thousand dollars. Stephanie said she never wanted to have to move to another town without having enough money to get started. I think she wanted to build it up to about two thousand." Rebecca's head drooped. "I can't believe they ran away."

"Do you know what the code is on Stephanie's cell?" Polly asked, putting her hand out.

Jeff put Stephanie's phone in it and Polly walked over to Rebecca.

Rebecca's lower lip started to quiver. "It's my birthday," she said. "Stephanie said they'd always remember that number, but since it wasn't anybody in their family, nobody else would know."

Polly swiped the phone open and pressed the four numbers, 0508. "That's it, honey. Thank you." She opened the recent call history and took her own phone out to record the numbers. "What's the 740 area code?" Polly asked.

Jeff looked up. "That's Ohio."

"She took a call from a number there this morning."

He shuddered and swallowed. "Now do you think it has something to do with her father?"

"I hope not," Polly said. She walked over to the front door and looked out. "Where is Stu? I thought he'd be here by now."

As if on cue, his vehicle pulled in behind hers and Polly pushed the door open.

"This is quite a gathering," Stu said, when he walked in. He took a look around, walked into the kitchen and back through the bedrooms, then came back out. "There's no sign of a struggle. They just picked up and left, right?"

Polly nodded. "It looks like it. Rebecca says they'd hidden some cash and a cell phone in the vent up there." She pointed above Rebecca's head. "It's gone, too."

"And they didn't say anything to any of you?" Stu asked.

"Kayla just said good-bye," Rebecca said. "It was like she was never going to see me again."

"Did either of them talk about where they'd go if they had to run away?" he asked, looking around the room.

Polly walked over to stand beside Rebecca, put her hand on her daughter's back and then looked at Jeff. "I don't remember her talking about somewhere else she'd want to live. Do you?"

He shrugged. "She talked about living where it was warm. But we both kidded about that. A beach in Hawaii or even Orlando where she could take Kayla to Disney World. But I don't know. She talked about seeing the mountains in Colorado and going to San Francisco. She had a lot of plans."

"What about when you were around, Rebecca?" Polly asked. "Did they ever say anything?"

"I don't think so." Rebecca nodded toward Jeff. "Yeah, they wanted to go to Disney, but that wasn't for a couple of years." She smiled up at Polly. "Stephanie said that I could go with them if you'd let me."

"Of course I would," Polly said. "I can't believe they lived around us for nearly a year and we have no idea where they'd go if they had to leave."

"Why did they have to leave, anyway?" Rebecca asked. She leaned forward to look around Polly at Stu.

"We'll check on that," he said.

"The first thing you should do is make sure her father is still in jail," Jeff said. "I can't think of any other reason for her to bolt like this."

Polly handed Stu the cell phone. "There's an Ohio phone number on there. Whoever it was called this morning just before she took off."

"You didn't call it?" Stu asked with a grin.

"Only because you showed up," Polly said.

Stu walked around Polly and stood in front of Rebecca. "Would you walk around the trailer with me?" he asked. "You've been here more than anyone else and if you see anything that might help us track the girls down, you'd help me out a lot."

"Yes!" Rebecca jumped up. "Thank you for letting me help. I feel so useless."

"Everybody does in situations like this," Stu said and guided her into the kitchen.

"How are you doing?" Henry asked Polly. "Have you started to hurt yet?"

She stretched the muscles in her back. "I'm okay for now. I'll probably take some aspirin before I go to bed tonight. Tomorrow will be worse than today."

"What did you do?" Jeff asked. "I should have asked earlier. I saw Eliseo bolt out of the parking lot this morning."

"She fell in a hole and found a body."

"Shut up," Jeff said with a laugh. "At your new house?"

"Behind the garage. I was hauling chunks of concrete and all of a sudden the ground gave way and I was in a strange little room that had been dug out underground." She spoke in a whisper. "And there's a full-blown tunnel, too. I think it leads all the way back to the house."

"Did you check it out?"

Polly glanced at Henry and grinned at his scowl. "No. Henry was going to be upset enough that I'd fallen in. I didn't want to push my luck."

"That's right," Henry said. "Heath and I will check it out. You aren't allowed in there until we can be certain that it's safe."

"But it's a tunnel!" she said. "If it's safe, we can have fun with it. You could shore up the walls in the room for a hideaway."

Henry gave a slow shake of his head. "We're going to live in that place for decades before you've finally finished with all of the projects you want me to accomplish."

"If you're lucky," she said.

"Whose bones were in that room?" Jeff asked.

"We have no idea," Henry replied. "Aaron called in the Department of Criminal Investigation. Apparently they have resources." He stepped closer to Polly. "I think she found something really old this time, though. There was also an old still in that room."

"Still?" Jeff asked. "Like moonshine?"

Henry laughed. "Could be. Maybe corn whiskey. Who knows, it could easily have been operating during Prohibition."

"Wouldn't it be crazy if the Bell House was a speakeasy?" Polly asked. "Maybe that's why it didn't last."

"If it was a speakeasy, they should have been raking in money hand over fist," Jeff said.

"Not if the law got hold of them," Stu said, coming back into the living room.

"Tell me you couldn't have been bought with some good, smooth whiskey," Henry said with a laugh. "Did you two find anything?"

Rebecca held up a teddy bear. "Kayla left Silver. Can I take him home with me? Please? If we find her, I know she'll want him back."

Polly looked at Stu and he nodded.

"Of course you can," she said. "But we aren't going to let any of these things go yet. Even if we don't see Stephanie and Kayla for a while, we'll pack it all up and put it in storage for when they come back."

"I don't think we'll need to come back in here," Stu said, "but if we do, should we contact you?"

Jeff held out the key. "I have this. I can let you in." He turned to Polly. "I'll check with the landlord. They're probably paid up through the end of the month, so we have some time. If not, I'll make sure they are." He set his jaw. "Those girls are coming home. No matter what. They certainly don't need any more chaos in their lives."

Stu headed for the front door. "As soon as I find anything out, I'll let you know. And if you hear from Stephanie or Kayla..."

"We'll call," Polly said.

He shook her hand, then Henry's and Jeff's. "Thanks for your help, Rebecca," he said and walked out the front door.

"Are all the lights off?" Polly asked Rebecca.

"We made sure." Rebecca moved toward the kitchen. "There's some meat and stuff in the refrigerator. Should we leave it or take it?"

"Let's plan on coming back in a couple of days if they aren't home yet," Polly said. "We can clean out the fridge then."

Rebecca's shoulders relaxed. "Thank you. I just can't believe this. Why would they leave without telling any of us?"

"Because Stephanie wants everyone to be safe from whatever she's scared of," Jeff said.

"I hope it's not her dad," Rebecca said. "He's a bad man."

"Yes he is, honey." Henry put his arm around her shoulder. "Let's get out of here. Why don't I take the two of you up to the diner for lunch? Jeff, you're more than welcome to join us."

He nodded and looked around the room one last time before leaving, as if the girls might just be hiding. "I'd best get back to the office. Thanks, though."

Polly checked the front door after pulling it closed behind them, then followed Henry and Rebecca to the truck. Rebecca climbed into the back and pulled her seatbelt on. Polly hoped this was fixed before her birthday. Last year, Rebecca hadn't told anyone about the date and spent it quietly with her mother. Sarah Heater was so close to the end of her life during those days that she hadn't had the energy to ask anyone to help Rebecca celebrate. Polly wanted to do something special this year, but with Kayla gone, she wasn't sure how Rebecca would respond. Her daughter had been through so much and she was still a happy young girl. It had to work out. It just had to.

CHAPTER THREE

Lunch was much too quiet. Rebecca was distracted and forlorn, breaking Polly's heart. How do you accept the fact that your best friend left town with no notice?

"Do you want to go over to the house and see the hole I fell into?" Polly asked.

"You fell in a hole?"

Polly chuckled. "Yeah. A big room. There was a set of bones and..."

Rebecca crinkled her forehead. "I don't believe it. You found a dead body at our house?"

Henry reached across the table and put his hand down in front of Rebecca's plate. "We're pretty sure the bones are very old." He looked at Polly. "I need to pick up my truck, too."

"That's right," she said. "I stole you from there. Do you suppose they're still taking the scene apart?"

"They'll be there for a while," he said with a smile. "But you can't work in that back yard until I'm sure there are no more holes for you to fall into. After that, Heath and I will clean up the rest of the concrete. I should have done that in the first place."

"If you'd fallen down there with your bobcat, you could have seriously hurt yourself," Polly said. "I can't believe you managed to break up that floor without falling in."

He nodded. "There but for the grace of God sometimes."

Polly poked Rebecca. "There's a tunnel, too. I think it leads from that room back to the house. And since we found a still there, I'm betting somebody made whiskey and sold it in the hotel. How's that for a story?"

"I can't wait to see it," Rebecca said. She pushed her plate back. "I'm done. Can we go now?"

"Henry isn't finished yet," Polly admonished. "Be patient. We have all afternoon."

"You mean I don't have to go back to school today?"

"No," Polly said. "Not today. You've had enough. What did you tell them in the office, Henry?"

"That we had a family emergency and she'd be gone for the rest of the day." He grinned at Rebecca. "I've got your back."

She laughed at him and then slumped into her seat. "I just wish it wasn't because Kayla is gone. How could she just leave and not tell me where she was going?"

"Something scared them pretty bad," Polly said. "All they could think about was getting away from whatever it was."

"Will you call Deputy Decker later to find out who called Stephanie on her phone?"

"I'll ask. I don't know how much he'll tell me, but I promise that I'll ask." Polly pointed at Rebecca's hamburger which was only half eaten. "Do you want to eat that later or are you really done?"

"Can I give it to Han and Obiwan?"

"That sounds great," Henry said, and put the last few bites of his hamburger on her plate. "There, that's enough bites of burger to make the boys happy."

Rebecca pointed to Polly's tenderloin. "You didn't eat very much of that either."

"That's not for the dogs, though," Polly said. She'd cut the sandwich in half, knowing Heath would finish it when he got home this evening. He always came in the house ravenous and no matter what she fed him, he was also ready for dinner when it was served.

"How was everything?" Lucy asked. She pointed at Rebecca's plate. "Your meal seems to have grown."

"We're taking it home to Obiwan and Han," Rebecca said. "And that's for Heath. He eats everything."

Lucy chuckled. "You have some lucky boys in your household. You take good care of them. Are you sure you don't want a sundae today?"

Rebecca's eyes grew big. "No, we're going over to the house to see the hole that Polly fell in. She found bones and a still and a tunnel."

"She did! I hadn't heard about that yet." Lucy smiled at Polly. "The grapevine failed me today. A whiskey still? How old do you think it is?"

"It has to be pretty old. Nobody has been in there for decades."

"My husband's granddaddy made moonshine back in the days of Prohibition," Lucy said. "More than a few farmers were doing that around here to keep their families fed. I'll have to ask him if he remembers any of the stories his father used to tell."

"We were wondering if Bell House was a speakeasy," Polly said. "We can't figure out why the hotel went out of business so fast." She chuckled. "I wonder if those bones belong to Franklin Bell. Nobody knows where he went either. It would be too bad if he died down there because no one knew where he was."

"Let me ask Greg tonight. If I find anything, I'll be sure to let you know. And maybe he can remember who some of the other families were that cooked whiskey. Who knows, there might be a really interesting story for you to tell over there." She picked up the plates. "I'll be back with your takeout in just a minute."

As she walked away, Polly leaned across the table. "I didn't know she was married. Have I ever met Greg?"

Henry shook his head. "No. He was in a bad accident. His lower body is paralyzed and he doesn't have much control of his arms. He also doesn't speak." His face grew soft. "But they have a good life. She's pretty wonderful to him and it doesn't seem to matter at all that he's different than the man she married."

"That's so hard. Do they need anything?" Polly asked.

"No, honey," Henry said with a smile. "They have a nurse that spends days with Greg when Lucy is working. And his old friends do what they can for him." He grimaced. "When he lets them."

Polly sat back as Lucy returned to the table. She put a plastic bag filled with the takeout containers on the table in front of Rebecca and set the ticket beside it. "Joe had a screwed up hamburger that he was going to throw away. He told me to give it to your dogs, so it's in the container, too." She winked and handed Rebecca a smaller, paper bag. "I heard about your friend leaving town this morning. I'll bet your heart is hurting. You'll find some cookies in there. They won't fix it, but maybe they'll help." She reached down and gave Rebecca a quick hug. "She'll come home. I know Polly and Henry, and they'll find a way."

"Thank you," Rebecca said, her eyes filling with tears. "I know they will. As long as we can find her, Polly and Henry will fix it."

"Stay out of those deep holes, now, okay?" Lucy tapped Polly's shoulder as she walked to another table.

"She's amazing," Polly said. "With all that she must have going on, she is always positive and happy."

Henry opened his wallet and put money on the table, then stood and stepped back while Polly and Rebecca got up and went ahead of him. The bell hanging on the front door clanged as they left and he took a deep breath. "I don't want to go back to work this afternoon, but I probably should."

"You could play hooky with us," Rebecca said.

"Let's go over to the house and show you the big hole in the ground, then we'll figure out what's happening next," Polly said.

~~~

Rebecca had been suitably impressed with Polly's big hole, though they couldn't get very close. The Department of Criminal Investigation was still working in the underground room,
~~~

mapping what they found and photographing everything in place before bringing it to the surface. After a short while, Rebecca grew bored.

Henry and his father had gone back to the shop to do some brainstorming about the best way to cover the hole and protect it from storms that threatened to come through later in the week. It sounded as if Henry wanted to actually keep the room. Polly couldn't imagine what he'd do with it. She loved that man. He might not be interested in rushing through the renovations of the house, but that only meant he wanted to do it right. If the Bell House came with a tunnel leading to an old still, he was going to make sure the tunnel and room remained for years to come.

"Can we just go home now?" Rebecca asked after they'd watched the activity for a while.

"You don't want to do anything else today? Since you don't have to go back to school, we could do something fun."

"I don't feel much like fun," she said. "I just want to go home and maybe hug the dogs."

"I understand," Polly replied. "Andrew will be here in a couple of hours."

"He doesn't know where I went either. I should have told him, but when Henry showed up, I just wanted to get out of there and see you."

"Let's go home then. Who knows, maybe Jeff has more news."

Rebecca drooped all the way to the truck. "This is the worst feeling ever," she said.

"Missing your friend?"

"I couldn't even prepare for it. I've moved before and left friends, but at least we had time to say goodbye. This is just..." Rebecca looked at Polly, her poor little face so sad. "It's too fast. And it's all wrong. They aren't going someplace better; they're running away for some terrible unknown reason."

"I know," Polly said. "We're going to do everything we can to find out where they've gone and bring them back safely."

"If they want to come back," Rebecca said. "Maybe they'll find a better place and won't want to come back, not even to see me."

"I love you, sweetie, but you're getting a little over-dramatic. You and I both know that Stephanie and Kayla wouldn't rush out of town unless it was for a drastic reason. It isn't about you."

"It feels like it is."

"Then you'd better check your feelings. You can be sad that Kayla's gone and you can miss her, but you don't get to make this worse just so you can get all emotional. Okay?"

Rebecca huffed.

Polly parked in the garage. "Go on upstairs. I want to talk to Jeff." She waited as Rebecca went inside and leaned back in the driver's seat. This was going to be a very long week. What a heck of a way to start it out. The morning had brought numerous questions and no answers. She hoped that answers started presenting themselves before more questions needed to be asked.

Her phone buzzed with a text from Heath. "*Do you mind if I go out with some friends for dinner after work tonight? I won't be late. We're just going for pizza."*

"Anybody interesting?"

She waited for a reply and though it took longer than she expected, he responded with, *"No. What do you mean?"*

"One of your girlfriends?"

That got an immediate response. *"I don't have a girlfriend. It's just a bunch of people."*

"Okay. Home by eight-thirty."

"Thanks."

Heath's social life had completely turned around these last few months. Last weekend was prom. She had expected him to settle on one girl as his date, but he ended up going with a large group of friends, some girls and a few boys. They'd gone to Ames for dinner, back to Boone for the prom and then when the after-prom activities were finished, many of them ended up at Sycamore House for breakfast. He and his brother had prepared the food, first asking permission to use the main kitchen downstairs. After sleeping most of the morning away, Heath had made sure everything was clean and back in place.

He'd spent plenty of time earning their trust and Polly found she didn't worry quite so much about him. It was hard to believe he was finishing his junior year in high school. She wasn't ready for him to leave.

Henry would scold her for thinking about those things. She should enjoy the moments they had right now and not dwell on what might happen in the future. Easier said than done.

Polly climbed out of the truck and went inside, passing through the empty kitchen to the main office.

"Hi there, Rachel. How are you doing in here?" she asked.

"It's okay. Today was kind of a slow day, so this worked out," Rachel said. "I called a friend of mine and she's going to come answer phones tomorrow."

"Thank you. Is Jeff available?" Polly nodded toward his closed door.

Rachel nodded. "He said that I was supposed to buzz him if you showed up. He wants to talk to you."

"No news about Stephanie and Kayla?"

"No," Rachel said. "It's just awful. What could have made them run like that?"

She pressed a button on the phone in front of her and Jeff answered, "Yes?"

"Polly's here. Can I send her in?"

"Yes, please."

Polly smiled and opened Jeff's door, then closed it behind her when she walked inside. Before Stephanie, Rebecca's mother had begun the task of clearing paper from Jeff's office. Polly could easily remember being unable to find a place to sit on his sofa because of the stacks of papers he hadn't had time to file. But over the last year, he and Stephanie had redecorated the office, turning it into a comfortable space. There was even room for a round table for small meetings. A large whiteboard hung on the wall behind the table and the rest of the walls were adorned with city skyline prints from around the world.

"Why are you hiding in here?" Polly asked.

"I can't concentrate as it is," he replied. "It's easier not to have to listen to all of the noise out there."

She glanced at the door. "It's quiet today. There's nobody in the building."

He gave a half-hearted laugh. "I caught myself listening to Rachel answer the phone, wondering if one of the calls would be Stephanie. And we had some people in here working on the furnace in the basement. I didn't have to deal with them. Eliseo did, but still. I couldn't help but pay attention because I don't want to think about what is really bothering me."

"I know," she said. "I have a girl upstairs who is just as useless."

"I don't even want to go home tonight. What if Stephanie tries to call the office and no one is here?"

"Now why would she do that?" Polly asked. "She's smart enough to know when the office is open. And she knows your phone number and Kayla knows mine."

Jeff glared at her. "Do you think they really do? Or are all of those numbers programmed into her cell phone? Do you know my number? Do you even know Henry's?"

Polly tried to come up with any of the phone numbers that she called regularly and couldn't. She shook her head. "That's terrible. I used to have everybody's phone number memorized. When did I give that up?"

"I just keep pleading with that phone to ring," he said. "All she needs to do is tell us that they're going to be okay. No, that's not all. They need to trust us to take care of them." Jeff slammed his hand down on the desk, making Polly jump. "Damn it, she needs to trust me to take care of her. That girl is one of my best friends and she just ran off without even telling me what was going on."

"I know," Polly said quietly. She leaned on the arm of the sofa, not knowing exactly what to say. She didn't realize that Jeff had been that close to Stephanie. As far as she knew, he saw Stephanie as a younger sister, someone to guide and help. But with all that they did together, it made sense that they'd become good friends.

He exhaled audibly. "Would you mind calling Stu?"

"Sure? What do you want to know?"

"I want to know what that call was that came into Stephanie's phone this morning. Who scared her?"

Polly took her phone out and thought about the huge number of contacts she had. Losing all of these numbers would devastate her. She scrolled through the list and called the sheriff's department, asking to speak with Stu Decker. It took only a few minutes before he came on the line.

"Hi Polly. You're asking for answers, aren't you?"

"Just that number. Do you know whose it is?"

"Yeah. It's not helpful. The call came from a convenience store in London, Ohio."

"What's in London?"

"We're still checking on a few things," Stu said.

"What's in London, Stu?" she asked again.

Jeff had started typing as soon as Polly mentioned the city name and turned his screen toward her.

"I'm waiting for more information to come in," Stu replied.

"The..." Polly leaned forward to read the screen. "Madison Correctional Institution? Did Stephanie's father escape?"

"We're still asking questions."

"You're being evasive. Do you think he called Stephanie and threatened her?"

Stu took in a deep breath. "After Joey escaped from the mental facility last year, I don't want to assume it's happening again. But it looks like that could be what happened."

"That poor girl. No wonder she ran. I can't imagine what he might have said to her."

"We don't even know if he's coming this way," Stu said.

"Come on," Polly replied. "If she ran, I think we can assume that she believes he's on his way to Iowa."

"We'll talk to Chief Wallers, too."

Polly sighed. "And damn it, he'll probably show up at Sycamore House because this is the last place she worked."

"Aaron would tell you to stay out of this," Stu said.

"I'll do what I can. Would you please let me know if this is all true? If I need to be prepared, I'd like to have some lead time."

"Okay," Stu said. "Talk to you later."

"Did you get all that?" Polly asked Jeff.

"Yeah. Bad guy coming to town. We're all going to die."

She chuckled. "I don't think it's all that ghastly." Polly flexed the muscle in her arm. "And he's never come up against a woman who isn't scared to death of him."

"Don't you even think about it," Jeff warned.

"I'll try not to, but we don't want anyone else around here to be in danger, either."

"The sheriff and the police can keep an eye on us. And if you aren't good, I'll tell Henry."

Polly smiled at him. "Now you're just being mean."

"I have to keep you safe one way or the other. You're always walking into something."

"Rachel says she has a friend who is going to answer the phones tomorrow. Are you good with that?"

Jeff shrugged. "She came by earlier. Kristen Travis. She does a lot of temp work, so she'll be perfect." He put his head down. "I don't want to hire anyone new for that position."

"You won't have to." Polly stood up and walked over to him, then rubbed his shoulders. "This is all going to work out. It just has to."

CHAPTER FOUR

"Let's see what you've drawn." When Polly got to the apartment, she found Rebecca at the dining room table. The television was on across the room, an untouched glass of water sat beside her, and she idly doodled in her sketchbook.

"Nothing. I don't feel like doing anything. Everybody says that when you're sad or missing someone, you're supposed to be way creative." Rebecca tapped on her temple. "I'm just blank. I can't think of a thing to draw."

"I suspect that creative people have to get past the initial shock of whatever it is that makes them sad before they can turn it into a beautiful expression," Polly said. "You're still in shock."

Rebecca turned in her chair to make eye contact. "Okay, I'm being really serious now, Polly. I know my birthday is coming up and I think that I should have my own phone." She put her hand up to stop Polly from speaking. "Hear me out. If I had a phone right now, Kayla could call me and tell me where she is and we could go get her. Then everything would be okay."

"I love you, sweetie, but we've had this discussion over and over. No phone until next year at the very earliest."

"But, what if she wants to call me and talk about whatever is going on?"

Polly grinned. "Then she will call my cell phone just like she always does. And that was a very nice try, but you having a cell phone wouldn't have changed the outcome of this situation in the least."

"It's just not fair," Rebecca whined.

"Life isn't fair and you'll get a cell phone when you get one. And guess what?"

"What?"

"Within a couple of years after you've had it, you won't even remember all of these days of not having one. But for now, the answer is no."

"What if I told you that's all I wanted for my birthday?"

"Then you're going to have a very boring birthday. Let it go, Rebecca. Please."

"Fine. Can I stay home from school again tomorrow?"

Polly took two ice cream sandwiches out of the freezer and sat down beside Rebecca, pushing one in front of the girl. "Now why would you need to stay home?"

"Because I won't be able to concentrate on my schoolwork if all I'm thinking about is Kayla and Stephanie." Rebecca ripped the paper wrapper on her treat and took a small bite off the end.

"Let's see," Polly said. She put her index finger on the divot in her chin and looked upward. "How can we help you concentrate at school? Oh, I know! I'll call your teachers and tell them that since you're having difficulty, you should be taking notes in each class because I'll want to see them at the end of the day." She paused. "No, I've got a better idea. I'll ask them to set up a video recorder so that we can go through each of your classes after school and make sure you didn't miss anything while you were sitting there. Does any of this work for you?"

"I just wanted another day to think about things," Rebecca said grumpily.

Polly reached over and rubbed her hand up and down Rebecca's forearm. "I know you do, sweetie, but sitting around here moping won't bring Kayla and Stephanie back. We're going to do everything we can to find them and help them know that Bellingwood is a safe place for them to live. However, that doesn't include you changing your life. You go back to school tomorrow and I'll go back to work at the Bell House. There's still a lot to do."

"What if you fall in another hole?"

"I hope I don't. But tomorrow is going to be a gorgeous day. Imagine sitting on a porch swing on a cool summer evening, drinking lemonade and listening to the cicadas buzzing."

Rebecca took another bite of her ice cream sandwich and gave Polly a long gaze. "You're weird."

"Was it the porch swing?" Polly asked. "I always wanted one of those."

"Nobody sits on their porches anymore. Not unless they're old."

"Oh, I'm sitting on my porch swing," Polly said. She poked Rebecca. "And I'm not old. We're going to play croquet on the front lawn and have foot races and everything."

Rebecca giggled.

"That's better." Polly leaned over to pull Rebecca into a hug. "It's going to work out. One way or the other, it will all be okay."

"Promise?"

"I promise."

Both dogs jumped up and ran to the front door.

"Must be Andrew," Polly said.

Rebecca patted her hair. "Do I look like I was crying?"

"You look just fine."

"Rebecca, are you in here?" Andrew yelled.

Polly stood up from the table. "We're here."

"What happened?" he asked, coming around the corner. "First Stephanie took Kayla out and then Henry came to get you. Did somebody die?"

"No," Rebecca started, then tears began to flow. "Kayla's gone."

"What do you mean, gone?" Andrew looked at Polly.

Polly pointed to the chair she'd just vacated. "Rebecca will tell you everything we know. Do you want something to drink?"

"Should we take the dogs outside?" he asked.

"No, I'll take them," Polly said with a smile. "You talk to Rebecca. Help yourself to anything in the kitchen." She walked toward the back door. "Come on, boys. Let's leave the young'uns alone and take a walk. Wanna go outside?"

At the magic word, the dogs ran for the back stairs and waited for Polly to catch up. She glanced at Andrew and Rebecca and smiled when she saw him put his arm around her shoulders. Yeah, yeah, yeah. They could get in all sorts of trouble, but sometimes a girl just needed her best friend to be there while she fell apart.

Obiwan and Han bolted for the tree line when she let them out the garage door. They were going to miss this place when she moved everyone to the Bell House. She'd feel more comfortable with them being outside by themselves at all hours of the day, but the dogs had invested a lot of time and energy marking their territory around Sycamore House.

Polly wandered down beyond the garden Eliseo was planting and toward the pasture. Han and Obiwan were far enough back that she managed to walk up to the fence without the horses realizing she was there. Demi was filthy from rolling in the dirt. That was a standard look for him. At least it gave Jason and his friends something to do when they arrived after school. Tom and Huck were the first to see her and ran as fast as their short little legs could carry them.

"Hi there, guys," Polly said, walking along the fence to the gate.

Nat brushed against Nan and then ran away from her. When she didn't respond, he pushed her again until she threw her head up and whinnied. Since that wasn't enough, he pushed again and she spun, then chased him around the fenceline. They pulled to a stop in front of the donkeys and Nan reached her head forward to sniff Polly's shoulder.

Polly held still, not wanting to startle the big horse. Nan wasn't very gregarious and this felt like a big moment. When Polly felt it had been long enough, she turned to face the horse and reached her hand out to stroke Nan's shoulder. "How are you doing, girl?"

Polly asked. "It's good to see you. I'm coming in, just give us a minute."

Han and Obiwan had caught up to her and were pacing back and forth in front of the gate, waiting to be let in. Polly opened the latch and stepped in behind them, then walked toward the barn. She grinned as she found herself surrounded by equines. The donkeys paced with her, Tom pushing her with his hips. Demi trotted over, followed closely by Daisy.

"Eliseo?" she called. "Are you here?"

The door to Demi's stall was open and Polly approached it, then called his name again. "Eliseo?"

"Right here, Polly." He came out of Daisy's stall. "What are you doing down here this afternoon?"

"Rebecca needed time with Andrew, not me. He lets her be all emotional and I tell her to stop it and face reality. She'd had enough of me."

"That's really bad news about Stephanie. I hope she's able to find a safe place from whatever spooked her."

"We think it's her father. It sounds like he might have gotten out of jail."

"They never get very far," Eliseo said. "The police in Ohio will find him."

"I hope so, but whatever he said scared her bad enough to run with everything she had. It's like she doesn't intend to ever come back to Bellingwood now that he knows where she's been living."

Eliseo stepped up to Nan and leaned on her, resting his head against her shoulder. "That would be too bad. She's made good friends here." He smiled. "How are you feeling? Any aches and pains after your tumble this morning?"

"I'd forgotten all about that," Polly said. "I'm okay now, but that might be different tomorrow morning when I get out of bed."

"I'm sure it will." He chuckled. "We have some good liniment down here. Just stop in and see us and we'll fix you right up." He walked over to the donkeys, who were still surrounding Polly. "You two go on back out and play. Leave her alone. She doesn't have anything for you."

When they didn't respond, he ducked back into the stall and took out their red ball. Giving it a toss, he whistled and everyone went running. Before long, Tom was pushing it with his nose while Huck chased him.

"Sam and I were thinking we'd bring Nan and Nat over to your new place one of these days with the cart. They'll help with the heavy work and we can haul the debris away after we're finished."

She sat down on one of the benches he'd placed under the roof so they could watch the horses. "It amazes me that you have them so well trained."

"They love to work," he said. "We put sweet corn in the field across the creek last week. If all goes well, we're going to have a great crop. We're planting more in another couple of weeks so we have plenty for Bellingwood Days. It's going to be a great summer and I want to be prepared."

"I'm going to have to get us all bonnets and hats, long dresses and breeches, aren't I?" Polly asked with a laugh. "I've never done a centennial celebration, but I saw pictures and everybody dresses up."

"Our horses will fit right in," he said. "Sam, Ralph, and I are talking about how we can show them off with some farming implements. They're already trained to do the work. We just need to have everything in place."

Polly shook her head. "I've been so focused on Bell House that I haven't given the centennial week much thought. I want it to be ready for the celebration, but I don't know what I want it to look like."

"You'll figure it out. You always do."

"Jason's got a girlfriend. Jason's got a girlfriend!" Scar Vasquez ran through the barn and skidded to a stop in front of Polly. "Oh hi, Ms. Giller. I didn't know you were here today."

Jason and their other friend, Kent Ivers, came barreling in behind Scar. "What's going on? Why are you here?" Jason asked Polly.

"Just out walking the dogs and thought I'd stop by to see the big kids. What's all this?"

Scar, short for Oscar, backed away from them. "It was nothing. Sorry, Jason."

Eliseo put his hand on Scar's shoulder and with a laugh, stopped him from ducking back into the safety of the barn. "Did you have something you wanted to tell me?"

"No sir. Not right now." Scar looked at his friend, guiltily. "I'll get the brushes. It looks like Demi's been rolling in the dirt again."

"They do every day," Jason muttered. "It's their favorite thing."

Polly walked over and touched his arm. "A girlfriend?"

"Not really," he replied.

"She wants to be, though," his friend Kent interjected. ""She told him today that she should have asked him to prom."

"I don't think Mom would have even let me go," Jason said. "She thinks it's only for upperclassmen."

"She's kind of right," Polly said. "There are some things that you get to do as you grow older."

"Well, it's stupid anyway."

"Is this girl older than you?" Polly asked.

Kent nodded enthusiastically. "She's going to be a senior next year. And if it weren't for Heath and his accident, Jason would never have gotten to know her. They talk every day and now they're texting after school, too."

Polly watched Jason's face flush two shades deeper. "What's her name?" she asked him.

Kent jumped back in. "It's Selena Morris. She even lives here in Bellingwood, so it's perfect. He doesn't have to drive all the way to Boone if he wants to see her."

"Come on, Kent," Eliseo said. "We have plenty of work to do."

"Do you like her?" Polly asked Jason after they walked away. "I mean, really like her?"

Jason nodded and shrugged, not looking up.

"Have you said anything to your mom?"

He looked up at that ... in shock. "No!"

"How about Andrew?"

"Not really. He's too busy talking about Rebecca this and Rebecca that."

"Of all the girls you know, is she the one you want to go out with?"

That question brought a look of confusion. "What do you mean?"

"I don't know," Polly said. "You know a lot of girls. Is Selena the one you want to date?"

"I guess. She's the only one who said anything to me. The others just act like they're part of the group or completely ignore me."

"Part of the group?"

"You know," he said. "We all just hang out together. Are you trying to confuse me on purpose?"

Polly shook her head. "Nope. I just want you to think about all of the possibilities. And I want you to have fun and get to know different types of girls while you're in high school. You're such an amazing young man. I want to see so much happen in your future."

He huffed. "Why are you letting Rebecca and Andrew be serious, then?"

Polly looked away, out at the horses and donkeys, at her dogs playing with Eliseo's two dogs. Why would Jason be any different than Rebecca and Andrew?

"That's a good question," she said. "I think everyone is different and the way they handle relationships is different, too. Henry and I didn't do all of the romantic, schmaltzy stuff when we got married, but Andy wanted that for her wedding. Sal and Mark will probably elope one of these days and tell no one. Andrew and Rebecca fit together. They make each other crazy and are each other's best friend. They force each other to be better at the things they love to do. And the truth is, if they break up and each find someone else to fall in love with, that will be just fine. I'll bet they will always be friends, though. You're different than Andrew."

"What do you mean?"

"Well, you didn't find a girl to be friends with when you were young. You found horses and Eliseo. Now you're growing up and girls are finally starting to pay attention to you. It's about time they realize how terrific you are, but I don't want you falling for the first one to bat her eyes at you because you're so ready to have a girlfriend, you can't stop yourself. You deserve a girl that will tell you the truth and be your friend. She'll make you as crazy-nuts as I make Henry and think you're amazing because of the things you do."

Jason scowled at her. "Why don't you think that's Selena?"

Polly had met Selena several times this last spring when she came over to the house with the group of friends that Heath spent time with. The girl was perfectly nice. She was polite and attractive and ... she didn't have much else going on. Someday she might find herself, but right now, she couldn't pay much attention to anything other than what everybody else was doing.

"It might be Selena," Polly said. "I'm not telling you that you shouldn't take her out. If she's asking, I think you should. It isn't every boy that has girls chasing him for a date. You should definitely take advantage of this."

"But you don't think she's girlfriend material?"

"I didn't say that either," Polly replied. "I'm just telling you that you are an amazing young man and you deserve an incredible girlfriend. Someone who thinks that you are a rockstar and then tells you that you can be even more than that. Because you are and you can."

"How do I get into these conversations with you?" Jason asked.

"I have no idea. I just open my mouth and then you keep talking to me."

He dropped down onto the bench. "I don't talk to anybody else in the world the way you make me talk to you."

"It's my superpower," Polly said. "Well, that and finding dead bodies. I did it again this morning."

His head shot up. "You did?"

"Yeah. Over at our house. In a hole in the ground. I fell in and landed on some bones. We think they're nearly a hundred years old."

"Who is it?"

"I have no idea. But there was a whiskey still in the same room.

I can't believe I didn't land on that, too."

"Are you okay?"

"I think so." Polly rubbed her lower back. "I'll probably wake up tomorrow morning moaning and groaning, but I'm pretty much okay. And there was a tunnel in the room that led back to the house."

"Wow," Jason said. "What were they doing with a tunnel?"

"Wouldn't it be cool if the old hotel was a speakeasy and they were making whiskey to sell during Prohibition?"

"You should totally do that for the centennial celebration this summer."

"Sell whiskey?"

"Yeah," he said, nodding his head. "Wouldn't that be cool?"

"No," she replied, shaking her own head. "It wouldn't. The law in the state would be down on me in a heartbeat. It's illegal to distill and sell whiskey without a license."

"So get a license."

"Yeah. No," Polly said. "We have a winery in town, we don't need a distillery."

"It was just a thought."

"We're going to have enough going on without trying to open a distillery. Sometimes I look at that house and think that I may never get to move in."

"It will be weird here if you're not around all the time."

"Yes it will, but maybe I'll actually come work here during the day if I live off site," Polly said.

"Everybody will miss you. Even the horses miss you when you don't come down very often."

"Now you're just making me feel guilty."

Jason looked up at her and grinned. "So we can quit thinking about me and girls now?"

"You're a rotten kid." Polly laughed and swatted at his shoulder. "You go on and help your buddies."

"I still don't know why I tell you everything that I tell you," Jason said, standing up. "But thanks."

Polly stepped in and gave him a hug. "I still love you so much it makes my heart hurt sometimes," she said. "I can't tell you how proud I am of you and who you're growing up to be."

She moved away before she made herself cry. "Now go to work. I need to gather my dogs and head back to the house. Good luck with your love life." Polly laughed out loud and then walked toward the gate. "Obiwan, Han. Come on! Let's go inside."

CHAPTER FIVE

Yesterday's fall had been a little rougher than expected. Polly had managed to sleep through the night, but woke up stiff and sore. It was only a few blocks to the coffee shop and the walk would help stretch her muscles enough to get her through the day.

When she opened the front door of Sweet Beans, the scent of coffee and baking stopped her long enough to breathe in deeply.

"It's that good, isn't it," a woman said, passing Polly in the doorway as she was leaving.

Polly laughed, a little embarrassed. "Yes it is. And it never gets old."

"Good morning, Polly," Camille said. "Your regular?"

"Yes please." She looked around the room and didn't see any of her friends. "Sal been in yet this morning?"

"Not yet," Camille said, shaking her head. "But we should see her any minute now. She's gotten on a pretty regular schedule."

"I think she's trying to get organized for the baby."

Camille put Polly's drink on the counter. "Have you heard that her mother is coming in for the shower?"

Polly put her hand on the cup. "No way. When?"

"Friday afternoon, I think," Camille said. "She called Sal yesterday morning to tell her that the plane ticket had been purchased."

"Poor Sal."

Camille nodded. "It's my fault. At least Sal blames me. I sent the invitation, not even thinking for a minute she'd come to Iowa."

"Where's she staying?" Polly asked.

"Ask Sal yourself."

The front doorbell jangled and Polly turned around. Her best friend strode in the front door, tall and glorious in black slacks with a red blouse that showed off all of Sal's features, including the perfect pregnant belly she carried.

"Did she tell you?" Sal demanded. "Sylvie said you were having a bad day yesterday so I didn't call, but did she tell you?" Sal pointed at Camille. "Did you tell her?"

"I did," Camille said with a laugh. "How are you this morning?"

"No better than I was yesterday morning, that's for sure. Can you believe it? My mother is coming to Iowa. What kind of fresh hell will she bring with her? Decaf today, Camille. We had a rough night and I'm not introducing any caffeine into our system today. Calm and steady, that's the ticket."

"Calm and steady?" Polly asked.

"Yeah, yeah, yeah. That's what Mark said, too. He told me that I'm so freaked out by my mother's arrival that I'm chasing the baby around in its bedroom." She pointed at her belly. "Poor baby. It doesn't even know yet how insane this woman can be. All it is getting is my emotional backlash."

"It sounds strange to hear you call it an it," Polly said. "I can't believe you two don't want to know the baby's gender."

"I have few enough surprises in life." Sal snarled. "Except for my mother. Let me rephrase that. I have few enough fun surprises in my life that Mark and I agreed this would be one of them. I'm looking forward to it." Sal picked up her coffee. "Thanks, Camille. You're a life saver."

She grabbed Polly's hand and drew her over to a table. "Tell me I'm not a horrible daughter."

"You're not a horrible daughter," Polly said. "Why?"

"I don't want her at the house. I called Grey and reserved a room at the hotel."

Polly chuckled. "That makes sense. She would make you crazy if she stayed with you."

"And I'm telling her that she can't come back to Iowa until I've been home with the baby for a couple of weeks. Is that awful?"

"Will you get away with it?"

"I don't know. But Mark said he didn't want us to try to figure out how to take care of a baby and deal with her shenanigans all at the same time. His mother said she wasn't coming down until Bellingwood Days. She'll stay with Dylan and Lisa."

Dylan and Lisa Foster had moved down from the Ogden's home in Minnesota long before Mark moved into town. Dylan owned Pizzazz, the pizza place across the street from Sweet Beans and Lisa owned a dance studio in town.

"She's not coming for the shower this weekend?"

"Oh yeah," Sal said, nodding vigorously, then she rolled her eyes. "That ought to be a trip. His mother epitomizes class and my mother is a snob. Want to have dinner with us Saturday night and help me avoid the awkwardness of it all?"

"No thank you," Polly said. "I want no part of that. You should see if your dad wants to come this weekend, too."

"I asked. He wanted to know if it was important to me. Which, in essence, meant that he wanted a weekend of quiet. He's a rat, but I can hardly blame him. He has to put up with Mom every day."

"Well, I look forward to meeting Mrs. Ogden. And it will be..." she hesitated. "It will be good to see your mother again."

"Liar."

"Hey, she likes me."

Sal nodded. "Yes she does. Lucky you." She took a drink of the coffee and put it down with a grimace. "Horrible decaf stuff. I can't even convince myself any longer that its placebo effect works. Camille?" She waved and waited for Camille to smile. "I tried. Can I have some tea with no caffeine? I give up."

"Chamomile?" Camille asked.

"That's not funny. How about some of that lemon ginger you made for me last week." Sal turned back to Polly. "Do you see what I've been reduced to?"

"But you still feel good."

"Of course I do," Sal said. "Stupid body seems to like being well cared for. When I'm finished having children, I'll teach it, though. We'll go straight out to black coffee and whiskey, steaks, french fries and chocolate shakes."

Polly sat back. "Finished having children? There are going to be more?"

Sal leaned toward her, then stopped and put her hand on her belly. "Don't tell anyone, but I like this. A lot. And I refuse to make my poor child be alone in the family like I was. Mark and I think that three or four kids would be fun."

"I'm sorry, what?" Polly sputtered with laughter. "Three or four kids. You?"

"You don't think I can?" Sal asked.

"No!" Polly exclaimed. "That's not it at all. You'll be a fabulous mom."

"Then what?"

"I don't know. It's just that you were always so career oriented, I assumed you'd be strutting around in suits and high heels, kicking up a storm with all of the businessmen and women you encountered. Babies never seemed like they'd be a part of that."

"I see no reason to get rid of the suits and high heels and as for being career oriented, babies don't need to change that," Sal said.

"You're right, you're right. I don't know what I'm thinking."

"Honestly, Polly, I don't think there's any better place than Bellingwood to raise kids and have a career that suits me. I've been picking up more and more clients all the time and it's work I can do from here. There will be times I have to fly out of town for meetings, but I do most of it over video conferences, and heck, since a lot of the clients are all over the world, that works best for everyone."

"I always pictured you in a big office building, rushing here and there, taking cabs to meetings on the other side of the city, meeting clients in coffee shops around town. I just have to change my vision of who you are."

"Polly, honey, I've lived in Bellingwood for a long time now. I'll never be in that kind of corporate America."

"You're right. I told you, it's my own problem."

"So what are we going to do about my mom coming to town?"

"We?" Polly asked. "What we?"

"Will you show her around Sycamore House and take us over to the Bell House? I want her to see what you've been doing."

"Of course. How long is she staying?"

"Just until Monday morning. She has all of her meetings, you know. She can sacrifice a weekend for her daughter, but not much longer."

Polly laughed. "I thought you didn't even want her here."

"Don't contradict the pregnant lady," Sal said. She stood up. "I'll be right back. Don't go anywhere."

Sal was gone long enough that Polly took out her phone. A text message had come in from an unfamiliar number and when she opened the app, she read, *"We're fine. Don't try to find us."*

It had to be from Stephanie. Polly replied. *"We're worried. We can help. Please don't run away from us."*

She hoped for an immediate response, but in a few more moments, Sal returned, carrying her cup of tea.

"What are you looking at?" Sal asked.

"Nothing. Just hoping for a response to a text."

"New boyfriend?"

Polly chuckled. "No. It's enough dealing with the fifteen I'm managing right now."

"No kidding. But what's up? You look really concerned."

"I think I just got a message from Stephanie."

"Your Stephanie? Is something wrong over at Sycamore House?"

"I can't believe you haven't heard. She and Kayla are gone. Stephanie got a strange phone call, we think it's from her father who was in prison for killing their mother and molesting

Stephanie for years. He escaped. She packed up everything and left town. Nobody knows where they're going."

Sal's eyes got huge. "Those poor girls. Do you think he's on his way here?"

"My luck, of course he is," Polly said. "It's not that I want them to feel threatened, but I also don't want them to leave forever. Jeff feels like he lost his right arm and Rebecca is a wreck." She shook her head. "I sound really selfish, but Stephanie and Kayla are important to us and I'm furious that they have to go on the run because their father is a murdering psychopath."

"And you haven't heard back?" Sal pointed at Polly's phone.

"Nothing."

"Do you want to talk about it?"

Polly shook her head. "Not really. It is what it is. If she'll give me a chance to help, then I'll do everything I can."

"I know you will," Sal said. "So how are things at your new house?"

"Other than the hole I fell into? The ground dropped out from under me and I tumbled in on top of some very old bones and a whiskey still."

"On top of them?"

"No, just into the room with them. I can't do anything over there now until Henry finds someone to check the back yard for any more rooms or tunnels."

"Polly, I swear you get into the craziest things. Everything was calm and quiet when we had pizza Sunday night." Sal looked around. "Isn't this just Tuesday?"

"Yeah, yeah, yeah. Whatever."

Sal took another sip of her tea and grimaced. "This is awful, too. I give up. What are you doing this morning?"

"I don't know."

"Mr. Gardner has some things at his shop for me to look at. Do you want to go with me? He said he might have something adorable for the nursery. Mr. Specek is going to refinish anything I find to match the crib." She smiled at Polly. "I can't believe you did that for me. I feel like I'm getting an heirloom, not just a crib."

"If you're going to have three or four babies, at least it will get lots of use. And I know Bill was happy to do it. He and Marie never complain about not having grandbabies, but at some level, they were kind of looking forward to doing baby things." She sighed. "At least they have Jessie and Molly. That little girl gets knitted caps and scarves, blankets and all sorts of cute things."

"Does Marie knit for Rebecca and Heath?"

Polly laughed. "Oh my gosh, yes. Neither of them will ever have to buy blankets."

"I was thinking that someday I might want to learn how to sew. Do you think the ladies next door would teach me?" Sal asked.

"Shhh," Polly said. "I want to learn, too. Maybe we should all do a class together. Learn how to sew, make some quilts."

"Quilts? That's a lot! But if I could learn how to sew clothes for my kids…" Sal shook her head. "I think it's the nesting hormones talking. I'd be awful at sewing."

"No you wouldn't."

"Yes, Polly, I would. I'd get mad at it and fling the sewing machine out the front door into a snowbank or maybe an oncoming car. And that would be just trying to sew a straight line. But do you really want to learn?"

Polly nodded. "I really do. Have you ever looked at some of the fabric they have in there?"

"Yeah?"

"And touched it and thought about how it could go together?"

"No?" Sal was laughing by now. "But it sounds like you have."

"I don't even have a sewing machine. It never seemed like something I needed."

"Your mother didn't have one? My mom did and she never ever touched it."

"I don't think so. I've never seen it, but there are still a ton of boxes from Dad's house in the garage. I wouldn't have to spend a ton of money to get started. If I learned, I could make curtains for the windows at the house and placemats for the table and quilts and..." She looked at Sal. "Stop laughing at me."

"I love you, sweetie, but are you kidding me with this?"

Polly frowned at her. "I don't have anything that I do. Rebecca sketches. Henry and Heath love working on cars. Andrew writes stories. You have a baby to plan for. Marie tried to teach me how to knit and I nearly poked her eye out with a knitting needle. I need something else."

"Because the new house isn't enough? Polly, you are going all the time. It's okay if you are idle for an hour in the evening. Come on. Let's go over to the antique shop and look around. Maybe you'll find something you absolutely need for your house." Sal picked up her two cups and carried them back to the sink behind the counter and dumped them out, then tossed them in the trash. "Sorry, Camille. My taste buds and I are having a disagreement this morning and they're winning."

Camille smiled. "Did I hear you say you're going over to the antique shop?"

"Yeah, are you looking for something?"

"I have a space about twenty-four inches wide that needs a small table or pedestal. If you see anything fun, text me a picture, would you?"

Sal glanced sideways at Polly. "Dang, I have to shop. This might kill me!"

They walked down the street to the antique shop. The bell tinkled as they walked in and Simon Gardner came out from behind a display of dolls.

"Good morning, ladies."

"Hello, Mr. Gardner," Sal replied. "Did you have any luck?"

"It's right back here. Follow me." He led them into the depths of the store and stopped in front of a beautiful old rocker. Beside it sat a short dresser and a side table. "What do you think?"

Sal turned to Polly. "What do you think?"

"Beautiful. I love the rocker."

"I've always wanted one. My friend, Judy, had a rocker in her house, but Mom said they were a waste of space."

"Why would she say that?"

Sal shrugged. "I don't know. She didn't like them. But I thought they were peaceful. And if I'm going to have a baby, I want one so

I can sit and rock it back to sleep at night. How about lamps. Did you find any?"

"Not yet," he said. "But I'm not about to give up. Not when I have such a great customer."

"I want all of these pieces," Sal said. "They look pretty good right now. I wonder if they'll need much work. The finish I chose with Mr. Sturtz was a pretty walnut."

Simon Gardner patted the rocker. "That's what these are."

Sal sat down in the rocking chair and leaned back, then started it moving. "Oh my goodness, this is wonderful. I feel calmer already." She waved Polly off. "You wander around and browse. I'm going to stay right here and rest."

"Aren't you supposed to be looking for a table for Camille?" Polly asked with a laugh.

"You go look. I want to rock."

"What kind of a table?" Simon asked.

"She said she has a small space on a wall; about twenty-four inches," Polly said. "Or a pedestal."

"I don't know how much she wants to spend, but I just brought in a beautiful glove chest. It's eighteen inches wide and about thirty-six inches tall. It's quite delightful."

"Let's see it," Polly said. "I'll send her a picture." She looked back at Sal as they walked away. "She really likes the rocking chair."

"I brought that in especially for her," he said. "She's become quite a good customer and understands the worth of beautiful pieces." He stopped and put his hand on a small cherry chest of drawers.

"This is a glove chest?" Polly asked. "I've never seen anything like it."

"It is meant to be placed near your front door to hold gloves and scarves. Many homes had a beautiful mirror hanging on the wall above it so you could ensure you were prepared before you left the house."

Polly sighed. "If she doesn't want it, I do."

He chuckled. "You have one already. It's in the attic of your home. It needs a little work, but would be a very pretty piece once it's restored."

Simon Gardner had spent several weekends digging around in the Bell House this last spring, cataloging the furniture and other items. Polly still hadn't managed to pull everything out that needed to be restored. The garage was filled with furniture she needed to make decisions about and that was just from the rooms on the main floor. Bill Sturtz and Len Specek had taken apart the bedsteads on the second floor, stripped them down and were refinishing them. The dressers and chests of drawers, vanities and other bedroom furniture were in a storage unit waiting to be cleaned up. It was all so overwhelming, Polly usually just ignored it.

"I think I took on too much with that house," she said. She snapped a picture and sent a text to Camille with the cost and a quick description.

"I'm sure it feels that way," he said. "My advice would be for you to move in and fix the rooms one by one. Then one day, you'll find that each room has become part of your family, just like the people who live there."

"That's awfully philosophical for someone who doesn't have to do the work," Polly said.

He laughed. "Yes it is. If I were a younger man, I would offer to assist you, but all I can do is advise you these days."

Sal grabbed Polly's arm, startling both of them when Polly jumped. "I need to head back to the coffee shop right now," Sal said. "Let's go." She nodded at Simon. "Write up a ticket for all of it and I'll be in tomorrow with a check. Thank you!"

She rushed Polly out of the shop.

"Why are we in such a hurry?"

"Because I need to go to the bathroom again. Now, come on. Move it!"

CHAPTER SIX

Stephanie hadn't replied yet, which was disappointing. The girl had been in the middle of some wildest thing at Sycamore House, but surely she realized everything always worked out in the end. Polly rolled her shoulder. Even if Polly took a few bumps and bruises along the way. The walk up to the coffee shop had helped and now, walking home, she was starting to feel more normal.

Traffic whizzed past Polly on the highway. She waved at a few people she recognized, then crossed to the Sycamore House corner garden when a break came. She sat on the bench and listened to the water trickling and moving in the pond. Spring had come early enough that the local gardeners had already planted and flowers were blooming.

Today was a perfect day. The sun beamed down, warming her face while a breeze brushed against her. Polly shut her eyes and allowed the moment to surround her. This was such a peaceful location and Polly never spent enough time out here. There was always something to do, or she was walking with dogs who loved tearing into the ground. Since Polly wasn't confident enough to replant anything, it was easier to just avoid it.

A horn honking drew her attention and she looked up to see Ralph Bedford waving from his wonderful orange truck. He was so proud of the paint job on that truck. She grinned. You could see that man coming from a mile away. She waved back and watched him head out of town. It was still surprising to Polly that she was part of this community. Even after four years, the ease with which people lived around each other was remarkable. Some days she felt as if she belonged here and was a part of the community, but there were still too many days like today when Polly felt separated from it all; as if she was gliding across the top of the town, dipping her feet in every once in a while, barely touching the activities and people.

Maybe it was the Bell House. During these last few months, when she'd spent hours and hours there, she'd been transported to a different era. Furniture and accessories all came from days long before she was born. And landing in a room with a body that came from generations past and a still that existed in her home's history was surreal. Polly barely remembered what she'd learned in high school and college regarding Prohibition.

There were evenings when her father would talk about the things that he'd experienced during his lifetime, things that Polly read about in history books. They'd gotten a good laugh at that. He told her about looking up at the sky in July of 1969 and feeling excitement and wonder as Neil Armstrong walked on the moon, and about his shock and revulsion at the news of Martin Luther King's death.

Where were the people who would have known about Prohibition in Bellingwood? Polly laughed at herself. The Bell House was one hundred years old. They were no longer living. But maybe there were people around whose parents had talked about those days. Beryl's Great-Aunt Evaline would have remembered the opening of the Bell House, but she never said anything to Beryl about it. She hoped Lucy's husband would be able to help.

It frustrated Polly that people didn't write out their memories before they died. Her dad hadn't given Polly enough stories before he was gone. So much history was lost the day he died. And for that matter, so much of Rebecca's history had been erased with her mother's death last year.

"Was that really a year ago?" Polly asked out loud. How did time move so quickly? Rebecca only had a few weeks left of being a seventh-grader and then only a year before she went to high school. Heath had just one year left before he was off to college.

Polly sat forward and dropped her head into her hands. She heard Henry in her head telling her to relax and take a breath. There was no need to rush time along any faster than it was already moving. And if she worried about losing the kids, she'd miss out on all that they had to offer right now.

"I hate it when you're right," she muttered, standing up. She waved at Eliseo, who was mowing the lawn behind the garage.

Walking to the front door, she picked up a few pieces of trash that had blown up onto the sidewalk and kicked bits of mulch back into the garden beds surrounding the building. A large number of cars in the parking lot told her something was going on inside. She didn't want to go into the office and meet one more person, but then she mentally kicked herself. Making those connections were the anchors that tied her to Bellingwood. The new receptionist was a friend of Rachel's, but Polly was darned if she could remember the name.

"Hello, Ms. Giller," the girl said. "How are you today?"

"I'm fine, thank you." Polly put her hand out. "I'm sorry. I don't remember what Rachel told me your name was."

"Kristen," the girl said. "Kristen Travis."

"It's nice to meet you, Kristen. Is Jeff in?" Polly pointed at the closed door that led to Jeff's office. "Does he have someone with him?"

"No. He's just working. I can buzz him if you'd like."

"I'll knock." Polly knocked on Jeff's office door and heard a gruff "Come in," so she slipped in and shut the door behind her.

"It's you," he said.

"Is that a bad thing?"

"No. I'm sorry. I'm frustrated."

"With Kristen?" Polly pointed toward the main office.

"Oh no," he said, shaking his head. "She's fine. I can't think, though. I keep worrying about Stephanie and Kayla. I wish they'd call and tell me that they're alive."

"I got this," Polly said. She swiped her phone to the text message she'd received and put it on the desk in front of him. "It has to be her. I sent a message right back, but she hasn't replied."

"The girl is killing me," he whined. "I don't want to be selfish about this, but does she know what she's doing to us?"

"I doubt she's thinking about anything but what's frightening her so badly. Her tunnel vision is completely focused on getting her and Kayla out of danger."

"Put a gun in my hand," he said, gritting his teeth. "I'll take care of that danger for her."

Polly smiled. Of all of her friends, Jeff was the last person she thought she'd ever see with a gun. But who knew? With as much fury as he felt right now, it might be a good idea for Stephanie's father to fear for his life. "Let's hope it doesn't come to that."

He gave a quick shake of his head, as if to clear the fog. "We have so much going on right now and I need her. When I'm out on a limb, Stephanie holds on to my pants leg so I don't fall off."

"Use this number," Polly said, showing her phone to him again. "Keep telling her those things. Make sure she understands how important she is to you ... to us. Remind her that Bellingwood is her home and we're her family." She tapped her index finger on the desk twice to get his attention. "But maybe you don't whine at her about how tough she's making your life."

"But she is." Jeff intentionally overdid his whine and leaned back. "I know, I know. You're right. I have an extra room in my apartment. She and Kayla could move in with me until this man is found and tossed back in prison. He'd never find my place. Hell, I'd let her work from there if she wanted to. And Kayla could just be sick or something while she took time off from school. Yes?"

"Anything you want," Polly said. "For now, though, keep communicating with Stephanie and hope that eventually she'll talk to you."

"At least I have hope now." Jeff clicked his mouse and said, "I talked to her landlord. She's paid up until the end of the month."

"What did you tell him?"

"Just that she had an emergency and had to leave town for a couple of weeks."

"And he didn't think that was odd?"

Jeff laughed. "Maybe, but when I told him that if anything came up while she was gone, I'd take care of it, he quit asking questions. He's probably heard stranger things. Dang, I want to get her out of that place and into something that looks nice to begin with. It would be good if she and Kayla could spend their money on fun decorations rather than trying to cover up crummy carpet on the floor, dingy walls and ugly linoleum."

"Stephanie is pretty frugal. She isn't going to make the move until she's completely ready."

"I know that," he groused. "That makes her really good around here, but she should do better for herself. I know they can afford it."

Polly shook her head. "Not if she's hiding that kind of money in the wall of her trailer. She's been socking that away rather than spending it."

"I hate that man for doing this to her," Jeff said. "And I'm not too happy with her mother for letting it happen."

"Some people can't hold up under that kind of pressure," Polly said quietly.

"But they were her daughters. She's supposed to protect them."

Polly just looked at him and smiled.

"I know. I know. Being angry at a dead woman who had no options doesn't help the situation. Is that what you're trying to tell me?" He stood up and paced over to the front window. "How are things coming over at the Bell House? Are you going to be ready to have people there for the sesquicentennial celebration?"

She wasn't prepared for the change in conversation and took a quick breath. "I don't know. I don't even know what we should be doing."

"Did you really find an old still?" he asked, turning to face her.

"Yeah and a tunnel leading back to the house."

"Maybe you should turn the front foyer into a speakeasy. The committee isn't limiting things to what happened a hundred and fifty years ago. We're celebrating the whole history of Bellingwood."

She nodded thoughtfully. "But I can't serve liquor without a license and I don't want to push Henry to finish something just so we can have a party. He's really busy. Since I fell in that hole, I don't even know if we can open the back yard to people until he's made sure it's safe. The front of the house looks pitiful without a porch and the back of the house is just destroyed. The only reason the inside doesn't look awful is because we haven't started tearing the walls out."

"You're scaring me," Jeff said.

"Scaring you? I'm terrified that I forced Henry into buying a money pit. When I think of all the things we have to do to bring that house around, I want to crawl back into that hole and hide my head. There isn't enough time left in my life to get that place to where it should be."

"Exaggerate much?" he asked.

"No. I can't do what needs to be done there and Henry is too busy to commit to it. We're never going to move in." Polly waved her hand. "I don't want to think about it. What's happening here during the sesquicentennial? Shouldn't I know about this?"

He laughed. "You'll know when you need to, but Stephanie had a great idea..." Jeff's voice trailed off. "Damn. She was really working hard on it, too."

"What is it?"

"We're turning the classrooms into classrooms from history. One will be set in the late eighteen hundreds, one in the nineteen fifties or sixties and then the computer room is going to be set up with all sorts of futuristic tech. She asked Elise for a contact at Iowa State and they're going to help us design some advanced presentation type of technology in there. After it's over, we're donating that to the elementary school in town."

"Miss Bickle-Pickle?" Polly asked. "She's going to let you?"

"She couldn't refuse such a great offer. Especially when the head of the school board is on my committee."

"Perfect. Are we doing the quilt show again?"

Jeff took a deep breath. "It's gotten too big, even for us. Especially if we want to do anything else. They're splitting it up this year among several different venues. Church sanctuaries and the elementary gymnasium will be the main showrooms. Most of the church halls will be serving food at one point or other throughout the week, and nobody wants food around those quilts."

"What are we doing in the auditorium?" Polly asked.

"It will be wild," he said. "Square dancing a couple of nights, regular dances on other evenings. One night will be a western-themed banquet." He shook his head. "Stephanie was working on all of that, too, getting people lined up to decorate during the day so we'd be ready in the evening. What am I going to do?"

"She's coming back," Polly said. "You have to believe that."

Jeff waggled his hand at the door. "You go now. I have a million things that I need to keep working on. The guys at the garage over there," he pointed northwest and Polly knew kind of where he was talking about. "One of them has an uncle who is a blacksmith and they want to set up a working smithy, but don't know where to find what they need." He laughed out loud. "Me. Talking to big, burly men about all of this. Tell me that isn't the funniest thing you've heard today."

"It's close," she said, standing up. "Tell me if you need me to do something."

"I need you to bring Stephanie back."

"I'll keep working on it." Polly put her hand on the door handle, turned back to say something more and stopped herself when she realized that he had already picked up his phone and was dialing. She waved, walked out and pulled the door shut.

"Miss Giller?" Kristen asked.

"Yes."

"Is he busy? I had, like, four phone calls come in while you were talking to him. Should I bother him?"

"Tap lightly on the door," Polly said, "Open it and slip the notes on his desk. And if he growls, he's just stressed. He doesn't mean it and will feel bad later."

"Stephanie leaving really messed things up, didn't it?" the girl asked.

"Jeff has grown to depend on her. I don't think any of us knew exactly how much." Polly held her hand out. "Here, give me the notes. I'll give them to him."

Kristen smiled in relief and handed her several slips of paper. Polly tapped on Jeff's door and opened it before he could say anything. He was still on the telephone, so she put the notes in front of him and backed out again, then walked back to Kristen's desk.

"He hasn't shown you how to send him information directly, has he?"

"What?"

"Just send him an email with each phone call you take." Polly pointed at the calendar. "Open that up and you should see his task list. Put each call and the number on the list with the time it came in. He lives off that thing, so he'll see everything you add to it."

"Thank you. He said something about the task list, but I didn't know what he wanted me to do."

"If you're here very long, he'll show you the rest of the programs we use to share information. It's pretty cool. But don't worry, he understands."

Before Polly could walk away again, Kristen put her hand out. "I have one more question."

"Okay?" Polly chuckled. "What else?"

"He said something about putting in hotel reservations if they call here, but I don't know how to do that either."

"Has anyone called?"

"Not yet. What should I do?"

Polly pointed at the phone. "Did he show you how to transfer a call over there?"

Kristen looked up at her wide-eyed. "I can send a call to the hotel? He showed me how to forward a call to him and the kitchen." She paused. "And to the barn, I guess. But I don't know how to send one to a whole different number."

"Don't worry about that today. That's a tomorrow thing at the very earliest." Polly looked around the desk and found a slip of paper. She wrote the phone number of the hotel down and said, "If you get a call for the hotel, just tell them to call there directly. Grey has enough help; they can handle a few extra phone calls this week."

The technology transformation that had taken place in the office at Sycamore house had happened over time and they'd all learned to adapt and use whatever they needed. Polly hadn't thought about trying to train someone new on things they used regularly. Jeff would have thought of it if he wasn't so distracted by Stephanie leaving.

"Thank you," Kristen said.

"Please don't be intimidated by all of this," Polly said. "It will come to you."

"By the time I learn it all, your regular girl will be back."

"We hope she'll be back soon, but it's nice to have someone else know what to do around here. Tell me, Kristen, do you like doing temp work?"

"I want a full-time job, but this is nice for now. At least I mostly work in Bellingwood this way. My little girl stays with my sister and her kids during the day. If I'm in town, I don't have to drop her off really early and sometimes I even go have lunch there."

"That's great," Polly said. She turned around and tapped on Jeff's door again.

"Yes?" he called out.

"It's me again," Polly said and slipped back inside.

"What now?"

She shut the door and sat back down. "Kristen needs a little more training," Polly said with a smile.

"I know, I know. Stephanie would usually do that kind of work."

"I have an idea and you're going to think I'm nuts, but hear me out," Polly said.

"What?"

"Stephanie needs a raise."

He chuckled. "I'm on board with that."

"She's doing a lot more than just reception work, isn't she?"

He nodded.

"Make her your assistant and have her start training someone to do her job. Maybe even Kristen."

"That's not a bad idea. She's doing so much more than when she started."

"Give her my office," Polly said.

"Wait. What? No. You need your office. We discussed moving the conference room over to the classrooms and turning that into a couple of offices."

"I'm hardly ever in my office these days," Polly said. "That's not really the way I work anymore. I can use Henry's office upstairs if I need to. Stephanie and I can talk about some of the bookkeeping functions that I usually do. She can take more of that on and all I have to do is go through what she puts in front of me and approve it. Right?"

"I suppose." Jeff wasn't totally on board with this yet, she could tell.

"Think about it." Polly smiled. "Maybe everything changes next year when we move out. Maybe we put the offices upstairs in the apartment and open the whole downstairs up to customers. Dream big, think way outside the box. What else would you like to do in our little empire?" She rubbed her hands together. "To the dark side I shall not turn, so great power we have at our hands."

He laughed. "Let's go slowly, though."

"Not too slowly," Polly said. "When Stephanie comes back, promote her and give her my office. We'll pack my knick-knacks up and store them for now. But she is coming back. Right?"

"That's a heck of a bonus for running away," he said.

Polly glared and Jeff put his hands up defensively. "I know, I know. I'm being good. It's the right thing to do. Let's just get her back home where she belongs."

CHAPTER SEVEN

Polly was growing nervous about getting the Bell House ready for the summer celebration. Now she had something else to think about. Moving out of her office was one thing, but the idea that she could turn her home upstairs into the offices for Sycamore House was really interesting. When she walked through the front door, she stopped and looked around. The space was immense and could be used in so many ways.

Han yapped at her while Obiwan paced at her feet. "I know. I know," she said. "You never get enough attention." Polly walked through to her bedroom and found the two cats curled up on the bed in a sunbeam. "You two are slugs."

She changed into her sloppy yardwork clothes and headed for the back door. When the dogs followed, she stopped them. "Not this time. One of these days you'll live there, but not yet."

Obiwan lay down on the floor in front of Henry's desk and put his head on his paws. Han, as always, didn't get it and followed her to the top of the steps. "Stay," Polly commanded. He gave her the saddest eyes he had and stood in place. "You're killing me," she said. "Go play with the rest of the animals, you aren't going with me." She pointed at Obiwan. Han gave another yap and sat down to watch her leave. This was the part she hated the most about coming home in the middle of the day and then leaving. They always made her feel guilty about that whole leaving again thing.

When she got to the house, she wasn't surprised to still see people working in the back yard. She knew better than to try to do anything back there, so she grabbed up her pruning shears, gloves and shovel to start working on the mess in the side yard. As she walked past the front door, Polly stopped and looked up at the house. "One of these days, you and I will be friends, but right now you're the bane of my existence."

Just before Polly turned the corner, she heard a large truck pull in and turned back to see who it was. It surprised her to see the name of a lumber company on the door and a huge load of lumber on the flatbed. She could barely contain the grin on her face as she walked back across the yard.

"Hello," she called out to the driver.

"Are you Ms. Giller?" he asked.

"Yes I am." She was a little confused as to how he knew she'd be here.

"Your husband ordered this and we're supposed to drop it in front of the house. Okay if we walk across the yard?"

Polly looked at the sad excuse for a lawn and nodded. "Sure. What is this?"

"It looks like you need a porch." He gestured at the open space. "There's enough here to make a very nice porch." He handed her a clipboard. "Since you're here, do you mind signing for it?"

She took the clipboard and backed up out of the way as they started pulling things from the back of the truck.

"What did you do?" she texted to Henry.

His response was immediate. *"Got a delivery there?"*

"How did you know I'd be here?"

"I told Gus to drop it in front of the house whether you were there or not."

"It's a porch, right?" she texted back.

"And there should be some windows with the delivery, too."

Polly watched those get unloaded and stacked against the house. *"I think I love you."*

"I know."

She chuckled. That would never get old. *"Thank you for this."*

"You're going to have to paint it."

"I'll do anything."

"Anything? I'm up for anything."

"You bet'cha, baby," she texted. *"Name the time and place and I'll be ready."*

"You're killing me. I have to get back to work."

"Ms. Giller?"

"Are you Gus?" she asked.

He smiled. "Talked to your husband, did you? He said this was going to be a surprise for you." Gus looked around, taking in the house. "There's a lot of work ahead for you here. Good thing you have someone like Henry to do it."

"I know," she responded, handing him back his clipboard. "And it's a good thing we aren't in any hurry. Henry has a lot of other things that will take precedence."

Gus laughed. "If you're looking for another contractor, I know a few in the area." He gave her a toothy grin. "Make sure you tell Sturtz I said that, okay?"

"I will. Thanks so much. You guys made my day."

"Any time we can make a pretty lady's day by dropping a load of lumber in her yard is a good day for us, ma'am."

Polly watched them back out and drive away, then wandered over to the pile of lumber. She wanted to pat it and tell it how happy she was that it was here, but thought that might be too much.

Another truck pulling into the driveway drew her attention. Polly had no idea what GPR stood for, so she waited for the young man to get out. She began to feel a little foolish when he didn't open the door right up and she realized that he was texting or checking email or doing something on his phone. So, she sent another text to Henry.

"What's GPR?"

"Nice timing," he sent back.

"What is it?"

"Ground penetrating radar. Barry owes me a favor. He's going to check the yard for more underground rooms."

"Really? This fast?"

"Tell me what you're doing at the house today?"

Polly wondered why he was asking. *"I was going to start ripping into the shrubs on the side of the house."*

"Exactly. You are on a mission and I can't keep you out of that place. It's easier to just get on it and know you're safe."

"Oh." She chuckled. He really did know her well. *"He's finally getting out of his truck. I'll talk to you later."* Polly sent the text and walked over to the young man who had studiously ignored her as he opened the back of his pickup.

"Hello there," she said. "Are you Barry?"

He stuck his head around the truck and said, "You Henry's wife?"

"I am. He says you're checking for underground rooms."

"Yeah. He told me you fell in one yesterday. Don't want that happening again. I'll check for telephone and cable while I'm here. Might as well know where everything is."

"You probably won't find much," Polly said. "No one's lived here since the nineteen-forties."

He nodded and stuck his head back into the truck.

"I'll be around," Polly said. "Let me know if you need anything." She waited a moment for a response and when none came, walked away.

"Chatty fellow," she texted to Henry.

He came back with, *"LOL."*

"You're chatty too," she muttered. "I hate texting that man when he's busy."

Two hours later, Polly retreated to her truck for something to drink and a break from the heat. Barry hadn't said anything to her yet and she had no idea how long he was planning to work. There was no way she was leaving before him, just in case he had interesting information to reveal. The door to her truck stood open and she rolled the window down on the passenger side. The cool breeze was relaxing and she leaned her head back and shut her eyes. Just for a minute.

"Are you Miss Giller?"

Polly popped her eyes open and sat up straight. "Hello there," she said and put her hand out. "Yes I am."

"My name is Pat Lynch," the older woman said. "I haven't had a chance to get down to meet you since we got back from Florida last month." She nodded down the street. "We live just around the corner there in the brown house with red shutters."

Polly nodded. "You spend winters in Florida?"

"Every year," the woman said with a smile. "But we miss home and our friends, so as long as we can make the trip back and forth, we will. Betty said you all bought this old place. It looks like you've taken on quite a task. It's about time someone decided to do something. My Albert used to trim the bushes along the sidewalk until he couldn't do that any longer. Don't know why the city didn't take better care of it." She chuckled. "Maybe they were scared of the ghost. That was quite a lot of excitement last fall."

"Did you know Mr. Bridger?" Polly asked.

"I sure did. His mama, too. Me and Albert, we've been married and living in our house for fifty-three years. We raised three kids and now we have eight grandkids and three great grandchildren. They're one of the best reasons for coming back to Iowa. Well," she said. "One of our granddaughters lives in Tampa. She has two babies, so we see her during the winter. Betty says you have a couple of older kids. But they aren't yours. Did you adopt them?"

Polly watched helplessly as Barry put his equipment in his truck. Without so much as a look her way, he climbed back into the driver's seat, backed out, and drove off. She turned her attention back to the woman standing in front of her. "Yes, we adopted both of them. Rebecca is in seventh grade and Heath is a junior in high school."

"It will be nice to have more young people in the neighborhood. We got old around here. But there is another young family that just moved in last summer. They're on the next block over, though. They have two little boys who go to the elementary school. Wilkens is their last name. Say, you look like you've gotten warm. Would you like to come over for something cool to drink? I'd love to have you meet my Albert. He doesn't get around as good as me these days, but he's still a witty man. I have to do all the driving. He'd put us in a ditch, mark my words. The government took away his driving license last year. Said his eyesight was going. I think it was just an excuse to make sure he doesn't drive. But that's okay. I can get us wherever we need to go. We have a cute little golfcart to drive around down in Florida." She chuckled. "It's kind of like a playground down there for old folks. Nobody drives those carts very fast, so if we run into each other, we just play bumper cars and bounce off."

"I'd love to stop by sometime, but not today," Polly said when the woman took a breath. "I need to go back to Sycamore House."

"Any time you'd like to meet my Albert or say hello, please feel free. We're just around the corner there in the brown house. It has red shutters, you know. Albert painted them before he had that last stroke. He came back pretty good from it, but doesn't get around like he used to. I suppose the next time we have the house painted, we'll have to hire it out." Mrs. Lynch put her hand on the truck as she turned herself around. "Stop by sometime. We'd love to see you," she called out as she walked away.

Polly pulled the truck door shut and breathed out, "Oh my. What a riot. And now, because I said I would, I have to leave." She backed out of the driveway, shaking her head. "I didn't talk to the people who are doing archeology in my back yard and I didn't talk to Barry."

She drove away from the house, confused at what to do next. It wasn't often that people got the better of her, but it had certainly happened today. Going home and leaving the dogs again was not an option. Once per day was her limit on that guilt. Heading for the coffee shop wasn't a good option either. She was a mess. Between the sweat, dirt and weeds, Polly didn't feel like she was appropriate for human consumption.

Wending her way through town to the highway, Polly headed west and then south to Boone. She dug down into the console and found a bottle of antibacterial hand wash that she'd jammed in there not long after Henry gave her the truck. That and a few napkins later, she was at least presentable enough to go through a drive-thru and make a quick trip to Hy-Vee to look at flowers.

That was a joke. They'd probably die before she even got them back to Bellingwood. She and Eliseo had a conversation about hardy plants. If they couldn't live on their own, he'd just be subjecting them to an early grave by leaving them in her care.

Every time she drove on this road, it brought a smile to her face. The fields were coming alive with crops, the ditches were green again and the sky was bright blue with a few puffy clouds.

Polly slowed to avoid something in the road ahead of her and then screeched to a stop as she got closer. She turned her flashers on, jumped out of the truck, and took out her phone as she ran around the front to the person half on the road and the shoulder.

"Hello, Polly?" Aaron asked tentatively.

"I'm on R-27. There's someone lying on the road." Polly closed the distance, looking around to see where they'd come from.

"Are they alive?"

"I don't know yet," she said. "Just a second." She knelt down beside the young woman and reached out to touch her. "She's still warm. I'm looking for a pulse." Polly brushed the woman's hair back from her neck and pressed her fingers on the carotid artery. "I can't find a pulse, Aaron, but I'm not sure. She's really beat up. I don't know if she was hit by a car or what, though."

"Someone's on the way. Can you stay with her?"

"Of course I can."

The young woman jerked and Polly jumped. "She just jerked. Tell me that isn't a dead person convulsion or something," Polly gasped into the phone.

"I don't think so. Check her again," he said.

"Miss, can you hear me?" Polly asked, leaning back in. There was no response, but she saw the girl's eyelids flutter. "Aaron, she's alive. Tell them to hurry."

"Don't move," Polly said, touching the girl's arm. "I'm going to get some blankets."

A low moan was the only response as Polly ran back to the truck. "Aaron, can I talk to you later? I need my hands."

"I'll be there as soon as I can."

Polly scrambled into the back seat of her truck and yanked out the towels and blankets she kept back there for the dogs. This was the second time she'd used them for something like this. She was never leaving the house without a pile of these again. She backed out of the truck and looked up as another vehicle slowed down to a stop behind her.

"Are you okay?" a young man asked, getting out of the passenger seat. He took in the scene in front of her truck and rushed up. "Can I help you? Did you hit her?"

"No," Polly said. "I just found her. The ambulance is on the way. I've already called the sheriff." She handed him a blanket. "We need to keep her warm. Take this and cover her legs."

"What happened?" a woman asked, running up. "Oh! The poor girl. Do you know who it is?"

Polly didn't say anything, just began layering towels across the girl's torso while looking her over. Bruises covered her face and upper arms, like a beating gone horribly bad. As the young man placed the blanket across her legs, he and Polly grimaced at each other over the cuts and bruises below her shorts.

"Help me," a weak voice cracked.

"I'm right here. My name is Polly Giller and I've called the sheriff. They'll be here to take care of you in a few minutes."

"Am I dead?"

"No honey, you're very much alive. I wasn't sure there for a minute, though."

"Polly Giller?"

Nervous laughter bubbled out of Polly. "Apparently, I find live people who need me, too," she said. "Don't worry. You're going to be fine." She sat down on the highway in front of the girl and slid her hand under the girl's hand that was resting on the asphalt. "Can you tell me your name?" Polly asked.

There was no response, so Polly lifted her hand, raising the girl's arm, which sent tremors through her body. Something was broken there, the pain waking the girl back up.

"What's your name, honey," Polly asked quietly, leaning in.

"Lynn."

"Lynn, as far as I know, you need to try to stay awake until the ambulance gets here. You scare me when you drift off."

"Sorry," Lynn whispered.

"No need to be sorry. I just want you to be okay. Did you get hit by a car?"

Tears leaked from the girl's eyes. "No."

"Are you from around here?"

"No," Lynn said.

It was obvious to Polly that Lynn didn't want to answer questions about what had happened, but Polly wanted to keep her talking. Then it occurred to Polly that if Lynn knew about her history with dead bodies, she'd just lied.

"What's your name?" Polly asked the young man, who was probably in high school.

He looked up at the woman, as if to ask for permission. She nodded after checking her watch.

"I'm Josh Kramer. This is my mom, Madeline."

"Thanks for stopping, Josh. This is Lynn."

He looked at Polly, then said. "Nice to meet you, Lynn. I'm sorry you're hurt."

"Are you from Bellingwood, Josh?" Polly asked.

His mother bent forward. "No, we're from Stratford. We had an appointment in Boone. But we're going to be too late for it now. I should call them." She walked back toward her car.

"I'm going to DMACC this fall," Josh said.

"Yeah? What kind of courses."

"Civil Engineering. I want to work outside." He breathed. "But I'm not a farmer. Dad drives a truck."

"That's great," Polly said. "I really appreciate that you stopped." She looked up and back toward Boone as she finally heard sirens. "Do you hear that, Lynn? Everything is going to be okay."

The girl had closed her eyes again and Polly couldn't see that she was breathing. "Lynn? Wake up. You have to talk to me. Come on, Lynn. Say something."

The ambulance and emergency truck pulled over in front of Polly's truck, with Aaron's SUV right behind. Two EMTs jumped out and ran over to Polly.

"She was talking to us and now there's nothing," Polly said, standing up to make way.

Josh stood up as well and stepped around the girl, nearly losing his balance on the grass at the edge of the shoulder. He looked down at the ditch and gave Polly a wry smile.

Polly watched Aaron walk toward them and moved around the vehicles to get to him. She was thankful this had happened here and not on one of the busier highways. They'd be fairly safe from oncoming traffic.

"What's happened, Polly?" he asked, looking at the EMTs who were working over the girl.

"We were talking and a few minutes later, she wasn't." Polly reached out and took his sleeve. "I thought I had her."

"Did she say anything?" he asked.

"Her name is Lynn. That's all I got. She has to be okay."

One of the EMTs turned to Aaron and gave him a slight nod in the negative.

"No," Polly moaned and sagged against him.

"Who is that?" Aaron asked Polly.

She turned to see Josh and his mother standing in the shade of her truck. Madeline had pulled her son close, wrapping her arms around him as they watched the scene unfold.

"They're from Stratford and just stopped to help me. I don't know their last name," Polly said. "Just good people."

"I'm going to talk to them. Go sit in your truck. Call your husband. Take a deep breath or two."

Polly's legs felt like lead weights as he walked her back to her truck. Aaron opened the door and gave her a hand as she climbed in. She leaned back again and shut her eyes. This was going to be a hell of a week.

CHAPTER EIGHT

Opening the door to her truck, Polly climbed in, shut the door, and leaned back against the seat. She watched the frenetic activity on the highway in front of her and found herself holding back tears. The sound of a sharp rap on the passenger window made her jump and she waited while Aaron climbed in with her.

"Will you be okay to drive home?" he asked.

She sat forward and rearranged herself in the seat so that she looked like she was more alert. "Yeah. It's only a few miles."

"This is different than you've ever faced before. Are you sure? I can get one of my boys up here to drive you back into town."

"Thomas Zeller died in my arms," she said. "None of it's ever really easy. Everybody thinks it's no big deal for me."

"That's because you want them to think that, Polly," Aaron said quietly. He took her hand in his and squeezed it. "You don't want anyone to feel sorry for you."

"You're right, there," she said. "They have their own things to deal with. I can handle this, but sometimes I need..." She paused. "I don't know what I need. My life moves too fast for me to sit around and feel sorry for myself. I didn't want to go home because if I leave again, the animals will make me feel guilty. The kids will be back in a while and I won't let them see me fall apart over this. Especially with Stephanie and Kayla gone. Rebecca doesn't need to worry about me. The truth is, I'll be fine. I just need a few minutes to huddle into a ball by myself and fall apart."

"Do you want me to call Lydia? She’d love to see you."

Polly smiled at him and shook her head. "Thank you, but I really will be okay and I'm sorry I said anything. I just wasn't expecting her to die." She gestured with her head at the car parked behind them. "How's the kid doing?"

"He'll be fine, too. I don't think he even knew what was going on. Thank you for letting him help, though. That will be a good memory for him - that he at least did something."

"I've never seen the girl in Bellingwood," Polly said. "Did you recognize her?"

"No. She isn't familiar. All she gave you was a first name?"

"Yeah. Lynn. But she knew that I found dead bodies. She recognized my name, so she has to be from around the area. Right?" Polly liked the feeling of his big hand around hers. He was calm and steady as she worked to regain her sense of stability.

Aaron nodded and looked up as one of the emergency workers waved to him. "I need to talk to these guys before they leave. Are you sure you're okay to drive?"

"It's only a few miles," Polly said with a reassuring smile. "I'll go straight home." She took her hand back, then said, "Oh. I think I heard from Stephanie this morning."

"You did?" Aaron had his hand on the door handle, but stopped to look at her. "Did she call?"

"No, I got a text from an odd number telling us they were okay and not to look for them. I've given the number to Jeff so he can keep texting her."

"All you need to do is communicate. We will do everything we can to keep her and her sister safe if they come back."

"I know that and so will we. Jeff offered to have her move into his apartment with him until this is settled."

"We're already keeping an eye out in case her father shows up.

Everybody is watching for him." Aaron waved back at the EMT. "I need to go now. You should be able to turn around."

Polly looked into the rear view mirror and saw the car behind her drive away. "Thanks, Aaron. I'll be fine."

"I'll call later to check on you," he said and got out of the truck.

As Polly backed away from the scene to turn around, it struck her that in less than an hour, people would travel this part of the road and never know what had just happened. Life was so fragile. In mere moments, that poor girl was gone. If Polly hadn't been there, she'd have died alone.

"One set of bones would have been more than enough," she muttered. "Can I be finished now for a while?" She came to a stop, then turned the corner leading to Bellingwood. When Polly drove into the garage, she turned the truck off and opened the door. Jumping down to the floor, she was surprised at how weak her legs felt and stumbled before grabbing the handle.

"Whoa," Polly said, standing upright. She made her way around the front of the truck and went inside, then up the steps to two happy dogs on the top landing. "I love you, too," she said. "Just let me get in the house." Obiwan and Han followed her into the media room. Polly looked longingly at the sofa. All she wanted to do was collapse, but if she fell asleep, she didn't want to be out here when the kids got home from school.

She finally made it into her bedroom and pushed the door shut enough for privacy with a gap for animals to pass through. Kicking her shoes off, she dropped onto the bed, reached over to Henry's side and grabbed the comforter, rolling it around herself. She knew the temperature in the house was warm, but she'd started to chill. Obiwan jumped up and put his head on her shoulder while lying down beside her and Han wandered around the floor, trying to figure out what was going on.

"I just need to be quiet for a minute," she said. "Just a few minutes. Okay?"

The phone in her pocket rang. Polly turned over to reach for it, saw it was Henry and answered, "Hey there."

"Aaron just called me. Why didn't you?" he asked.

"Don't yell at me," she said. "I'm sorry."

"I'm not yelling. I didn't mean that. Where are you?"

"In bed with Obiwan."

"Are you okay, honey?"

"I don't think so, but I will be. Don't worry."

"Do you need me to come home?"

"No," she said. "I'll be fine. Don't worry." She felt tears start to choke her. "Talk to you later." Polly quickly hung up before she cried all over Henry and put the phone on the table.

"Yes I do," she said to Obiwan. "I need him to come home." She pulled her dog closer and finally relaxed enough to sob into the nape of his neck.

"I wanted her to live," Polly said. "She shouldn't have died. Why did she die?" Polly cried and cried by herself with the dogs on her bed. Obiwan wiggled around to get in front of her and nestled in her arms, while Han tucked himself in behind her legs. Polly yanked tissues from the box beside her bed, blew her nose and forced herself to slow her breathing. Tears continued to leak from her eyes so she yanked a few more tissues, dabbed at her eyes, then rolled her head on her neck, trying to relax.

~~~

Polly woke up with no idea what time it was. She sat straight up, knowing that she needed to get everyone moving for the day, confused though, at the sound of the television. She checked the time on her phone and was even more confused. Two o'clock. She took a couple of deep breaths, looked around for the animals and when she found none, looked down at her clothes and realized that she'd fallen asleep in the middle of the day. But who was watching television and why were the dogs okay with that?

"Obiwan?" she called tentatively. When he didn't come running into the room, Polly headed for the kitchen and peeked into the media room.

"What are you two doing here?" she asked Rebecca and Andrew.
~~~

"Half day, remember?" Rebecca said. "Where did you come from?"

"I was in my room." Polly scratched her head. "Did you take the dogs out?"

Andrew waved his hand over his head. "Took care of it already. They're good to go."

"Thank you," Polly said. "Did you at least have lunch?" She realized that she was starving. "I'm going to have a sandwich."

Rebecca came over to the dining room. "Are you okay? You look kind of out of it and you never eat lunch this late."

"I'm fine," Polly said. "Thanks. It's just been a weird day."

"Weird day, like fun weird day or dead body weird day?" Rebecca asked.

"I hate that you even know to ask me that," Polly replied. "But yeah. I found a girl on the highway going down to Boone."

Andrew clicked the television off and ran over to join them. "You found someone? Was it bad? Was she hit by a car? How long was she there before you found her? How old do you think she was?"

"Stop it," Rebecca said. "And grow up, would you? Somebody died."

Andrew frowned and said, "I'm sorry."

"It's okay," Polly said. "But I don't want to talk about it."

The two kids looked at each other, surprise evident on their faces.

"Was it someone you knew?" Rebecca asked quietly, reaching out to take Polly's hand.

"No, that isn't it. I'm feeling overwhelmed by everything right now."

"Because Stephanie and Kayla are gone, too. Right?" Andrew asked.

"That must be it." Polly said with a smile.

"Everybody's asking about them at school," Rebecca said. She scooted past Polly into the kitchen. "I can't believe Stephanie didn't tell anyone where they were going. Not even the secretary knows and she knows everything about everybody."

Polly picked Leia up off the counter and snuggled her face in the cat's neck. Leia tolerated it for a few minutes, then pushed out of her arms so Polly would put her down. Instead of returning the cat to the counter, Polly lowered her to the floor and Leia took off. "What are you doing?"

Rebecca looked up. "I'm making you a sandwich. You aren't running on all cylinders."

"If I'm not going back over to the Bell House, I should probably take a shower."

"We could help," Rebecca said.

Andrew looked at the two of them. "Help Polly take a shower?"

"No, silly," Rebecca said. "We should go to Bell House and help her work."

He groaned.

"You'd do that?" Polly asked. "Awesome. Let me put my shoes on."

She was in the dining room, laughing to herself, when she heard Andrew whisper to Rebecca. "What did you do?"

"I don't know," Rebecca replied. "I never dreamed she'd take me up on it."

"We'll run up to your house so you can change into old clothes, Andrew," Polly called. She'd been tempted to tell them she was kidding, but the more she thought about it, the better the idea sounded. Maybe she could work off some of this funk by hauling bushes and shrubs out of the dirt.

Rebecca came into the living room. "You're really going to take me up on that?"

"Why not?" Polly asked. "It's a beautiful day and I'm not a fan of you sitting in front of the television all afternoon."

"We could work on our homework..." Rebecca's voice trailed off as she realized how hopeless that sounded.

"I won't work you very hard," Polly said. "I promise. Just come with me."

"Okay," Rebecca said with a sigh. She stuck her head back into the dining room. "I'll be back. If we're really going, I'd better change my clothes."

Polly chuckled as she sat down on the bed to put her shoes on. She made a quick call.

"Hello there," Sylvie said. "Is my boy giving you trouble?"

"Only a little bit. We're running over to your house so he can change clothes, then we're going over to the Bell House and work in the yard. I doubt that we'll be back by the time you get off work, so you should pick him up over there."

"If I want him back, that is," Sylvie retorted. "Actually, I'm at home. I was going to call and see if you wanted me to take them off your hands for the afternoon. I'd rather pull weeds with you all. I'll bring his clothes and meet you. How does that sound?"

"He'll love that," Polly said with a laugh.

"Is it evil and rotten that I think it's hilarious?"

"We'll just be evil and rotten together. I'll see you over there."

Polly hung up and slipped the phone back in her pocket, then finished tying her shoes and went back out to the living room. Rebecca hadn't emerged yet - more than likely taking time to make sure that her sloppy clothes looked just perfect. The poor girl went back and forth between treating Andrew like a brother and a boyfriend. Polly and Henry never knew which Rebecca would show up.

"Your mom is meeting us at Bell House," Polly called out. "She's bringing your clothes."

"Noooo," Andrew whined. "Do I have to go?"

"Yep. Now it's a full-blown plan in process. Gather up your things, because you'll go home with her after we're done."

"And just when I thought I was going to have a relaxed afternoon," he muttered loud enough for her to hear.

Rebecca came out of her room, dressed in a pair of shorts and a nice t-shirt.

"You look nice," Polly said.

"Thank you. I think it's always important to look nice."

Polly chuckled. "Even when you're going to work in the dirt?"

"Especially then. No reason to look like a slob."

"I guess so. Are you ready?"

"Can I take my sketchbook?"

"You can put it in the truck, but I doubt that you'll have much time. We have lots of debris to haul."

Rebecca ran back into her room and grabbed a bag. "Just in case."

The dogs weren't any happier this time when Polly left, but she and the kids managed to get out and into the truck without too much trouble. She drove to the Bell House and pulled into the driveway, thankful that the team from the DCI was gone.

"I want to look in the hole," Andrew said, jumping out of the truck.

Rebecca followed him. Polly wanted to tell them to be careful, but stopped herself. They were always being told what to do and if there was one thing she knew about Rebecca; it was that the girl was careful.

"Polly, this is cool!" Andrew yelled.

"It's a hole," she replied.

"But it had bones down there. It's like a room in the ground."

"It *is* a room in the ground, you moron," Rebecca said.

"But..." Andrew started, then said, "Never mind."

Sylvie pulled in and Polly waited for her friend.

"Your mom's here," she called back to Andrew.

"Okay."

Sylvie walked around the truck with a plastic grocery bag filled with clothes. "Where is he?"

Polly pointed. "He found the hole."

"That's pretty cool, you know?" Sylvie said. "A hidden room with a tunnel. You just never know what you'll find in these old houses. I know Andrew hoped that there would be something awesome in our house. He spent weeks scouring every inch of the basement for a hidden room."

They walked through the open breezeway to the other side of the garage.

"Can I go down there?" Andrew asked. "I could jump in."

Sylvie looked at him. "How would you get out?"

"How did Polly get out? Did she use the tunnel?"

Polly shook her head. "Eliseo had to bring a ladder."

He looked around. "Where is it? Let's check this out."

"I don't know where it is, but no, you're not going down there," Sylvie said. "Now, here are your clothes. Go into the garage and change. We have work to do."

"Man, I never get to do anything fun," he complained. Andrew stomped his feet as he walked toward his mother and when she didn't let him take the bag, looked up at her. "What?"

"You know what." Sylvie raised her eyebrows.

"Yeah. Sorry."

Polly turned around at the sound of another vehicle pulling in and was surprised to see Henry's truck. "Just a sec," she said and ran back to the driveway.

"Hi there," he said when he got out of the truck. "What are you all doing over here?"

"I was in a funk, so we came over to work it out on the yard. What are you doing here?"

"Heath is meeting me to get those windows carried inside and start building you a porch."

"Now?" Polly pulled him into a hug. "Already?"

"It's as good a time as any. Will that help your funk?"

Polly didn't let him go. "You have no idea."

"I've been thinking on this whole house renovation thing and I have a couple of ideas I want to pose to you." He took her hand and they walked toward the lumber.

"What?" she asked. "Don't keep me in suspense."

"What if I bring water and electricity in and we let Heath and Hayden move in this summer and rough it while they do demolition? We'll pay them over and above, but it wouldn't cost nearly as much as hiring subcontractors. Dad and I will teach them how to do the work and maybe we could turn the garage into a shop with some of your dad's tools and equipment."

" That's a great idea," she gasped. "Have you talked to them?"

He shook his head. "I wanted to talk to you first, but I know Hayden was considering hiring on with a road crew again and I'd just as soon put him to work here so he can be close to his brother."

Polly leaned on him. "I had the worst day going and you just made things a whole lot better." She reached up and kissed his cheek, grinning at the stubble. He hadn't shaved for a few days. "Thank you."

"I know better than to let you sit on a project for too long. It starts stressing you out. If I don't keep up with you, it worries me that you'll just move us over here before the house is ready and I'll be stuck with cold showers and no heat this winter."

"You aren't going to make the boys take cold showers, are you?" she asked.

"They won't have air conditioning for a while, so they'll be thankful for cool showers, but no. We'll make sure there's a bathroom that works and electricity in part of the house for them."

"I met one of our neighbors today," Polly said. "Pat Lynch?"

He shook his head. "I know they live around here, but I don't know them very well. Her husband is Al or something? Dad probably knows them. Their kids were older than me."

"She's talkative. I'm supposed to go over someday so I can meet Albert." Polly grinned. "*Her* Albert. I don't know if she's always called him that or if she was just laying claim in front of the new woman in the neighborhood."

Henry laughed. "You're a bit of a threat, you know."

"Barry the radar guy was here. He's not talkative. And he left without telling me anything. Did he talk to you?"

"He's odd," Henry agreed. "He likes to do his thing and get out. You probably freaked him out by being here. I suppose you tried to talk to him."

"Like any normal person," Polly said. "It was difficult, though."

"I don't know if I want to tell you what he found."

"Why not? Is it bad?"

Henry shook his head. "No, but I was kind of thinking I'd like it to be a surprise. Can you wait?"

" That's mean." Polly swatted his arm. "Are we safe in the yard?"

"Let's just stay in the front yard. Okay?"

"He found another room, didn't he?"

"I'm not telling. Just stay out front until I can investigate. Will you try that?"

She scowled. "I'll try. But I don't like it."

"You have plenty of work to do on the side of the house over there and we're going to be busy all week building this porch. And besides, I think they're bringing in students from ISU tomorrow to finish in that room. Real live archeology."

"At my house," Polly said. "That's just weird." She nodded. "Okay. I'll be good. Now can I help you haul these windows somewhere so they're safe?"

CHAPTER NINE

"Resting your weary head?" Jeff asked when he walked into her office.

Polly looked up. "No, just deep in thought. Did you hear anything more from Stephanie?"

"Not yet, but I won't give up. What happened to you yesterday? I didn't see hide nor hair of you and there was some rumor floating around that you found another body."

Polly sighed. "I did. A poor girl on the highway. She was alive, Jeff. And then she wasn't. That was one of the rougher ones I've dealt with. I'm telling ya, right now I feel like the world is all upside down and I don't know how to get it back to where it belongs. This bit with Stephanie and Kayla is a mess. Why won't she talk to us? She should know better than to run away. You and I are the best fixers around."

"The same thoughts I've had for the last couple of days," he said. "And I go back and forth from worrying about them to being mad at her for making such a rash decision. Then I'm back to worrying again."

She nodded. "How's Kristen doing today?"

"We spent more time training and she's picking it up. You got me thinking yesterday and if Stephanie does come back and I give her more responsibility around here, training someone like Kristen is the right thing to do. She's a nice girl. Very pleasant on the phone and with people who come in the front door." He frowned. "If Stephanie doesn't come back, maybe we're training her replacement."

"Let's not think about that yet. Are you going to be here for Rebecca's party Sunday afternoon? I know that's a lot of extra time for you to spend in Bellingwood."

He smiled at her. "Maybe I'll move in with you for the weekend."

"Rebecca hasn't said anything to me yet about the party," Polly said. "She'd usually be asking a million questions and telling me what she wants to have happen, but it's like she doesn't want to think about it without Kayla here."

Jeff reached into his pocket and pulled out his phone. "That's a great idea."

"What?"

He finished typing and looked at her. "I just laid a little guilt on Stephanie about Rebecca's party. They'd already bought her gift. I didn't see it at the trailer, so maybe they took it with them."

Kristen tapped on Polly's door. "Mr. Lindsay, there's a phone call for you on line one. Do you want me to transfer it in here or to your office?" She paused. "Or would you rather I take a message?"

He stood up. "I'll get it in my office. Thank you, Kristen."

She smiled and backed out as he walked out of the door.

Polly leaned back and looked around, thinking back to the day that Doug and Billy helped unpack her knick-knacks and Star Wars memorabilia. She'd been so excited to have an office of her own in a business she was going to create. Things had changed so much in the last few years. Sometimes it was hard to remember all that had happened.

It wouldn't take that much to pack it all back up. Maybe she could take over one of the rooms at Bell House when they were finally settled. The library there would be a great place to work.

Maybe she'd take time to do some writing of her own, among the books that had filled her life with so much. That would be a wonderful room with her books on deep, dark wooden shelves interspersed with Star Wars characters and toys. She rolled back and put her hand on top of the R2D2 that she'd gotten as a shower gift. The Millennium Falcon could hang from the ceiling. Kessel Run - twelve parsecs.

That would be the last room to come together, though. Bedrooms would come first. No, the kitchen had to come first. At least that way they'd have a place to gather as a family. Then the bedrooms and then a living room. She was going to miss the intimacy of the apartment. They were always passing each other as they moved from room to room, but that would end as everyone claimed their own place in that immense sprawling house.

"Ms. Giller?" Kristen stood in her doorway again.

Polly rolled back to her desk. "What is it, Kristen?"

"Mr. Lindsay is busy and I have a woman on the phone who wants to rent the entire addition for a month. Do we do that?"

"Absolutely. You can send the call in here if you don't want to take it."

"She was asking about a discount since they're renting the whole place."

"We can always be flexible," Jeff said from behind Kristen. "Put her on the speaker, and you and I will work through it together." He grinned at Polly and waited for Kristen to step back out.

Polly leaned back. She'd signed checks and sorted through the mail. It felt good to sit still and she wasn't ready to head back over to the Bell House quite yet.

They had worked until dusk settled in last night. She and Sylvie tore through the bushes, finishing that project. Andrew and Rebecca weren't quite as excited about working with them as they were about helping Henry and Heath on the front porch. But a lot of work had gotten done and Polly felt good about their progress.

Eliseo had done his best to convince her to remove the arbor walkway. There was no good purpose for it. Last night, Polly finally got on board. It led from the hidden gate in old Mr. Bridger's yard to the back yard of the Bell House where he'd planted the marijuana crop, but unless Franklin Bell had originally owned the land that belonged to Jim Bridger, she couldn't understand why the arbor was ever built. If it had been in an area that regularly saw traffic, she'd have left it alone, but it was just taking up space.

Sylvie had started pulling the vines off the arbor while Polly cleaned up the brush from beside the house, but they went home before she got too far on it. Polly had half a mind to ask Eliseo to bring the horses over again and pull the thing loose from the ground; roots, vines, posts and all.

"Got a minute?" Jeff asked.

"Sure. Who was that?"

"It's pretty cool," he said. "A writer's workshop wants to rent the space for the entire month of June."

"Okay. Just four rooms?"

"That's for the organizers and leaders. They also want to rent the back classroom and the computer room."

"It seems a little late to be planning something like this."

He chuckled. "June of next year."

"Oh!" she said with a laugh. "That makes more sense. I couldn't figure out how they'd line that all up."

"It's already filled for this June."

"With what?"

"Everything we have is filling up for June and July, in anticipation of the Sesquicentennial."

"That's weird. It's a month early."

He shrugged. "A family is taking the top for both months."

"Descendants of one of the founding families?" Polly asked.

"Got me. Stephanie took the reservation." His face scrunched up in annoyance. "I'm angry right now. She'd better turn that car of hers around right now and come back to Bellingwood."

"Tell her that," Polly said, pointing to his pocket. "Rather than telling me, every time you get mad or worried, tell her. Annoy the heck out of her."

"Rather than you?" he asked.

She pushed a drawer shut in her desk and turned off her monitors, then stood up and walked toward him. "I didn't say that. But I'm leaving to go rip out an arbor. When I come back, I expect you to have found Stephanie and convinced her to return so I don't have to keep hearing about this."

"What?" Jeff looked at her in shock.

"I'm kidding. But it would certainly help if you could just take care of that for us."

He backed up as she walked toward the door. "You're always entertaining, Polly."

"It's my best thing." She walked out and turned back. "Have a good day, you two." Polly walked on upstairs to change into work clothes again. The animals begged to follow her, but she managed to get in and out again.

Her first stop was at Sweet Beans. Camille looked up when she walked in. "You look like you're working hard," Camille said.

"Heading over to the house to rip out an old arbor. One of these days I'm going to have control of that yard so I can think about something else."

"Sylvie told me the other day about how much work you've put into all of the different places in town." Camille waved her hand around the shop. "Even this. You've taken on big projects."

"This might be the one that does me in," Polly said. "I was too stupid to know it couldn't be done when I bought Sycamore House. Then Henry convinced me that the inn would be no problem, and I was only partly involved in the coffee shop. Now I'm fully aware and fully involved and I have no idea where to find the end of it."

"You'll be working away and one day you'll realize it's all finished," Camille said. "If you need someone to paint walls, though, I can help with that. I finished up our dining room last week. That was the last room."

"How's it going?"

Camille shrugged. "It's great living with Elise, but owning a home is hard work. There are so many things that I didn't know I needed to know." She grinned. "And now I know. Believe it or not, I replaced fixtures in the bathroom by myself. And, I put new guts in my toilet. By. Myself."

"That's awesome."

"I also discovered how easy it was to replace a toilet seat. Who knew?"

"So you're the queen of bathroom repair now."

Camille put Polly's coffee on the counter. "Don't be getting all crazy on me. But I can install a new shower head, too." She chuckled. "Elise helped and we're going to do hers this weekend. You should come over sometime."

"Whenever you're ready for me."

"Maybe not yet. I'm replacing the carpet in the living room next month."

"By yourself?"

Camille shuddered. "No. I hope that when that's done, I'll be finished with most of the major changes. I'd like to sit in the living room some evening without looking around and finding one more thing that needs to be cleaned up, fixed or changed. And it's my own problem. I didn't like the brown outlet covers, so I changed everything to ivory. I wanted a ceiling fan in the living room, so I had that installed a few weeks ago."

"You'll like that this summer," Polly agreed. "I'm glad the two of you are enjoying the house."

"Elise is so quiet. She works all the time, so she's never in the way. And she does sweet things like buying flowers and leaving them in a vase on the kitchen table. If I'm not around and she makes a meal, she'll put one together for me with instructions on how to re-heat it."

"Wow, that's really thoughtful. I didn't know she was like that."

"She says she isn't," Camille said with a laugh, "but she's trying to remember to do things. Elise told me that if a thought flits through her head, she puts it on a sticky note and looks at it until she does it. The first flowers took her three weeks to finally get done, but then she found a shop in Ames that she drives by on her way home, so it's easier for her to do it now."

"You two are good for each other."

Camille leaned over the counter. "Don't tell my mother, but I'm going out on a date Thursday night with a professor friend of Elise's."

"She set up a date for you? Who is this girl and what did you do with my Elise?"

"I think she just needed someone in her life who treated her like a normal person. I also think she was ready to be more involved, too."

"So is this a blind date? Or have you met him?"

"Blind date," Camille said. "That's why I'm not telling Mama until it's long past."

"I can't wait to hear about it. I didn't do many blind dates." Polly didn't want to tell her that every blind date had been awful. Maybe Camille would have better luck. Those things had to work out for some people.

"It should be fun." Camille looked up when the doorbell rang again. "That's a big bakery order for the bank. I need to take care of this."

Polly nodded. "See you later." The first sip of her coffee brought an instant smile to her face. Sometimes it was the simplest things. She went back out to her truck and, feeling like the coffee had given her extra courage, dialed the sheriff's office in Boone and asked for Aaron.

"You didn't dial my cell phone, so I have to assume that this isn't one of those calls," he said.

"Nope. Just sitting in front of Sweet Beans and wondering if you know anything more about the girl from yesterday."

He didn't say anything and Polly could almost see him take a deep breath before responding. She wasn't generally this forward, but that death had really shaken her up.

"We don't have much more information yet," he said. "The autopsy isn't scheduled until later this afternoon. Even then, we won't have a full picture for about a week."

"No ID or anything? Where she came from? Missing person reports? Anything?"

"We're working on it, Polly. You know that."

"What about the bones from the Bell House? Anything on those, yet?"

Aaron sounded more relaxed at the change of subject. "Those are at a lab at Iowa State now. We don't have the resources to investigate something that old. I think you'll find that this is a perfect case for the forensics students there."

She blew a breath out. "So I know nothing. About anything. I'm not a fan."

"I understand that. As soon as I have any information that I am free to tell you, I will."

"That means I have to go find it for myself. I'm sorry to be grumpy about this, but I'm ready for something to be solved."

"It's been a rough week. But these mysteries always unravel."

"I still don't know if there's hidden gold in Bellingwood somewhere," she grumbled, thinking back to earlier this year. She'd never really thought they would find the gold that Beryl's ancestor had stolen, but a little part of her had hoped.

Aaron laughed out loud. "What would you do if you found it?"

"I'd fly to Hawaii until the house was completely redone and all of my things moved in."

"I see."

"But I'd probably find bodies washed up on the beach and their law enforcement wouldn't be nearly as nice to me as you are. Maybe I'd be safer if I just flew to the moon."

"NASA would never understand how bodies fell out of space for you to find up there," he said.

"Yeah, yeah, yeah. I'm trying to stop feeling sorry for myself, but I seem to be failing. This is going to require more turned up ground, I can tell."

"Turned up ground? Stay away from the cemetery, Polly Giller."

She chuckled. "Got it. No, I'm tearing up the yard today. As soon as I can get all of the bad stuff out and Henry finishes the front porch, Eliseo will help me level the yard and make grass grow."

"Then good luck with your day and I'll call if I find out anything that I can tell you."

"Thanks, Aaron." Polly took another drink from her coffee, dropped it into the cup holder, turned the truck on, backed out and headed for the Bell House. She was going to accomplish something today. Even if it was just ripping down that arbor.

When she pulled into the driveway, she took another drink, then picked up her gloves and walked over to stand in front of the house. They'd put the floor joists in last night and she could see the shape of the porch. This was going to be wonderful when it was finally built. Henry was pretty good to her, jumping on it so quickly.

While she stood there, she heard a strange sound coming from the street and turned to see Eliseo driving Nan and Nat from the wagon.

"What are you doing here?" she asked, a huge smile on her face.

"We've come to help. Remember?" he replied. "We're going to take that arbor down and then haul it away." Eliseo pointed at the porch. "Looks like they got a good start on it last night."

"Really?" she asked weakly. "That's wonderful. I'd forgotten."

He jumped down and unhitched the horses from the wagon, then patted Nan's shoulder as he walked toward Polly. "These are your horses and they're hard workers. They hauled rock for me last summer. This will be much easier."

"I hope so."

Eliseo led the horses around to the side where the covered arbor stood and scratched his head. "When we pull this up, that brick is going to come with it, I think. Why don't you go look for the wheelbarrow?" He pointed toward the garage.

She nodded and walked away. Polly wasn't even sure where the wheel barrow had gone after she left it on Monday. It wasn't by the rock pile they'd created so she opened the garage in hopes that someone had parked it inside the front door. She turned her phone's flashlight on so she could peer around the piles of furniture she'd dragged out of the house. This was just one more overwhelming amount of stuff she needed to deal with. But no wheelbarrow.

Polly closed the door on the garage and walked around back, careful to stay away from the hole she'd fallen into. The wheelbarrow was nowhere to be seen there, either. Henry wasn't going to be happy if someone stole it. It was her own fault, though, not putting things away. She was leery about walking too far into the back yard. If Henry wouldn't tell her whether or not there were more rooms underneath the ground, she had to assume there were. With her luck, she'd fall into another one and that would just be embarrassing.

A loud crack reverberated around the house as she walked back to the front of the garage. He'd done it without her. Then she realized that he'd sent her away so he could take care of things without her getting in the way. Polly remembered where she'd last seen the wheelbarrow – on the other side of the house where they'd been working last night.

Eliseo stood beside the horses with as big a grin as she'd seen, his eyes lit up in glee. "That was fun," he said, patting Nat. "We want to do it again. Oh look." Eliseo pointed at the wheelbarrow. "It was right here."

"You're rotten," she said, pushing it over to where he was standing. "You sent me away."

"I wasn't sure if it would work and I didn't want you to be hurt if anything went flying. We're going to drag this across the yard to the wagon. I'll be back to help you dig out the rest of the bricks."

Polly watched the structure as the horses pulled it across the lawn, leaving branches and leaves in its path. One more thing dealt with. She might get through this yet.

CHAPTER TEN

Construction was exhausting. They'd spent another evening at the Bell House, working on the porch and Polly was pretty sure this manual labor was going to kill her. Then she laughed. Once upon a time, she had been pretty sure that hefting bales of hay would kill her. All that had done was make her stronger. It was amazing, though, how quickly she lost those muscles when Eliseo came on board. But she wasn't going to offer to do it again.

Henry and Heath were relaxing in front of the television. Last fall and winter it had been football, then it was NASCAR and basketball, hockey, and now baseball. She was glad they enjoyed watching the games together. Rebecca had come into the bedroom with Polly to watch something, but was finally in her own bed. With Kayla gone, Rebecca was sticking close to Polly. She went into her room at nine thirty without any prompting and the last time Polly checked, her light was off. The poor girl was trying to stay engaged with the world, but had to work at it.

Obiwan stretched out along Polly's back and she held still when his claws tangled up in her hair. She reached around, tugged them loose and then scooted up on her pillow, away from danger. She reached up to turn the light off and swiped her phone open to look at the time. A buzzing startled her and she realized that it was ringing.

"Hello?" she asked softly.

"I want to come home, Polly," Kayla said.

"Oh honey." Polly turned over and sat up in bed. "Where are you? We want you to come home, too."

"I'm not supposed to tell you. Stephanie let me call because I wouldn't stop crying, but I can't tell you where we are."

"Can I talk to Stephanie?" Polly asked.

"No. She won't talk to anybody. She wants you to tell Jeff to stop texting her."

"I'm not going to do that. He misses her terribly. You both are very important to us. Rebecca is lonely without you."

Kayla cried some more. "I keep telling Stephanie that Rebecca is the only best friend I've ever had."

"Are you two safe?" Polly asked.

"Yeah. It's a nice hotel. There's a swimming pool and everything. Stephanie said it's like a vacation."

"That's a good way to look at it. But I really want to talk to her."

"She doesn't want to. She says she's afraid you'll talk her into doing something stupid like coming back to Bellingwood."

"That's not stupid, Kayla. We're your family and we love you. We'll do everything we can to keep you safe."

"Stephanie says that isn't enough if he's out of jail. He'll find us if anyone knows where we are. She says that it's like he can read minds or something. Can I talk to Rebecca?"

"She's in bed and her light is off. Can you call tomorrow? A little earlier?"

Kayla must have put her hand over the phone because the question she posed to Stephanie was muffled.

"Stephanie says this is the only time I can call. Please? I need to tell her that I'm sorry I left without talking to her."

"Oh Kayla, please let me talk to Stephanie."

"Would you wake Rebecca up first? I just want to tell her that she's my best friend and I'll never forget her."

Polly was already walking toward the door. She knocked on Rebecca's door and opened it. "Rebecca? Are you sleeping?"

"No," came Rebecca's voice in the dark.

"Kayla is on the phone and she wants to talk to you."

Rebecca sat straight up in her bed, her body silhouetted in the light from the street. Polly strode across the room and handed over the phone, then covering it, said, "Stephanie won't let me talk to her. See if you can either make that happen or find out where they are. Anything. Please?"

"Hello?" Rebecca said into the phone. "Kayla?"

"I miss you, too," Rebecca said and then listened. "We're so worried about you. Does anyone know where you are?"

The conversation alternated between pauses and Rebecca speaking. She talked about kids at school and working at the Bell House. She told Kayla about the body in the ground and then about Polly finding a girl on the highway. She asked Kayla in fifty different ways where they were, but never got a clear response. Stephanie had that story on lockdown.

"You have to finish seventh grade," Rebecca finally said. "How are you going to do that if you don't go to school?" She listened and then said, looking at Polly, "You can live here at Sycamore House. Nobody can get in and Polly will make sure we get to school every day and she'll pick us up so you're safe. She'd even ask one of the cute deputies to keep an eye on us when we're walking from the school to her truck. If you come back right away, Andrew and I can help you make up your schoolwork. I'll bet the teachers won't even make you do some of it if they know what you've been through."

She listened again and then said, "But I don't want to hang up. You can't go away again. I want you to be here for my birthday party. It's no fun without you. This isn't fair." Rebecca started to cry. "I can't lose one more person in my life."

Polly sat down on the bed and put her arm around Rebecca's shoulders.

"I'm sorry," Rebecca said to Kayla. "Mom would tell me that I'm being dramatic. I know this isn't about me. But I don't want to go to eighth grade without you here. You have to come home."

As she listened to Kayla, Rebecca took a deep breath. "Okay. I know. I love you, too. Call me again, will you?"

She handed the phone to Polly, who jammed it to her ear. "Kayla?"

The phone clicked off as she listened and the phone call was over. Polly dialed it right back and slumped when the call was rejected. They could keep doing this all night, but Stephanie would just turn the phone off.

"How are you doing?" she asked Rebecca.

"Better, I think. At least I know that she's out there. Do you think they'll call back?"

"I don't know," Polly said. "We'll keep trying. Stephanie told Kayla to have me ask Jeff to quit texting them. I think he's getting to her."

"Good," Rebecca said. "I know I shouldn't say anything bad about her, but she's being stubborn and it's going to hurt Kayla's future."

"We can never understand the horrors of what Stephanie faced with her father," Polly said. "And we can't expect her to make decisions based on our view of life. She can only do what she thinks is best to protect both herself and her sister. I would do whatever it took to make sure you were safe, even if it meant that I had to go on the run with you."

"We'd take Henry, though, right?" Rebecca asked. "Because we need him."

Polly laughed. "Okay, we'll take Henry, too. Now, lie down and try to get some sleep. Morning comes whether we're ready for it or not."

"I've never asked you to do this before, but would you stay here for a while?" Rebecca asked. "Every time I start to go to sleep, I think about Kayla being gone and then I wake up again."

"Scoot over," Polly said, thankful for big beds in this house. She lay down on top of the blankets and snuggled up to Rebecca, wrapping an arm around her, blankets and all. "Now relax your toes, one by one." Polly deliberately slowed her breathing. "Next think about relaxing the top of your feet and then your ankles." She continued to breathe, speaking softly and slowly as she encouraged Rebecca to relax her body. It was a trick her father had taught her years ago on the nights she was too nervous to sleep because of a test. He'd sit beside her bed and talk her through her muscles, relaxing each one until she drifted off. They never got much further than her fingers before she was out like a light.

Tonight, Polly felt Rebecca relax against her before they even got to the girl's knees. That didn't take long. She let herself relax, smelling the freshly shampooed hair against the pillow. Polly didn't want to move. This moment felt too special. If Rebecca never asked her to comfort her like this again, it would be okay because she had this moment and would never forget it.

~~~

Polly woke up to darkness and silence in the house. The cats had fallen asleep at the end of the bed, but the dogs were elsewhere. She peeled herself away from Rebecca and waited quietly while her daughter roused, turned over and fell back to sleep. Polly left the bed and tiptoed across the room, shuddering when her toe hit a stack of books on the floor. No matter how many times Polly asked Rebecca to clean her room, it was never going to be free of clutter.

Slipping out of the door, she pulled it shut, leaving enough room for the cats to move in and out, then went across the living room into the kitchen. Polly was restless and had no desire to lie down in her own bed, then toss and turn until she wore herself out. If she remembered correctly, there was still a container of chocolate chip cookies in the freezer. Polly opened the refrigerator door for light and then opened the freezer. Just as she put her hand on the chocolate chip cookies, she realized that there was something even better - a piece of frozen chocolate cake left over from last weekend when Hayden was here. She chuckled. That was perfect. With that and a glass of milk, Polly headed for
~~~

Henry's office. At least there she could turn lights on and not worry about disturbing anyone, and Henry's office chair was quite comfortable.

Henry was tidy. His desk was tidy; his truck was always tidy. Because he was always cleaning up after her in the house, Polly's shame took over and she did her best to clean her own messes before he got to them. Never once did he say anything to make her feel guilty and maybe that was the worst of it. He was much too nice about her failings, accepting them without judgment.

She laughed to herself. Women would think she was crazy for complaining and Polly knew that it was her own guilt that made her want him to get annoyed about her messes, but she had what she had. He wasn't going to change and be less nice to her, so she'd just have to make do.

Polly turned around in the chair. Tucked into a corner of one the shelves he'd built in here was the old lock box that had belonged to her father. She wasn't sure why she felt a need to connect to him tonight, but in this box held the things he'd believed to be important. She put the box on Henry's desk and stared at it while taking a sip of milk.

Rats. She'd forgotten to grab a fork, but that wouldn't stop her. Polly picked up the cake and took a bite, leaning over the desk as crumbles spilled out of her mouth. With one hand holding the cake, she patted around the side of the desk for Henry's box of tissues. When her hand hit it, she yanked out three and placed them under the cake before putting it back down. Two more tissues to wipe her lips and she was set. Instead of throwing them in his trash can, though, Polly needed to remember to take them back to the kitchen. Those animals could find the scent of food wherever it was hidden in the house and before she got up the next morning, they'd have shredded tissue all over Henry's office.

She turned the key in the lockbox and opened the top, letting it fall back on the desk. The last time she'd dug through these things was when they were trying to understand who Ruth Ann Marshall was ... before she revealed herself as Polly's birth mother.

Polly put her hand on top of the pile of papers and

photographs in the box and shut her eyes. Those revelations had been horrifying, but she'd learned she could get through just about anything. Especially with Henry standing beside her. One of his zippered hoodies was draped around the back of the chair and Polly lifted it off and put it on, tugging it across her chest. She brought the fabric up to her nose and breathed in the scent of him. Did he have any idea how much she loved him?

Did Polly's parents love each other like that? They must have, but they hadn't had much time together. Polly remembered her mother, and while those memories were wonderful, it was her father who had been there for everything Polly experienced. All through the end of her elementary school years, junior high, high school and college. He'd kept an eye out for her with boyfriends, making sure she always knew how important she was to him and that no boy had better treat her less than she deserved. He'd sat through concerts and gone to parent-teacher conferences, never complaining that he had to do those things alone.

But his life hadn't revolved around her either. He was busy with the farm and loved spending time in his shop. Polly wasn't comfortable thinking about him with other women, but he'd let her know there were a few along the way. He had just never found the one who was so special to make his wife. She wondered if he had lived longer what might have been different. They were just becoming friends, rather than father and daughter, when he died. Polly still felt as if there was a wealth of knowledge about him that she'd never uncover.

As much as he would have loved being part of Sycamore House's renovation, he wouldn't have been able to contain himself at the opportunity to work on the Bell House. She smiled. What fun it would have been to have him there with her every day. When he got older, she would have asked him to move in, but until then, he'd have had his hands in everything they did to restore that old house to its former beauty.

She brushed a tear from her cheek. Sometimes she really missed him. Tears didn't come as often anymore, but every once in a while, something reminded her that he was gone. Polly pulled out the passport that she'd wondered about three years ago. She still had no clue as to why he'd traveled to England and France and wondered if she would ever know. The necklace of her mother's was still in its box and she rubbed her thumb over the clasp. Photos of her family when she was a child. Polly couldn't help herself and turned to glance back at the bookshelf again, seeing the photo album that Ruth Ann had given to her. That could stay where it was. Maybe someday she'd be able to look at it again and not be disgusted at what that woman had tried to do. She'd insinuated herself into Polly's family many years before, and then tried to do so again with Polly two years ago. Never again would she be allowed near those that Polly loved.

Polly touched the folded edge of a love letter that she knew by heart. Her father had written beautiful words to his bride to be. She opened an envelope filled with dried rose petals from the bouquet he'd given his wife and daughter when they came home from the hospital. Everett had saved the sweetest things. Polly picked up a manila envelope, knowing without looking that it contained certificates from all of her music contests. He loved to hear her practice, even when it was just scales. Polly always thought he was a little nutty about that, but it certainly had kept her returning to the flute night after night. He was a very smart man. She hadn't tried that tactic with Rebecca yet. Practicing was still a challenge. Polly needed to take her flute back out pretty soon and get ready for the summer band.

Her fingernail snagged on the ragged edge of a piece of paper and she lifted a small stack of papers. When she couldn't find what it was she'd touched, she flipped the stack over and saw a piece of paper caught in the tape of an old family picture.

"What's this?"

"What's this, is right."

Polly nearly jumped out of her skin at the sound of Henry's voice. She looked up at him guiltily as he walked into the office. "I couldn't sleep and was thinking about Dad."

"And eating chocolate cake at my desk, no less."

"Milk, too." She held up the glass with a grin.

"What sent you into Rebecca's room? Did something upset her?"

"I'm sorry," Polly said. "I forgot to tell you." She shook her head. "No, that's not right. I just fell asleep. Kayla called and wanted to talk to Rebecca."

"Were you able to find out where they were?" he asked. "Did you talk to Stephanie?"

"No. Poor Kayla wants to come home, but Stephanie is terrified. She's just not thinking right and I don't know how to help her if she won't let me. I can't get past her fear."

He walked over to stand beside her and stroked her hair. "I think it's a good sign that she let Kayla call Rebecca, don't you?"

"But it's not enough." Polly leaned against him. "I just wish I knew where they were."

"Give her time. The longer she has to think about the choices she's making, the better decisions she'll make. The first choice to leave Bellingwood was made out of fear. Stephanie needed space to think. She's a smart girl and will figure it out." He reached over and closed the box, then put it back on the shelf. "Come to bed with me. The dogs miss you."

"Just the dogs?" she asked.

He laughed. "So far. If they knew you were in here eating dessert, they'd be jealous too." Henry picked up the tissues and empty glass, then swept chocolate cake crumbs into his hand. "You're a slob," he said with a laugh.

"And you love me for it."

"More than I can say."

CHAPTER ELEVEN

Henry turned to Polly. "Do you have plans this morning?"

She'd sent him questioning looks all through breakfast since he was generally out of the door long before the kids left for school, but he was still here.

"Uhhh. No?" she said. "Wanna mess around?"

He laughed out loud. "Always, but I have a small surprise for you over at Bell House."

"I was going over anyway," she said. "Me and the rake. We're about to get cozy-friendly." Polly flexed her arm. "I'm building these muscles back up. You'd better be careful."

He waggled his eyebrows at her. "I'm always careful, baby." He dipped his head in mock shame. "That *so* didn't work, did it?"

"Nope, but I appreciate the effort."

Henry picked the plates up from the table and carried them into the sink in the kitchen. "How can I help you get out of here?"

Polly looked around and shrugged. "I'm ready to go now, I guess. Are we in a hurry?"

"Maybe a little."

"Do I have time for coffee from Sweet Beans?"

He glanced up at the clock on the wall and rolled his neck. "Only if you don't spend time chatting with everyone you see there. Can you do that?"

"One truck or two?" she asked, heading for the back door.

"Better take two."

"Then I'll race you." Polly ran down the steps and through the doors to the garage. She hit the button to raise the garage door as she raced to her truck. After she backed out, she hit the button to lower it again and giggled. Fair-shmair. He didn't need his fix as bad as she needed hers.

Picking up her phone, she dialed the coffee shop and when Sky answered, she breathlessly gave him her order. "Can you hurry this for me? I hate to ask, but I'm racing Henry to the Bell House."

"It will be ready when you get here," he replied with a laugh. "The two of you are weird. He just called me, too. Said I was supposed to give you his coffee."

"That fink," she said. "I'll be right there."

She pulled out onto the highway, waving at Henry as he backed out of the garage, trying her best to drive within the speed limit. Polly knew that when challenged, she would do anything to win. Running into pedestrians in downtown Bellingwood or getting picked up for speeding by people she knew was not a precedent she wanted to set.

When she got to the coffee shop, Polly gritted her teeth and cursed since the parking spaces in front of Sweet Beans were filled. "What in the hell?" she yelled. "All of a sudden, today, you all want coffee? We're never this busy!"

She parked in front of Pizzazz and ran across the street, then pulled up short when the normal allotment of customers was inside. "Where is everyone?" she asked Sky at the counter.

"There's a retreat at the quilt shop next door," he said, gesturing with his head. "They started early this morning. We had quite a rush there for a while. Lucky for us, they thought to tell us it was coming. That's why you get to see my pretty face today." He held out two cups and Polly put money on the counter, then took them from him.

"Thanks. I'll talk to you later. In a rush," she said and ran back to the front door.

"Good luck!" he called.

As she ran across the street, Henry stopped to let her pass and waved. She walked to the driver's side and waited for him to roll the window down, then handed him his coffee. "That was mean, making me pick yours up, too."

"I'm dawdling, so you won't be late," he said. "Hurry!"

"I'm hurrying. But why?" she asked.

"You'll see. Go on, get going." He waved her in front of him and she ran to her truck, jumped in and jammed the coffee into a cup holder.

Henry drove on down the street, tapping his brakes as he slowed his truck while waiting for her.

"He is such a weirdo," she said, backing out and following him. He pulled over to the right, put his hand out and waved her around. As she drove by, she shook her head and laughed. Henry just waved again.

Several cars were parked on the street in front of the Bell House when they arrived, but there was room for her to pull into the driveway. She parked, took up her coffee and jumped out, waiting for Henry to do the same.

"Now what was I in such a rush to get here for?" she asked.

"Come with me." He took her hand and led her behind the garage to where there was a group of people already in the room-sized hole in the ground.

"What's going on?"

"Just wait." Henry walked over to an older man, shook his hand and then beckoned for Polly to join them. "This is Professor Argual from Iowa State. He and his students are here to help me with the surprise."

Polly shook the professor's hand and then the man stepped forward. "Go ahead, James." He walked to the far wall of the room and motioned for Polly and Henry. "I think you can see better over here."

"What is this?" Polly whispered.

"You'll see."

She looked down into the room and realized that the students had dug out lines surrounding a rectangle in the wall. "Is that a...?"

Henry nodded.

James slipped what looked like a trowel in the right side of the space they'd delineated and ran it up to the top and around, then down to the bottom. Once he was satisfied that it would come free, he pushed the door and surprisingly, it swung open to the inside of another room.

"It worked," he said, loud enough for them to hear.

"What's in there?" Polly asked. Her feet moved before her brain and she headed for the ladder that had been dropped into the room.

Henry stopped her. "Let them do their job."

"But I want to see." As soon as it came out of her mouth, she knew it was ridiculous and stepped back. Turning to the professor, she asked, "Wouldn't the air be awful in there?"

He nodded. "With the images we received from the GPR, we knew that it was as close to the surface as this space, so early this morning, we poked holes in the ground to allow the atmosphere to clear." He smiled. "It also has the added benefit of allowing natural light into the room." The professor bent over. "Ella, what do you see?"

"Not much, professor," a girl called back. She stepped into the doorway. "No more bones, that's for sure. "Empty kegs and shelves of empty bottles. He had quite a production going on here, whoever it was."

"It has to be Franklin Bell," Polly said.

One of the other young people pressed past Ella and climbed the ladder enough to hand something to his professor. "We just found a stack of these. Thought you'd find it interesting."

Polly stepped over to see what he'd been handed and Argual passed it to her. "You'll like this," he said.

She found that she was holding a label for Franklin Bell's Corn Whiskey.

"Bell's Whiskey
Distilled and Bottled in Bellingwood, Iowa
Better than Good, A Balm for the Soul
None finer for medicinal purposes."

"This is fabulous," she said. "Are any of the bottles full?" She turned to Henry. "That would be some seriously aged whiskey."

James came back out into the main room and looked up. "We didn't find any actual whiskey in there. Maybe the poor guy drank it all before he died."

Polly nodded, a little disappointed.

Then Henry took her aside. "They're going to be here for a while and after they've been through that room, they'll leave things as they are for us. You can do whatever you want with the bottles and kegs."

"Really?" she asked.

"Another group of students is coming over this afternoon from the engineering department to make sure the tunnel is safe and these kids will trek through it, checking to see if there's anything else of interest."

"That would be terrific," she said. "Can you believe it, Henry? This place had to have been a speakeasy. How fun is that?"

Professor Argual put his hand on her elbow. "It's good that you look at it that way."

"It's history. Whether it's good or bad," Polly said, "it's history. Prohibition was a pretty significant time for America. Women finally started insisting on their rights and before anyone knew what was happening, they were voting. Just like men. It's hard to believe that women had to..." she paused. "And some still have to fight for equality." Polly hugged Henry. "I love you."

"I love you, too. What's that for?"

"You're just a good guy."

The professor looked at them and smiled when Polly realized that she'd said all of that in front of a relative stranger. "If you'll excuse me," he said, putting his hand on the ladder. "I want to get a look at this."

Polly and Henry walked back to the front of the house and when they got to his truck, she reached up and kissed him. "I forget sometimes how lucky I am to be married to a man that has never thought of me as less than anyone else."

"You shouldn't ever have to think that you're lucky to have that," he replied, touching her nose with his. "It disgusts me that any woman would worry about a man treating her that way. Anyone treating anyone that way." He gave his head a quick shake. "I can't think about it or I get too angry."

"Like I said," Polly replied. "I'm lucky."

"So am I." Henry put his hand on the door handle of his truck. "Am I safe to leave you here alone? Promise you won't go down there until someone tells you that it's safe?"

"Because I'm a poor weak woman?"

He laughed. "Hoisted with my own petard. I asked for that one, didn't I?"

"I'll be good and I'll be safe. Thank you for setting this up for me. It was fun. I can't wait to do something with that label."

"Because you will do something, won't you. Tell me you haven't already researched how to run a whiskey distillery."

Polly bit her lip with a grin.

"You did," he exclaimed.

"Yep. And it will never happen. It's harder to get a license to distill whiskey than it is to brew beer or make wine. I'm just not *that* interested in restoring history. But I think Lydia, Andy, Beryl and I could come up with something fun with the bottles and labels."

"Okay," he said, nodding. "I'm heading to work. Heath and I will be back again this afternoon."

As he drove away, Polly wandered over to the porch. Much of it would be finished by early next week if they kept up this pace. There were so many interesting and exciting things to be done here, but danged if they weren't all going to exhaust her. She walked back to the garage, opened the door, and took out the rake Eliseo had brought over. That side yard wasn't going to clean itself and he was planning to come over with the horses to run a tiller through the entire yard. At least they now knew where it was safe to traverse. She shuddered at the thought of one of those horses falling into a hole in the ground.

While Polly raked the yard, she thought about the bones she'd found on Monday. Those had to belong to Franklin Bell. No one knew what had happened to the young man. All of a sudden, one day, he was gone. She didn't believe for a minute that he'd drunk all of the whiskey in that room. It was too well sealed for him to have been in and out of it prior to dying. If it was Franklin, he was the one who built this place and would have never allowed himself to get trapped in that room.

She took out her phone and dialed the sheriff's office in Boone again, this time asking for Anita Banks.

"This is Anita. How may I help you?"

"Hi Anita, it's Polly Giller. What's up?" As soon as the words were out of her mouth, Polly wanted to take them back. What a silly thing to say to someone.

"Not much. What's up with you?"

Polly chuckled. "Now that we have the pleasantries out of the way. I was wondering if you could tell me anything more about those bones I found on Monday."

"You've been busy this week and it's only Thursday," Anita said. "Tell me you're done."

"I hope so. I was ready to be done after I climbed out of that hole in the ground. Do you know how he died? Was it even a he?" Polly asked.

"Let me see what I can find," Anita replied. "I just need to shut these two windows and open this program..." Anita cursed.

"What's wrong?"

"Damned computer. I keep telling them that if they want me to be a goddess, I need the proper tools. But those idiot IT boys think they know more than the cute girl. Because obviously, I'm an airhead."

Polly laughed again. Anita was far from being an airhead and those who treated her poorly would likely find themselves in a basement room, pecking away on old Royal manual typewriters.

"There," Anita said. "I let it know who's the boss. Now, give me a minute to log in and find what you need. Are you going to invite me up to see this place someday?"

"You're welcome to come any time," Polly said. "If you want to see it while things are in chaos, come now. If you want to see it when it's all finished, though, that could take some time."

"I heard some of the boys say there was a tunnel leading back to the house. Is that true?"

Polly nodded, caught herself and said, "It sure is. We're hoping to have that opened up in the next week or so. Some kids from the university are working to make sure it's safe and to make sure that they've found anything of importance. There's another room filled with empty bottles and barrels. They may not find anything else, but at this point, who knows."

"Here we go," Anita said. "They know that it was a male, probably in his late twenties or early thirties. Yada, yada, yada. Here it is. Two bullet holes. One in his skull and the other would have gone through his chest. One of the comments here is that it looked like an execution. Wow, Polly. You certainly find them."

"Is there any way of knowing when his death occurred? Was it really a hundred years ago?" Polly asked.

Anita took a moment and said, "They are waiting on more tests, but initial estimates point to the early nineteen hundreds."

"Do they have genealogical information on Franklin Bell to compare this to?"

"They sure do," Anita said. "There's a note here. They've sent out requests for any photographs of the Bell family to the Bellingwood library, our newspaper here, and the genealogical society in Boone, too. A student is going to attempt a skull reconstruction. That's kinda cool. I think that's all for now."

"That's great," Polly said. "Two bullet wounds. Do they know what kind of bullets?"

"Hmmm," Anita said. "Reading. Reading. No, they have the bullets, but haven't finished identifying them yet. There's another note about looking for some historical weapons. Guess that one hasn't been answered yet."

"That's fine. Makes sense. Thank you so much."

"No problem. Do you need anything else? Wanna talk to Sheriff Merritt?"

"I've talked to him enough this week. But Anita..." Polly stopped. She was probably going too far now. "Can you tell me anything about the girl I found on the highway?"

"I can't," Anita said.

"Because you'll get in trouble?"

"Well, that and because we don't know anything yet. They scheduled the autopsy, but then the coroner broke her hand in a softball game."

"Ouch. That probably sets you back."

"We aren't all that busy," Anita said, "but yeah. It's too bad. We all hate it when we know there's a family out there who has no idea what happened to their kid."

"So you don't know if she's from around here?"

"We don't yet. Nobody's reported her missing and I have a program watching the regional missing person reports."

Polly took a breath. Something had been preying on her mind and though it was probably preposterous, it wouldn't hurt to say it out loud. "Have you looked at reports from Ohio?"

"Why Ohio?" Anita asked, then she made a sound in her throat. "Oh. That's a good idea. It's doubtful, but we shouldn't rule it out."

"If he's everything that Stephanie says he is, I wouldn't put it past him," Polly said. "And if this is real, I need to stop begging Stephanie to come back. She's right and should stay far, far away from here until we catch him."

"We?" Anita asked. "That kind of talk will have Aaron dropping you into protective custody."

"Whatever. But if it is true, that means their father is already in Iowa and looking for them. He's not a nice man."

" I'll talk to Aaron and let him know what you said." Anita took a breath. "Polly, we really need to talk to Stephanie if he's in town, though. She's the only one who can tell us anything that would give us a clue on how to track him down."

"You're right, but that will be a difficult conversation to have with her. She's worked so hard to put him out of her head and has done everything she can to reduce his exposure to Kayla. I hate asking her to remember details about the man who treated her so badly."

"We can have a counselor here if that will help," Anita said.

"She has a therapist and Jeff is her rock. I don't know what I can do, but I'll try."

"Let me know when you're giving tours at the whiskey house," Anita said. "You always have interesting things going on in your life."

"I do wish it were quieter some days."

"Stay out of trouble. If Aaron needs anything more, I'll have him contact you."

Anita hung up and Polly stood there, staring at the ground. She almost wanted that poor girl she found on the highway to have been killed by Stephanie's father. That would mean there was only one deranged killer around. If it was anything else, well, she didn't want to consider that possibility.

CHAPTER TWELVE

No matter how much Andrew whined about blisters on his hands or Rebecca pleaded to just be allowed some free time since she worked so hard at school during the day, they were going over to the Bell House with Polly. They'd been under orders to finish their homework as soon as they got home from school and then they were expected to help.

There was no arguing with Polly. She wasn't leaving them alone and she needed as many hands to work as possible. Sylvie was all for it and brought work clothes every day for her son, knowing that if she didn't, he'd find a way to leave them at school to get out of helping.

Most of it was just adolescent complaining, but sometimes Polly wanted to put her hands over her ears and sing loudly to avoid hearing one more whiny voice. Maybe she should just try that someday. Today, though, she'd ordered them to change clothes. She wasn't putting up with their noise any longer. Andrew was shocked. Polly didn't often yell at him. That was okay, she'd work with the shock for a while. When it wore off, she'd try something different. Rebecca was learning where Polly's limits were. There were times she pushed past them, but this afternoon she acquiesced. Polly knew that it probably had a lot to do with Kayla being gone. The phone call last night had, at the same time, made Rebecca feel both better and worse.

When the kids joined her in the dining room in their work clothes, she hustled them down the back steps and out the door to the truck.

"What are we doing today?"

"Working on the porch with Henry, and I want to finish cleaning all of the junk out of the yard so Eliseo can bring the tiller over and start making grass grow again."

"I get the wheel barrow," Rebecca said.

"Ah man," Andrew whined. "That means I have to pick up the junk."

"I think you both pick up junk," Polly said. "We have plenty of gloves."

"I want the pink ones," Rebecca called out.

Polly watched Andrew in the rear view mirror. He nearly opened his mouth to argue, then clamped it shut. He caught her eye and grinned. "I get the black ones."

She pulled into the driveway and waved at Heath, who was rolling Henry's portable air compressor across the lawn. Polly was unnerved at the speed with which Henry sent nails into boards with his nail gun. The first few times she'd been around him, she backed off, sure that one was going to fly out and nail her right in the heart. Henry hadn't argued or done anything other than wait for her to live through the experience a few times. It was still strange to see him travel down a board at such high speed, but at least she was comfortable letting Andrew and Rebecca work in his vicinity.

He'd asked about her father's nail guns, showing her the boxes where they were stored. She didn't have a memory of her dad using them when she was in the workshop, but as she'd grown older, she was generally too busy to spend much time there.

Andrew saw people at the back of the house and took off running before she could stop him. "Go ahead," Polly said to

Rebecca. "They found another room this morning. I haven't talked to them since earlier today. Maybe you'll learn something new."

Rebecca ran to follow Andrew, and Polly wandered over to the porch. "Hey there, hotstuff," she said, hooking her arm into Henry's. "How was the rest of your day?"

He shook his head. "Randy punched a hole in a wall because he was jacking around with a two by four, then Ernie drove over a pile of wood, popped two tires, and managed to spit something up that poked a hole in a gas tank."

"Crap!" she exclaimed. "Are they fired?"

"Not today," he said with a grimace. "Mark thinks it was just a full moon. I'm about done with Randy, though. He's starting to cost me money."

"Ernie?"

Henry shrugged. "Bad day for him. He felt terrible. Then, when I was driving over here, Dad called and said that Mom saw a doctor today and he's worried about her blood pressure. That's got everyone in an uproar because Jessie thinks it's Molly's fault."

Polly slipped her hand down to take his, stoking the top of it with her thumb. "I'm sorry. What does your mom say?"

"That she'll figure this out and nobody is taking Molly away from her."

"Is your dad upset?"

Henry huffed out a breath. "Probably more than Mom. He started talking about moving back to Arizona and said something about this not happening if they'd been there."

"Oh no," Polly said. "That made you feel really guilty, didn't it."

"Gah." Henry sat down on a floor joist. "I love having them be part of the business, but I want them to be around for a long time. If being here for me shortens those years, I'll make changes right now."

Polly stood over him, still holding his hand. "Have you talked to your mother about this?"

He shook his head.

"So you don't know what her doctor said. You don't know how bad this is or anything."

"Hmph," he said. "No."

"It could just be that she needs to take medication and better care of herself, right?"

Henry didn't say anything.

"Right?"

He looked up. "I let Dad scare me. But I want her to be okay for a long time."

"Do you want to go talk to her?"

He nodded at the porch. "I need to work on this."

"Can I go talk to her?"

Henry stood back up. "Is it crazy of me to want you to fix this?"

Polly chuckled. "Not at all. You keep an eye on the kids. Don't let them bother the people out back too much and make them clean up the rest of this yard. It shouldn't take them any longer than an hour to finish. I'm going to take a ride over to the house and see for myself how Marie is doing. And then, if everything is okay, I'm going to go out to the shop and calm your father down. I'll let you know what I find out."

"It's just high blood pressure, right?" he asked plaintively.

"Right." Polly reached up and kissed his cheek. "And thank you for letting me stick my nose in this."

He kissed her cheek. "Go, before I realize how ridiculous I'm being and make you stay here."

She ran for her truck, waved and backed out of the driveway. This was probably one of the sillier things she'd done lately. Marie was going to think they'd all lost their minds. Family was so strange. They could yell at each other about the oddest things, but when it came to having a frank conversation about something like high blood pressure, that was too difficult.

It only took a few minutes to get across town. Polly drove into the parking area of the shop and turned off her truck, then took a breath. She headed for the back door of the house and stopped when she saw Molly and Marie in the back yard. Molly was in a cute little swimsuit, playing in a sandbox that Bill had made two weeks ago. Marie looked up from her lawn chair when she heard Polly's footsteps in the grass.

"Polly!" the little girl screamed.

Marie helped Molly get out of the box and released her to run to Polly. "What are you doing here today?" Marie asked as Polly bent down to scoop up Jessie's daughter.

Polly brushed sand from Molly's bottom and then kissed her cheek. "How are you?"

"Sand." Molly pointed at the sandbox.

"Do you want to go back in?"

Molly shook her head and snuggled into Polly's neck.

"I guess she wants a hug," Marie said. "Do you have a minute to sit?"

"I'm here because your husband and son are worried," Polly said. She took the arm of a second lawn chair and dragged it over to the sandbox.

"About me?" Marie asked. "Because of the doctor's appointment?" She rolled her eyes. "Those men."

"Bill seems to think that if you'd gone to Arizona, this wouldn't be a problem and now Henry's worried that you're going to die an early death."

Marie laughed out loud. "And neither one of them had the courage to talk to me about it. I tried to tell Bill that it was no big deal, but he is intent on worrying about me. My parents have high blood pressure and so does my brother. It was bound to happen. I don't know how I've done so well for as long as I did. We'll start the medication; I'll check it regularly and make a few alterations in my lifestyle and then move forward."

"I told Henry that he was worrying too much, but one of us needed to talk to you or he wouldn't sleep tonight. It's bad enough when I don't sleep, but that's not normal for him."

"He could sleep through anything," Marie said.

Molly settled down into Polly's lap and leaned against her, putting her thumb into her mouth. Polly looked up at Marie.

"Honey, thumb," Marie said.

When Molly didn't remove it, Marie nodded at Polly, who gently tugged the thumb out of the little girl's mouth. Molly resolutely put it right back in and Polly took it out again, then held her hand. She tried not to chuckle at the pouty lip that popped out, but before long, Molly relaxed against her again.

"Her nap was disturbed because of my appointment," Marie said. "I tried to schedule it so as to not disrupt her, but they just didn't have another time."

"Everything else is okay?" Polly asked.

"Healthy as an old lady horse. I told Bill that nothing was prying me away from this little girl. For heaven's sake, she's the one who keeps me so healthy. I haven't been so active since Lonnie and Henry were kids. I'm going to miss having a baby around as this one grows up. She changes so much."

Marie was always so careful about not making them feel guilty for not having babies, but every once in a while, Polly felt a little guilt for depriving her mother-in-law of the joy of being a grandmother.

"I understand you had some excitement at the new house," Marie said. "Henry told us that there was an old whiskey still down there."

"This morning they opened a new underground room and found barrels and empty bottles." Polly grinned. "They also found some labels that Franklin Bell must have had printed. It's strange to think that my house was part of history. We read about Prohibition and here I am finding it."

"You should talk to my father sometime." Marie's parents were world travelers. Polly had only met them a couple of times, though they had a home in Bellingwood.

"He isn't old enough to have been alive when the Bell House was built," Polly said.

"No, but *his* parents were. And they were a bunch of story tellers. If you get him started, he'll probably have plenty to tell you about the early days of Bellingwood."

Polly chuckled. "That would be great. Are they coming back for the Sesquicentennial?"

"They wouldn't miss it. Mom will dig out her bonnet and skirt and Dad will regale the city with tales; half made up and the other half true. You have to guess which is which and more than likely he doesn't even know any longer. But honey, didn't Henry tell you they were coming home this week? They want to meet your family and when I told them Rebecca's birthday party was on Sunday, they moved up their travel plans. I asked Henry to invite you all over to dinner Saturday night."

Polly had a hard time keeping her laughter in check, not wanting to wake Molly. The little girl had turned into a cuddly, warm ball on her lap and as long as Marie didn't say anything, Polly was going to continue to keep the child quiet.

"That's why he didn't have a problem with me coming over to talk to you about your high blood pressure," Polly said.

"What do you mean?"

"Because he had completely forgotten to tell me about the invitation and by making you do it, he knows I'll have calmed down by the time I see him again." Laughter rumbled in her chest and Molly squirmed against it, then settled back in to sleep.

"I'm so sorry," Marie said. "I should have called you myself, but it all happened yesterday and he stopped by this morning. I just assumed he said something."

"Please don't worry." Polly smiled. "I'm not upset. I'm looking forward to seeing your parents again. Can I bring anything?"

Marie shook her head. "Of course not. Mom and I have a great time in the kitchen together. She'll want to make something exotic and I won't have nearly the ingredients for it, but she'll make it up as she goes. Dad will hold court in the living room. I can almost see him striding up and down the length of it as he engages everyone in his stories. Bill will hide upstairs until he absolutely has to come down."

"He doesn't get along with your parents?"

Marie screwed up her mouth as she thought about how to respond. "That's not it, exactly. Bill always feels common around them. My parents don't think of him that way, but because they are educated and have been all over the world, he always tries to measure himself against their lives." She gave Polly a sad smile. "The thing is, my father would love to know the things that Bill knows - like how to create beauty with his hands. And though this was my parents' home, they aren't connected to people in town any longer. They know people, but they have no strong sense of community here." Marie shrugged. "They don't know you and to be honest, they're not close to Lonnie or Henry either. Oh, they're the fun grandparents that my kids loved to talk about, but there were never hugs or sitting on their lap or snuggling up against them on Christmas morning while we sang Christmas carols. Dad knows what they missed out on, though he wouldn't have changed his life. And he thinks the world of Bill for providing that for me. But Bill is still uncomfortable."

"I guess I'm lucky," Polly said.

"What's that, dear?"

"Because I have you here. Both of you."

"Yes you do and I promise you that I'm not going anywhere."

"Do you think your parents will ever settle down in Bellingwood?"

"Someday maybe they'll have to," Marie replied. "They can't travel forever, though it feels like they're going to try their very best to do so."

"Do you miss them?"

"I don't think so. This has always been their life. I got out of it as soon as I was able, but I've never known anything different with them."

Jessie came around the corner of the house and saw her daughter on Polly's lap. "Hi there," she said in low tones.

"Hi yourself. I have a snuggly baby." Polly stroked Molly's hair. "She's pretty cute."

"I just came out to see if she needed anything." Jessie smiled at Marie. "I needed a break. Your husband and Les are spraying finish in there today and even the air purifier isn't cleaning it up."

"Pull up a chair, honey," Marie said.

Jessie grabbed the closest chair. "Have you heard anything from Stephanie?"

"That's right," Marie said. "You've had a really rough week. How are things working out at the office?"

"We have a good temp girl," Polly replied, "but we miss

Stephanie, and Rebecca misses Kayla. She called last night to tell us they were safe."

"Do you know where they are?" Jessie asked.

Molly must have finally heard her mother's voice because she came awake and started to work up to tears. Jessie leaned over and took her daughter from Polly and patting her, put her back to sleep in her own arms.

"They won't tell us," Polly said. "And I guess I don't blame Stephanie for that. If their father is nearby, it's probably not safe for them to be here. I just hope that he's found soon so everyone can get back to normal."

Jessie kissed her daughter's head. "Do you think he's here?"

"I don't know what to think. He might be. But then again, he could still be hiding in Ohio. Right now it's all up in the air."

"I can't even begin to think about how bad that was for Stephanie," Jessie said. "Nobody should treat their daughter like that."

Polly smiled and nodded. Jessie's mother had nothing to do with her and she hadn't seen her father since he'd come out to Iowa to find her. Neither Jessie nor Stephanie had lived through a normal childhood, but at least they'd both found people in Bellingwood who stepped in as friends and family. Polly was so grateful to Marie Sturtz for what she did for Jessie and Molly. When Jessie had needed a solid rock, Marie was there to provide it.

"I'm glad she got out of there," Polly said. "Now I just want her to come home."

They all looked up as Bill Sturtz came into the back yard. "It looks like I found the garden," he said.

Marie chuckled. "What?"

"All the prettiest flowers are right here in my back yard."

"You sweet talker, you."

"Jess, you should go on home with your tired baby," he said. "Len and I are going to be spraying in there for the next couple of hours. If the phone rings, they can leave a message and we'll handle it tomorrow."

Marie hopped out of her chair. "Let me round up Molly's things. You stay right there."

"I can do it, Marie." Bill stepped in front of her. "Just tell me what I need to do."

She pushed him back. "William Sturtz, you're a wonderful man and I love you, but if you get fretful about my blood pressure, you're going to send it sky high and then you and I will have a long talk. I am fine. The doctor says I'm healthy. Don't you dare turn this into something that it isn't. Got it?" She pecked his cheek with a kiss and swept past him.

He turned and looked sheepishly at Polly and Jessie. "Am I in trouble?"

Polly laughed. "If you weren't so cute, you'd be in trouble all the time, I'm thinking."

"Maybe you and your family should meet us at Davey's for dinner tonight. I don't know that I want to stay at home alone with her until I figure out how to get out of this one."

"We're working over at the new house," Polly said. "And we'll be sweaty messes by the time we're through. I think you're on your own tonight."

He lifted his eyes to the sky. "Heaven help me."

Marie came back outside with a backpack. "Here you go, Jessie." She put it on the ground in front of Jessie's chair and then sat back down and looked up at her husband. "You go work and don't come in the house until you decide that I'm going to be fine. Got it?"

"Yes ma'am," he said and sauntered off. Polly watched him leave and laughed when he turned back around and stuck his tongue out at his wife.

"You two still have a lot of fun, don't you," Polly said.

"Every day."

CHAPTER THIRTEEN

Every day this week, Polly woke up stiff and sore. It was finally Friday. The weekend was too busy for more construction. At some point her muscles would be back in shape, but she had another day of aches to wash away under a hot shower.

Sal was already driving to Des Moines to collect her mother from the airport. She had begged Polly to meet them for a late lunch at Davey's and then give a tour of Sycamore House and the Bell House.

With all that had been going on over at the Bell House this week, Polly looked forward to watching Mrs. Kahane traipse through the yard to show her the Prohibition hideout and storage they'd uncovered. Students from the university had found their way to Bellingwood all week, and last night they'd pronounced the tunnel quite safe.

Andrew was beside himself. He'd been allowed to walk through the tunnel just before his mother picked him up and it was as if his brain found a new high speed. He'd babbled to Rebecca about the stories he could tell and she'd grown excited with him at the possibilities.

Henry planned to reinforce the doorways on both ends before too much traffic passed through there. He'd also talked to a few of his vendors about the best way to shore up the walls of the rooms where they'd found the still and the barrels. Since the holes had already been dug and the earth had long since settled, he and Polly were dreaming about what to build on top of that space. They'd discussed a patio, but with a large back porch attached to the house, it didn't make much sense. At this point, anything was possible.

Polly turned the water off in the shower and rolled her shoulders. She had no idea how she'd been so lucky as to find someone like Henry. There was nothing he couldn't do and when he told her to dream big and they'd either figure out how to make it happen or scale back from there, she could hardly contain herself. The Bell House was going to take a long time to get to where she was happy with it. Henry had to remind her on a regular basis that they were in no hurry. That worked most of the time, but when she got excited, all she could see was the finished project and she wanted to be there right now.

By the time Polly got to the kitchen, Henry was gone for the day. He liked being able to let his crews leave early on Friday afternoons, so that meant his day started before everyone else's.

"Have the dogs gone out?" she asked.

Heath was in front of the television eating his breakfast while Rebecca had her nose in a book at the dining room table.

"Hey. Family," Polly said, louder than she'd spoken the first time.

"Yeah. They went out," Rebecca said.

"What are you reading?"

Rebecca tipped the book up and then back down before Polly could focus on the title.

"Is that for a class?"

"No. Just some of my friends are reading it. It's okay. I got it at the library."

"What are you watching, Heath?" Polly asked, loud enough for him to hear.

"ESPN. No biggie."

"Why don't you come over and join us?"

Rebecca looked up; startled. "Are we having a family meeting or something?"

"No. I just wanted to spend time with my family before the day started." Polly went into the kitchen and poured herself a cup of coffee, then looked around. "What did you guys eat for breakfast?"

"I just had some juice," Rebecca said.

Heath dropped into a chair at the table. "What's up?"

"Did you eat anything?" Polly asked him.

He shrugged. "I'm not that hungry."

"For heaven's sake," she said and opened the cupboard. Pulling out cereal boxes, she put them on the peninsula and then took milk out of the refrigerator. "You two are eating something before you go to school. No argument. Heath, come get bowls and spoons. Rebecca, put your book down and grab the cereal and milk." She took a drink of coffee and then pulled the toaster away from the wall, making sure it was plugged in. "I'm going to make toast and you're going to eat it."

"You don't have to do all that," Heath said.

"What are your plans tonight?" Polly asked. He'd worked hard this week with Henry putting the porch on at the new house and though he'd offered, tonight they were taking a break. The weekend was going to be busy enough without starting it out with more construction.

Heath moved past her with the bowls and spoons. She took down two clean glasses and put them on the peninsula, too.

"Rebecca," she said, louder than she intended.

"What?"

"Put a bookmark in your book and close it."

"But I'm almost to a stopping point."

Polly laughed. She'd been there too many times to count. It wasn't going to work on her, though. "Just think about how exciting it will be to go back to that. Close the book."

Rebecca jammed a piece of paper in the book and slammed it on the table.

"Rebecca?" Polly warned.

"Sorry."

"So what are you doing tonight, Heath?" Polly asked. "Anything fun?"

"I dunno," he said. "We were supposed to go over to Morgan's house, but her dad got the flu or something. Nobody has any money to go out."

"Bring 'em here," Polly said. "We'll buy pizza. And we'll leave you all alone. I promise." She couldn't think of anything better than hiding in her bedroom, reading a book and snoozing while Henry watched television.

"What about me?" Rebecca asked. Her shoulders slumped and she dropped her head. "It's my birthday weekend."

"You're right," Polly said. "Heath, you can't have any of your friends over tonight."

Rebecca looked up at her in confusion. "Why not?"

"Because it's your birthday weekend."

"I didn't mean that. I just kinda thought Kayla would be around and we'd do something."

Polly hugged her shoulders. "I know that. But we're going to have a wildly busy weekend with a lot of people celebrating different things. You're going to meet Henry's grandparents tomorrow night and I know they're looking forward to meeting both of you. Sal's baby shower is tomorrow and your party is on Sunday. Beryl is taking you out for lunch tomorrow before the shower. There is so much going on." She turned to Heath. "Do you want to bring your friends here?"

"Yeah. That'd be great," he said. "Six thirty okay?"

"That's fine. And as for you, little Miss, you have a couple of options. I could talk to Jessie about you..."

"Could I spend the night with her and Molly? That would be awesome. I haven't been over there in a long time. We could stay up late and watch movies and she could do makeup and my hair. Please, please, please?"

"I'll talk to her. If that's what you want to do and she's available, you're set."

"Beg her," Rebecca whined. "That would be the perfect start to my birthday weekend." She clasped her hands together in front of her face, "Oh please."

Polly chuckled. "I'll see what we can do." She walked around the table and put her hand on Heath's shoulder. "If you think about it, text me today and tell me about how many are going to show up."

He nodded, his mouth full of cereal. "I will," he said once he'd swallowed. "Thanks."

~~~

Polly smoothed a phantom wrinkle in her skirt as she turned to look at her back in the mirror. Everything was in place and she was fit to be seen with Lila Kahane. The woman was as judgmental as could be, but so far, Polly had escaped much of her criticism. It was funny. She encountered these same people every day in Bellingwood, but gave them no thought. She didn't care what they thought of her and when some of the women she knew made snide comments about what she wore or how Rebecca dressed, she just ignored it. They weren't her friends, they didn't impact her life and she didn't have time for their petty behaviors. But for some reason, Sal's mother was different. Polly knew it was probably because Sal was always concerned about her mother's perceptions and that rubbed off. The thing was, Lila loved Polly and could never say enough nice things about her. Polly had caught Sal sticking her tongue out more than once as her mother gushed over something Polly said or did.

The number of times Polly had to dress up to this degree during the day were limited now that she owned Sycamore House, but she still had a few nice things from the days she worked in the Boston Public Library. She slipped her feet into blue pumps that matched her skirt, checked one more time that everything was in place, and headed for the back door. When she opened the garage door, she laughed out loud. Only in the Midwest could she dress as she had and then drive a truck to
~~~

lunch. Polly had to hike her skirt to climb up into the cab and that made her laugh all the harder. This was the life. Lila Kahane would never understand its appeal.

She pulled into a parking space at Davey's and was relieved to see that Sal's car wasn't already there. Being late was an incredible sin in Lila Kahane's eyes. It wouldn't matter that you were three minutes early. Mrs. Kahane had her own clock and judged everyone's timing accordingly. Polly used the extra moments to get out of her truck as gracefully as she could manage. Maybe a more flared skirt the next time would be a better idea. She went inside, told the hostess there would be three of them and when asked if she wanted to be seated, Polly chose to wait instead.

She didn't wait long for Sal and her mother. Both women were tall. Where Sal preferred deep reds and rich tones, her mother accented her beautiful silver hair with blues and sumptuous grays. They caused heads to turn no matter where they were, both entering a room with an air of authority and grace.

"Polly," Lila said, giving her a light hug and touching her cheek to Polly's. "It's good to see you. Living in the country has done wonders for you." She patted both of the younger women's faces. "For both of you. You look so healthy." Lila pinched Sal's cheek and said, "All of that color in your faces, extra meat on your bones and you look comfortable in your lovely clothes."

Wham. Polly wondered what the car ride up from Des Moines had been like for Sal.

"Is this your party?" the hostess asked Polly. When given an affirmative nod, she continued. "Right this way."

Lila Kahane led out and Sal drifted behind, grabbing Polly's hand. She opened her eyes wide and shook her head, mouthing, "Oh my lord!"

Polly tried not to chuckle and barely contained it when Lila turned around. "Hurry, girls. Don't make me walk by myself."

"Yes, mother," Sal said. She squeezed Polly's hand and then dropped it, walking around the table to sit beside her mother.

The hostess handed out menus and then asked if she could get anything from the bar for them.

Lila spoke up first. "Please bring me a tall glass of iced tea. Pour the tea over the ice, please, do not put the ice in after you've filled it with tea. I would like real sugar brought to the table in a bowl, not any of that packaged stuff and in another dish, bring four lemon wedges. Be sure to wash the lemons before you slice them." Then she looked at Sal and Polly.

Polly had always known Sal to be picky when she ordered food in a restaurant, but she watched Sal process on what her mother was doing.

"I'll just have water," Sal said.

Polly smiled at the hostess. "Water is fine for me, too. Thank you."

"Is there anything other than steak to eat here?" Lila asked.

Sal took a breath. "Open your menu, mother. It's a very nice restaurant with a large selection."

"So you don't have a chef who specializes in interesting entrees," Lila said. "Just run of the mill food." She looked through the menu, turned to the back, then opened it again and glanced through it before putting it down. "I guess a cobb salad will have to do."

"Mother," Sal said.

Polly nudged Sal's foot with her own. "I think I'll have a salad as well," Polly said. "But their pepper steak salad is very popular."

Mrs. Kahane picked her menu back up. "With a raspberry vinaigrette? That sounds lovely."

It nearly killed Polly to not snort a laugh, but she kept a straight face and didn't even wince when Sal kicked her under the table.

"You should also have a salad," Mrs. Kahane said to her daughter. "I can't imagine how much work you'll have to do to take off all the weight you put on during pregnancy."

"My doctor says that I'm doing just fine with the weight I've gained, mother. I'm not worried."

"Of course you aren't. You're young and don't see things through hindsight like I do."

Sal smiled and closed her menu. "I've seen pictures of you

while you were pregnant with me and just a few months after I was born. You never experienced much weight gain. How could you possibly know about this?"

Lila pursed her lips and glared at Sal. "I do have friends and they talk about the issues their daughters go through."

"I'm my own person and you do not need to compare me to the lazy slobs who belong to your friends," Sal said. She looked up when the waitress approached with their drinks. "The tea and all its special fixins' are for my mother."

After the girl was finished putting drinks down, she asked, "What may I get for you today?"

"First of all," Lila said. "I want you to make sure that I am the only one who sees the bill for today's meal. I will take care of it."

"Okay," the waitress agreed, her pen poised.

"I will have the pepper steak salad with raspberry vinaigrette. Be sure the dressing is on the side and in a real dish, not a plastic cup. I'd like the steak to be medium rare, not beat to death on the grill or griddle or whatever you cook it on and I can not abide onions. Whatever you do, make sure that there are none on my salad. Do you have all of that?"

"Yes ma'am. Dressing on the side, medium rare, no onions." Without waiting for a response, the waitress turned her body to face Polly. "And you?"

"I'll have the same, but with onions and the dressing directly on the salad," Polly said. "Thanks."

"And for you, Miss Kahane?"

"I feel like steak today, too," Sal said. "But I want a New York strip, medium rare, baked potato with butter and sour cream and whatever your vegetables are for today. Oh, and a cup of corn chowder. You can just bring it out with the meal."

"Anything else?"

Sal looked at her mother, who was doing her best not to look shocked, but she was too well-mannered to say anything.

"That should be fine," Sal said. "And thank you."

"Are you sure you'll be able to eat all of that?" Lila asked. "That's an immense meal."

"What I don't eat, I'll take home to the pups," Sal said.

"Salliane," Lila scolded.

"Mother," Sal retorted in the same tone of voice.

Lila turned her attention to Polly. "I'm looking forward to seeing your little Sycamore House. Sal says that you have quite a nice business going on here. That's wonderful, dear."

"I enjoy it," Polly said. "There is always something interesting happening in the building."

"And you've taken in two young children to care for?"

"Rebecca will be going into the eighth grade this fall and Heath will be a senior in high school," Polly replied. "They aren't so young, but they're mine and I love them."

"Tell me about this new house that you're renovating. It used to be a speakeasy? I attended a lecture several years ago on women who brought about Prohibition. It was fascinating information."

"The house was originally built as an upscale hotel, and I believe the owner thought he could make extra money by selling whiskey. They also had musical groups come in from the larger cities in the Midwest. We don't know anything for certain except that he was distilling whiskey over there."

"You certainly have your hands full. And you're happy with your husband?" Lila wrinkled her forehead. "Tell me why you didn't take his name. Is it purely for business reasons?"

"The business had much to do with it, but it was personal as well," Polly said. "I suppose some might call me an independent girl, but I've always been Polly Giller and since I wasn't expecting Henry to take my name, he didn't think it crucial that I take his."

Lila laughed a pert little laugh and dabbed at her lips with the napkin. "You girls and your newfangled ways. I just hope Sal decides to give the child a solid foundation before it's born."

Sal took a deep breath and looked up in relief as the waitress approached with a large tray. She neatly placed their plates in front of them and stepped back. "Is everything to your liking?" she asked, looking directly at Lila. She had taken extra time to make sure that each request of Lila's was correct as she put things on the table.

"This looks fine," Sal said and held up her glass. "Could I get some more, please?"

"I'll be right back with a pitcher."

Polly knew this meal could go one of two ways, so she quickly took a bite of her salad and when it was just as she expected it to be, looked up at Lila. "This was such a good choice. It's one of my favorite dishes here. I love the blend of flavors. How does yours taste?"

Sal shook her head and smiled at Polly as they waited for Mrs. Kahane to take a bite.

"It's very good, dear. Thank you for recommending it to me." She put her knife and fork down, wiped her hands on her napkin and turned to Sal. "How is yours?"

Sal hadn't done anything other than cut into the steak. "It looks perfect. I'm sure it's fine. Mother, you should hear what Polly's been up to this week. She found another body, you know."

"Other than the bones with the still?" Lila asked, turning her focus to Polly.

Polly kicked Sal under the table again and smiled. This was going to be a long afternoon.

CHAPTER FOURTEEN

"Everything is good here. Let's take the dogs for a ride," Henry said. "It's a beautiful evening."

Jessie had picked Andrew and Rebecca up after she left work. They were going to have a pizza and watch movies until Sylvie collected her son. Heath and Polly had made a quick run to the store for extra junk food and soda pop for his party and all he needed to do was be downstairs to bring up pizza when it arrived. He was pretty excited about the evening.

"I don't feel comfortable leaving the kids all alone in the house."

Henry laughed at her. "We'll only be gone a couple of hours and there are so many adults downstairs that know us and care for our kids, we have nothing to worry about." He smiled. "And consider this another step in showing Heath that we trust him."

"But I don't want to set him up to fail," Polly protested.

"We've already talked to him about being responsible and keeping an eye on his friends so they're responsible, too. These are good kids and we'll be back long before the party's over. Then you can send me to our room and I'll go peacefully.

"Fine." Polly relented. It didn't sound like Henry was giving up easily. "But what about dinner?"

"We'll figure it out as we go," he said. "Come on."

They went out to the dining room where Heath was re-stacking cups and plates for the third time.

"Are you really okay with us being gone for a while?" Polly asked.

He shrugged. "It's fine. Not like anything's going to happen. We're just going to play games and eat.

"Okay," Polly said. "Have fun."

She patted her leg and Obiwan jumped up from where he'd been lying in the kitchen. "Come on, boy. We're going for a walk."

Han ran to the back stairway and waited, dancing in place until Polly and Henry got there. Henry snagged two of their longest leashes and herded the dogs into his truck's back seat, then held the door for Polly.

"This is almost like a date," she said with a smile.

"Consider it exactly that."

"Where are you taking me?"

"You'll see."

She buckled in and leaned back in the seat, scratching Obiwan's head as he reached forward to lick her face. "I know, I know. It's so exciting. You've been stuck at home all week long with nowhere fun to go. Now sit back where you belong."

"So Rebecca's going to be gone all night long?" Henry asked as he backed out and headed for the highway.

Polly grinned over at him. "All night. Gonna get me drunk so you can have your way with me?"

"Like I need to get you drunk for that."

"You could try it."

"I know you," Henry replied. "At first you're giddy and happy and horny and then? Then you're asleep."

"That's me. A useless happy drunk. Poor Henry."

She looked over at him when he made a familiar turn. "Are we going to the Bell House?"

"Patience, my dear." He put his hand on the console and waited for her to place hers within it. They interlinked their fingers and he gave her a gentle squeeze. "I know this has been a tough week." Then he chuckled. "And today you got to spend time with Sal and her mother."

Polly shook her head. "That woman is a trial to Sal. She's just one of those people who sees the world in a very different light. Her rules are so odd and yet she has no concept that people don't see things the way she does. It's funny to watch Sal, though."

"What do you mean?" Henry took his hand back as he turned into the driveway of their house.

"What's that?" Polly asked, pointing at the porch.

"Just a little surprise. Let's put the leashes on the dogs so they don't wander off. I keep thinking that even though there is so much to do in the house, we should focus on finishing fencing so we can bring them over more often."

Though the sun was still up, candles had been lit along the edge of the porch floor and a quilt had been tossed across the raw wood. Polly snapped the leash onto Obiwan's collar, while Henry did the same for Han and she jumped out of her side of the truck, then met Henry as he waited for her. The dogs rushed ahead, sniffing and stopping to check out every inch of the yard they could reach.

"How did you do this?" Polly asked.

"Here, hold Han for a minute."

She took the leash and stood, staring at the porch in awe. This was so sweet. Henry ducked into the side door of the house and came back with a large picnic basket, then taking Han's leash, he led them all to the porch. He dropped Han's leash over a post that had been placed in the ground next to the quilt and then took Obiwan's and did the same.

Polly sat down on the quilt and took the basket from him, then opened it. "Where did you come up with all of this?"

"I asked Mom to help. She and Molly prepared dinner, then Jessie and the kids brought it here and set things up. Did I surprise you?"

"This is amazing. You are always doing things like this for me. What's this?" Polly took out a pink rose.

"That's from Mom's garden," Henry said. "I can't believe she already has some blooming. You know, I know she worried that I would never find the right woman to marry, but neither of us could have seen you coming."

"I'm not sure quite what to say to that."

"Don't you know that you changed all of our lives when you arrived in Bellingwood? I was on my way to being a second rate carpenter. I probably would have worked for other contractors for the rest of my life. Sturtz Construction would never have been a big deal. But then you showed up and not only am I running the business, but it's growing and I have more confidence in my work than ever before. And then, there's Mom and Dad. They're having the time of their lives with people they never thought they'd get to know. Mom has Jessie and Molly and you and Rebecca and then Heath and Hayden. Do you know that she and Molly go over to Ames every once in a while to have lunch with him? Just to make him feel like he's part of the family. And Dad is building things that he'd never thought he would get a chance to build. He says that he's doing better work now than ever before. And Polly, it's all because you showed up and fell in love with me."

"You're exaggerating," Polly said. "I believe these things were going to happen and I showed up just because the timing was right." She pulled out a package. "What are we eating tonight?"

"It's just sandwiches," Henry said in way of apology. "I didn't know how long it would be before we got here and since there's no microwave, I wasn't sure how I'd heat something up."

"This one is peanut butter and jelly," Polly said with a laugh.

"That's from Molly. But Mom did pack a cold bottle of wine and some glasses for us."

"Oh, so you *are* planning to get me drunk and have your way with me."

"Look up there," Henry said, pointing at the sky. "It's a falling star."

"I wish I may, I wish I might have the wish I wish tonight," Polly said and closed her eyes. When she opened them, she asked, "You wanna know what I wished for?"

"No," he said. "Don't tell me or it won't come true."

"It comes true all the time. I wished that we would continue to have as much fun as we do now."

Henry leaned across the basket and kissed her lips, causing Polly to drop the sandwich and put her arms around his neck, holding him close. He reached up, caressed her cheek with his hand, then brushed his thumb under her chin. "I love you, Polly."

She put the basket behind her and scooted close to him, then leaned against his shoulder, breathing deeply as he encompassed her in his arms. "I love you so much and I think you just made me fall in love with our porch."

Polly felt Henry's laugh resonate against her and allowed herself to relax into his arms as he rested his chin on top of her head.

~~~

Even after her protests about leaving the apartment, Polly had been reluctant to leave the Bell House. They'd returned to a house filled with noise and excitement; kids spread out everywhere. Some were gathered around the television playing video games, a group at the dining room table was playing Polly's old Sorry game and when she walked through to the living room, she laughed to see that they'd pushed the sofas back to play Twister.

Jason introduced her to a girl that he had told her about before, insisting they were just friends. He, Scar, Kent and the girl, Mel, had found a corner and were playing Scrabble. Funny thing was, Selena Morris was nowhere to be found.

She looked around for some of the girls she'd seen at other parties, but didn't recognize many. Heath assured them that the apartment would be cleaned up before everyone went home, but Polly wasn't worried. He was having a great time and whatever mess was left over was worth it.

Polly was certain she'd remember none of the people Heath introduced her too. For as much as she loved meeting people, she had the worst time remembering names. If she met them more
~~~

than once, her odds were much better and she hoped that some of these kids would be around for a long time. Henry had recognized some of the family names, but agreed with Polly that he'd not remember any of the kids' names tomorrow morning. There were just too many, too fast.

The dogs created quite a stir when they came bounding into the media room. They made their way from person to person, sniffing in greeting and allowing the kids to pet them and snuggle as they pleased.

Polly watched the activity for a few minutes, just to make sure things were going smoothly and adult intervention was unnecessary. She double checked the bedrooms and bathrooms, remembering a few parties she'd been to in high school. Back in her day, someone was always sneaking out to be alone with a boyfriend or girlfriend. The only thing she couldn't do was check the rest of Sycamore House. If kids had come to the party and then snuck to any one of the hideaways in the building, there wasn't much she could do. When she asked Heath if everyone was where they were supposed to be, without hesitation, he confirmed that to be true. She had to trust him.

By the time she got back to her bedroom, Henry and the cats were already settled in, him in his easy chair in front of the television and the cats sprawled out on top of the bed, as close as they could get to him without actually being on top of him. Henry had adapted quite easily to being a dog person and he didn't mind the cats, but they knew better than to climb all over him. He just put them on the floor over and over until they quit bothering him.

"How's it going out there?" he asked.

"They're having a good time. Did you see Jason with that girl, Mel?"

"I saw a girl playing a game with him and his buddies. What are you trying to tell me?"

"I don't know." Polly kicked her shoes off and then looked guiltily at Henry before picking them up and putting them where they belonged. That was one of the things she planned to demand when they moved into the Bell House. Her own room that she could mess up and never clean. She flopped across the bed, lying on her stomach and peered at the television to see what Henry was watching. "The news channel?"

"There's nothing else on."

"Reruns would be better than this. All they do is tell us what we're supposed to be angry about."

He switched the television off and stood up. "What would you rather do?"

Polly pursed her lips. "I'd rather do *that,* but there are way too many people in the house."

"We are kind of trapped in here." He flopped himself on top of her, scattering the cats.

"What?" Polly gasped.

"TV is boring, we can't mess around, I'm stuck in a room with you. What else should I be doing?"

She attempted to roll over, but Henry had dropped all of his weight on her torso, making it impossible for her to move. In fact, breathing was becoming a much sought after commodity.

"Can't breathe," she moaned.

Henry lifted himself up just enough for her lungs to work and Polly made another attempt to flip him off her, to no avail.

"What in the world are you doing?" she asked, laughing, now that she finally had enough air.

"I told you. Something."

"What do you mean something?"

"It's just something."

Polly attempted to slide off the edge of the bed and Henry dropped down across the back of her legs and caught her ankles.

"Have you lost your mind?" she asked.

He started tickling the bottom of her feet and Polly squirmed to avoid his grip.

A light knock on the door and it came open, startling both of them. Henry rolled off Polly, barely catching his breath from laughter and Polly lifted her head to see Heath standing in the doorway, looking as perplexed as any poor young man might in this situation.

"I'm sorry," he said and pulled the door shut again.

"Heath, no," Polly called out, sliding all the way to the floor. She was this far gone, she might as well humiliate herself completely. "Come on back in, we were just messing around."

He opened the door again and kept his head down.

"It's really okay, Heath," Henry said, climbing off the bed. "We just got a little bored."

Polly had gotten to her feet by this point and sat down in Henry's chair. "We're sorry we're weird. What's going on?"

"Livia's mom just went into labor and they're going to the hospital. She needs a ride home fast so she can watch her little brother."

"Do we need to take her?" Polly asked, jumping up.

"Well, I can, if that's okay. Jason said he'd hang here until I got back. Do you mind?"

Polly turned to Henry, who shrugged. "Go," she said. "Get her home and come back."

"Do you care if I stop at the convenience store on my way back and get some ice cream? We're going to make sundaes."

Henry walked to the door. "I'll go get ice cream. I need to do something."

"Okay," Heath said, looking back and forth between the two of them. "Thanks. I'll be right back."

Polly tucked her feet up underneath her in Henry's chair and patted her legs for Luke to come up. He sat down on the floor, lifted a leg and cleaned his toes instead.

"Fine," she said and switched the television back on. "Well, that was embarrassing." Leia jumped back up on the bed, looked over at Polly and without warning, leaped across the expanse, startling both of them when she landed in Polly's lap.

Buzzing in her back pocket forced her to disturb the cat as she pulled out her phone.

"Hello?"

"Polly, it's Kayla. Is Rebecca there? Can I talk to her?"

"Oh, honey," Polly said. "She's over at Jessie's tonight. Where are you?"

"I'm not supposed to tell you."

"This is another new number. I didn't recognize it."

"Stephanie bought another phone today. She said that dad would figure out a way to find us because Jeff keeps texting and calling."

"Is she there?" Polly asked. "Will she talk to me?"

Kayla must have put her hand over the phone, because Polly heard muffled sounds. "She says you'll just try to talk her into coming back and we can't."

"She's right. I will try to talk you into returning, but most of all, I want to know that you're safe. Are you?"

"Yeah. I miss school and I really miss Rebecca. I can't believe I can't go to her birthday party. You're still having it, aren't you?"

"Absolutely. I wish you could be here, too. Please. Can I talk to Stephanie?"

There were more muffled sounds and then, "Hi Polly. It's me."

Polly breathed a sigh of relief. "Oh, Stephanie, it's so good to hear your voice. Are you two safe? Do you need anything? Do you have enough money? Are you getting enough to eat?"

"We're fine. You guys really just have to let this go. As long as my dad is out, he's not only a threat to me, but everybody else. He'll do anything he can to get what he wants. And he told me he wants ..." Stephanie paused and Polly heard a door click shut. "He told me that he wants Kayla. Polly, he told me that he dreams about having her every night. Can you believe that? Why would he say something like that to me?"

"Because he wants to scare you, honey."

"Well it worked. I'm terrified. I won't let him get near her."

"I get that. But you have a host of people here in Bellingwood that feel the same way. You don't have to do this alone."

"Yes I do. You all have your own families and your own lives to take care of. This is my family and nobody cares about Kayla like I do. I won't let him hurt her."

"Stephanie." Polly took a breath. "How long have you been part of my life?"

"I don't know exactly."

"Long enough to know that I have a tendency to take care of everyone. Remember, I'm the one who brought Heath Harvey into my house and that was after he threatened me."

"But he's your family."

"He wasn't when that happened and sweetie, you've been part of my family since that night Kayla came home with Rebecca after school. The thing is? Jeff is absolutely devastated that you're gone. Girl, he loves you to pieces."

"He's just my boss."

"Stephanie Armstrong, you know better than that. You should be ashamed of yourself."

"I know. You're right. He and I are friends."

"And he needs you. I mean, how many stalking texts have you gotten from him?"

Stephanie laughed. "I lost count."

"Don't you think the two of you would be safe at his apartment?"

"But I don't want to put him in any danger, either. Polly, you don't know how bad my father is. Nobody does."

"It's enough to know that you are scared of what he'll do. That's all any of us really need to know. Stephanie, this isn't about him. I don't give a hoot in hell about that man. I care about you and Kayla. He can be as scary as he wants, but we won't let him hurt you."

"You won't be able to stop him."

The conversation wasn't going to resolve. "Can you tell me where you are?" Polly asked. "Are you staying in a nice place at least? Eating at some nice restaurants?"

"We're doing fine," Stephanie said. "I'm not ready to tell you where we are or where we're going."

"Honey, you have to stop going. Bellingwood is your home and Jeff and I are your family. We might be a weird little family, but we are family. And you know I don't take that word lightly. Think about Kayla. She needs to finish the school year. Taking a week off is one thing, but it will be really difficult for her to make up the time she's gone if you don't come back."

"I know," Stephanie said softly. "I've been thinking about that."

"Look, you can stay at Sycamore House in the addition or you can stay at Jeff's apartment in Ames. Who would think to look for you there? We can figure out how to keep Kayla safe when she's at school. I'll pick them up after school and get them back here safely. We can do this. And who knows, your father might not even be in the neighborhood."

"Oh he's there," Stephanie said. "I checked my messages on my old phone. He's left me a bunch, telling me what he's going to do to Kayla because I kept her away from him."

"You know he's in town?"

"Yeah. Somewhere around there. He said he found our trailer and he went in and lay down on our beds so he could smell us."

"Oh, Stephanie, I'm so sorry." Polly wanted to be sick. She couldn't imagine what Stephanie was feeling. "I have a difficult question. Have you saved those messages?"

"Damn straight," Stephanie said. "Once he's caught, I want to have all the evidence I can to put him away for life."

"Good for you. I'm proud of you for taking charge, you know. But remember, you don't have to do this alone."

"I have to go now. Kayla's in the other room."

"Can we talk again?"

"Okay."

"Promise?"

"Yeah. I promise."

CHAPTER FIFTEEN

Drifting in and out of sleep the next morning, Polly finally pulled herself fully awake. They'd been up much too late last night chatting with Heath, who was wired higher than a kite. It made her smile to realize how far he'd come this last year.

He and Henry were already gone this morning and since Jessie was going to make sure that Rebecca got to Beryl's house for her art lesson, Polly had nowhere to be until Sal's shower this afternoon. Then her heart lurched. She also had dinner tonight with Henry's grandparents. There was no reason for that to make her nervous, but it did. All she knew about them was that they traveled the world and met extraordinary people. Somehow it made her feel so commonplace. She understood what made Bill so uncomfortable around them.

Did they like a good McDonald's hamburger or were they above that, only eating foie gras and duck confit? The thought of either of those items turned Polly's stomach. Maybe living the international high life wasn't all that special.

But it was. They'd seen things she would never get an opportunity to see. They'd climbed the Eiffel Tower and had even met the Pope in Vatican City. They'd gone to Rio for Carnival and ridden on elephants in India. Marie had hated that life, but it was surprising to Polly that Henry was so willing to stay at home. He told her that he'd never had anyone to travel with, but he seemed to be as content as she was with living in Bellingwood.

Rebecca's heart was more attuned to travel. While they weren't traveling as a family this summer with all that was going on, next summer had to be different. However, Polly could hardly wait to give Rebecca her birthday present. She'd been planning it for months and it was killing her to wait.

Henry and Heath were at the shop finishing their gift for Rebecca. They wouldn't let Polly in on that secret either. She wasn't sure who was more ready to burst for tomorrow's fun: her or Rebecca.

As for the shower, Polly and Sal had long since managed that gift. Polly had hired Bill Sturtz to build a crib for the nursery and then she helped Sal refinish a few pieces they found at Simon Gardner's antique shop earlier this spring. Polly did all of the work, since Sal was afraid of getting too near the chemicals, but between the two of them, they'd started an absolutely adorable room for the baby. The pieces Sal had purchased this week would finish it. Since Sal and Mark didn't want to know the gender before the birth, Sal was using bright primary colors against the dark walnut furniture. Rainbows and balloons made it one of the happiest rooms Polly had ever seen.

What Sal didn't know was that Sylvie, Camille and Elise had asked Bill to make a bassinet for the baby. When Sal was trying to think of everything she might need, that never occurred to her and Polly was under strict orders to keep her in the dark about it.

So many fun things were happening this weekend; it broke Polly's heart that Stephanie and Kayla weren't here to participate.

Han came bounding into the bedroom and leaped on top of Polly.

"What?" she whined, rolling over so he'd slide off.

He licked her face and put his paws out, his butt in the air; sure signs that he was ready to play.

"Why didn't Henry take you?"

The dog wagged his tail and bounced his front paws at her, growling in play. This silly thing wasn't giving up. She had Obiwan trained. Yes, Han was quite well trained when you gave him orders, but the rest of the time, he was a big, dumb goofy dog.

He bounced his paws again and spun around on the bed, then nosed at her face.

"Fine. I'm up." Polly tossed the blankets off and then grabbed them again and snuggled back in. May's weather was all over the place. Two weeks ago it had been cold and rainy and in the fifties, last week the temperatures were in the seventies and they had sunshine. But this morning it was back in the fifties and the sky was gray and threatening. Spring in Iowa was always entertaining.

Han refused to let her settle back in. He draped himself across her waist and stuck his nose in her face again. She could feel his bottom wagging with excitement.

"I don't do this very often, do I?" she asked. "Okay, okay. I'll suffer in the cold. Now get off me."

She pushed him aside, threw the blankets back again, shivered and sat up.

After a shower, Polly pulled on a pair of shorts and a sweatshirt, thankful again for radiant heat coming up from the floor. She chuckled. That was one thing she'd miss when they moved to the new house. There was no way she'd be able to talk Henry into redoing all of the floors. Maybe he'd just do their bedroom. But then she'd feel guilty that the kids didn't have it in their rooms and they'd miss it in the kitchen and living room. Yeah. She was just going to have to go without.

Henry had left the coffee pot on in the kitchen and there was enough left for a mug while she brewed a second pot. As she filled the pot with water from the sink, she looked out at the sycamore trees lining the drive. Leaves had started popping and after three years, the trees were branching out. They weren't nearly as big as her dreams told her they would be someday, but they were still beautiful. Polly looked across the street at the swimming pool's parking lot. If there was one thing she hated, it was that there was a public parking lot across from her house. Two cars were there this morning and with all the talk about Stephanie's father being in town, Polly worried. She'd been staked out before by people parking in that lot.

Parking spaces at Sycamore House were filling with people preparing for a wedding reception this evening. Sylvie would already have the cake here and Rachel would arrive later this morning to begin preparations for the meal. She and Jeff had an amazing staff.

With her coffee mug in one hand, Polly opened the refrigerator to look for something interesting to eat for breakfast. She opened the freezer and chuckled at the amount of ice cream. The sundaes had been a hit, but Henry had bought way too much. However, he'd managed to slide a box of ice cream sandwiches in as well. She looked around, chuckling at herself. There was no one here to see her, so she took one out, peeled the wrapping back and went out to the living room to eat her ice cream on the sofa. It was good to be alone on a Saturday morning.

Polly had no more gotten her feet up on the coffee table when a knock came at her front door.

"Who is it?" she called out.

"It's me. Jeff."

She looked around guiltily for a place to hide the ice cream and then decided to just own it. Unlocking the door, she frowned at him. "What are you doing?"

"I need to talk to you."

"Okay. Come on in." Polly brandished her ice cream sandwich. "Want one?"

He laughed and patted his stomach. "No. Get thee behind me. I'm doing good."

"Yes you are." She locked the door behind him and said, "Sit. What's up?"

"I know where Stephanie is."

"Okay. Where is Stephanie and how do you know this?"

"I'm a bad stalker boy," he said, dropping his head. "I should be ashamed."

"What did you do?"

"I went through the search history on her computer."

Polly sat down and nodded. "That's a great idea. What did you find?"

"Well, she was looking at hotels and I think I know where she went."

"And you're just going to taunt me with this information? Spit it out. Is she far away?"

He bent over and lowered her voice to a whisper. "I think she's only in Omaha."

"Why are we whispering?" Polly bent close to him.

"Because I don't want anyone else to hear."

She sat back up. "I'm all alone this morning. So, you found where she's staying in Omaha?"

"I think so. She did searches in Minneapolis and Sioux Falls and then she checked out Kansas City and Omaha. She hit a hotel's site in Omaha three times just before she took off."

"I talked to her last night," Polly said quietly. "She isn't ready to come home." Polly grinned. "And we both think you're a stalker."

Jeff sat straight up. "What did you talk about? Are they okay?"

"They're fine and I offered to wire her money if she needs it. They've gotten another cell phone. Jeff, her father absolutely terrifies her. He threatened Kayla."

"That makes sense," Jeff said.

"He left really terrible messages on her old cell phone. I can't imagine where he found her number, but she's saving them for the police."

"Did you tell her that they could stay with me?"

"More than you've told her?" Polly asked. "Of course I did. And I told her that they could stay here at Sycamore House or anywhere they felt safe."

"You know that it kills me she won't let me help her through this. We've been through just about everything else together."

"Stephanie believes that she is keeping us all safe by leaving town," Polly said. "I hope that she got to Omaha and stayed there, rather than moving on somewhere else."

"Ach," Jeff said, looking down at the floor. "I didn't even think about that. I was just so excited to find something ... anything that might help us find her."

~~~

Polly checked herself in the mirror one last time, then stopped at the dining room table to pick up the package Rebecca had wrapped for the shower. Beryl had taken the girl out for lunch after their lesson and the two would come to the coffee shop together.

"See you later," she said to the animals as she headed out the front door. It might be Rebecca's birthday weekend, but so far Polly felt like she'd had a fantastic treat with all of those hours by herself. She'd spent time reading and sprawled out on the sofa in the living room and the other sofa in the media room; she'd watched television and spent way too much time with her computer. So far it was a great day.

Enough cars would be parked around the coffee shop that Polly decided to just walk up. It was only two blocks and though it was cool, the rain had stopped, clouds had passed and the sun was out in full force.

There was no reason to arrive early. Camille and Elise were decorating. And at that, it wasn't very extravagant. Sal insisted that there were to be no silly baby shower games. She was not measuring her waist for anyone, and she'd made Camille promise that any decorations had to go home with people today; she didn't want anything to end up at her house. Sylvie was in charge of the goodies, Polly was footing the bill for any drinks people wanted from the coffee shop and other than that, it was simply an opportunity for people to get together to celebrate Sal's baby.

Sal and her mother were already at the Sweet Beans when Polly walked in.

"Hello, Polly," Lila Kahane said. "It's good to see you again."
~~~

"Are you having a nice weekend in Iowa?" Polly asked.

"It's very quaint."

"Mom, stop it."

"What?" Lila asked. "I didn't say anything negative. I just said that it's quaint."

"But we all know what you mean." Sal hooked her arm through her mother's and gave Polly a quick shake of her head. "Have you met Mark's mother yet, Polly?"

"No I haven't." Polly nodded toward a voluptuous, gorgeous woman talking to Lydia Merritt. "Is that her?"

"Yes. Isn't she amazing? Come on." Drawing her mother along with them, Sal led Polly over and said, "Kathryn? I'd like you to meet my friend, Polly Giller. Polly, this is Kathryn Ogden."

Mark's mother turned to Polly with a radiant smile and put her hand out to take Polly's. "I've heard so much about you, it's nice to finally meet you face to face."

"It's nice to meet you, too, Mrs. Ogden," Polly said.

It was easy to tell that the woman was a dancer. She held herself upright with grace and strength; every movement seemed to glide into the next. She wore a simple, deep blue wrap dress and her dark hair, sprinkled with hints of gray, was pulled into a loose pony tail.

"Your friend, Lydia, was just telling me about the house you are renovating. You found a still this week?"

Polly laughed. "We did. It's been fun to re-learn the history of Prohibition while I tried to figure out what it was we had there. Those were exciting times in this country and to think my house had a small part in it. Next thing you know, someone will tell me that Al Capone slept in one of the bedrooms."

"Wouldn't that be terrific?" Kathryn said. "Do you think it's possible?"

"From the looks of the empty bottles and labels we discovered, the business was in full swing. I'm hoping to find someone whose family was involved, just to get some more information."

The front door bell rang and Beryl waltzed in with Rebecca in tow. Beryl was in full regalia, wearing a long purple dress, a raspberry beaded belt hanging low on her waist. An immense beaded brooch held a raspberry scarf in place on her shoulder and a bright purple wide-brimmed hat adorned her head.

"Hello all," she called out.

Rebecca caught Polly's eye and grinned. She'd been caught up in Beryl's colorful frenzy, but instead of purple, she wore a shorter, blue dress with a gold chain at her waist, a gold, teal and pink scarf slung around her neck and a gold beret on her head.

"Excuse me," Polly said to Kathryn and Lila, "that's my daughter."

Before Polly could walk away, Lila Kahane stopped her. "Is that really Beryl Watson? The artist?"

"Have you heard of her?"

"Oh my, yes. Anybody who is anybody knows of Beryl Watson." Lila turned on her daughter. "Why didn't you tell me you knew Beryl Watson?"

"I didn't assume you'd know who she was," Sal replied.

"You must introduce us."

Polly gave a quick shrug and walked over to where Beryl and Rebecca were talking to Elise. "You two look fabulous," she said.

"Don't we?" Beryl did a quick spin. "We skipped our lesson this morning and did some shopping. Rebecca needed something fun and wild in her wardrobe. Did we succeed?"

"You certainly did." Polly hugged Rebecca to her. "You really look great. I love this style on you."

"Beryl calls it boho casual," Rebecca said, then she whispered to Polly. "I don't think she really knows what that is, but I like it." She tugged at the scarf, then patted the beret. "I want more things like this. And this dress is so cool." She spun around and the dress lifted in the breeze she created. "It's comfortable, too."

"You're really growing up," Polly said. "I need to quit thinking of you as a girl and remember that you're growing into a young woman. It's killing me, you know."

They turned around when Joss came in the front door, followed by Sandy Davis.

"No babies?" Polly asked, greeting each of them with a hug.

Joss huffed a laugh. "Not if I can help it. Their dad is over at the new house with them. He thought this would be the perfect time for them to get used to it while there is no furniture there. I think it's great. Whatever he wants to do."

"And you?" Polly asked Sandy.

"Benji's mom. He's in Des Moines today. Hopefully I won't be gone too long. I think she wants to go shopping this afternoon, so I can't strand her with the baby."

Camille tapped a knife on a mug to get everyone's attention.

"Hello everyone, and welcome," she said. "We'll start soon, but please order whatever you'd like to drink from the coffee shop. It's on us. Our own Sylvie Donovan and her crew baked the delightful treats for this afternoon. Sal will be seated at this table," and she pointed at a table near the bathroom. "If you put your gifts there, we'll have a little fun and get to it. Thank you for coming."

"Really?" Sandy asked. "Free coffee? Oh my goodness, you have no idea how much I was looking forward to being here today. Just so I could buy a coffee. Thank you."

Polly laughed. "We all have our addictions, don't we? This is one of my worst."

Lila had not left Beryl's side since the moment Sal had introduced them. Beryl finally put her hand on Lila's arm to stop the woman from talking. Taking Polly's arm, she drew her aside. "Do you really like Rebecca's outfit?"

"Oh Beryl, it's fantastic. Did you two go to Ames? By yourselves?"

Beryl scowled at her. "I knew just where I was going. We didn't get lost once. I promise."

"Thank you for making her feel so special."

"I can't wait until tomorrow's party," Beryl said. "She's going to be so surprised."

Polly nodded. "So you met Lila Kahane?"

Beryl quickly glanced over her shoulder. "Apparently Sal is more like her father than her mother. Though I believe I've given the woman a year's worth of name-dropping. Good heavens, she's shallow."

"You're so funny," Polly said. "Here you finally have an adoring fan show up in your back yard and you're not interested in her adulation."

"It would be one thing if she'd actually purchased something of mine. As it is, she's trying to drop names with me of wealthy people in Boston who own my work. Honey, I already know them." Beryl nodded at a cluster of women. "Who's the babe?"

Polly followed her gaze. "That's Mark's mother, Kathryn Ogden. Isn't she gorgeous? And she's as nice as they come, too."

"Well, that explains that," Beryl said. "This child of theirs has great potential for beauty." She scrunched up her face. "I certainly hope it isn't an ugly baby, though. Have you ever had to stand over someone's newborn and lie about how cute they are? It's not fun. Lydia's Marilyn? She was one seriously ugly infant. I was scared she'd never grow out of it."

"Beryl," Polly hissed in a whisper. "Stop that."

"Her next two weren't very attractive either. But Lydia and Aaron loved them like they were perfect. They must have seen something in them that I couldn't see."

"You're dreadful."

"At least Andy's babies were cute. They had those little round cheeks and button noses that you just wanted to squeeze..."

"I got so tired of you squeezing my babies' noses," Andy said, coming up behind Beryl. "I was just sure you were going to wear them off."

Beryl reached out and tweaked Andy's nose, causing the other woman to jump back.

"Don't ever change, Beryl," Polly said. "You're one in a million."

CHAPTER SIXTEEN

Sal finished opening her gifts, and then after people ate their fill and congratulated her, the shower broke up and women drifted out of the coffee shop. Some of them left with the adorable mason jar centerpieces that Camille and Elise made. Sylvie had brought up ten jars from Sycamore House's stock. They'd originally used them at the barn raising and hoedown three years ago and Polly was afraid they'd never see the bottom of those boxes. Filling the jars with M&Ms would have been enough, but they'd attached the lid to the outside of the jar with bright ribbons, and stuck a wooden skewer into it with a gift card to Sweet Beans from Sal.

Since Rebecca was sitting by herself at a table while others were cleaning up, Polly walked over and dropped into a chair beside her. "Had a long day?"

"Yeah. I need a nap. We didn't sleep very much last night. Molly was too excited and kept waking up."

"I need to stay; do you just want to walk on home?"

Rebecca yawned. "Do you mind?"

"No, that's fine," Polly said with a smile. "You don't even have to take the dogs out. Henry and Heath might be home, but ignore them and go lie down. We're supposed to be at Bill and Marie's by six thirty." Polly picked at the sleeve of Rebecca's dress. "You should wear this. It's wonderful."

Rebecca looked down at herself. "It was fun with Beryl this morning. A clerk thought she was my grandma and we didn't tell anybody anything different."

"Wouldn't she be a crazy grandma?" Polly asked.

"I told her that if I had to pick one, she'd be it." Rebecca leaned in. "But then I told her that she didn't act like any grandma I'd ever known. She was too cool. I think Beryl liked that."

"You're a smart girl."

"You should have seen that store, though. Polly, they had the coolest clothes."

"We'll have to go back sometime."

Rebecca's shoulders dropped and her face fell. "I like shopping at Goodwill with Kayla because we always have so much fun finding things to wear. We could never take her where Beryl took me. The clothes are expensive." She looked at Polly. "It isn't fair that they don't have any money."

"They're doing better than they were, honey," Polly said. "Stephanie is really frugal. I know how much money she makes and she could afford to shop at some of those stores once in a while. But she doesn't want to and honestly," Polly raised her shoulder, "I don't blame her. At your age when you're still growing and your body is changing it just feels weird to spend a lot of money on something you won't wear very long."

"Sal wouldn't agree," Rebecca said with a laugh. "I don't see her in the same clothes very often."

Polly laughed and then snorted a little. "You're right. Maybe I have a strange attitude toward clothing. It's something I wear. That's all. Sal sees clothing as part of her presentation to the world. But you're stuck with me. Sorry to say."

"That's okay," Rebecca said, patting Polly's arm. "Most of the time it's just fine. I don't pay too much attention to what I wear, but sometimes it's really fun to get to buy fun things and dress up. I feel like I'm a different person." She put her hand on the back of her head and struck a pose. "Like maybe a world traveler or a spy or maybe even a famous artist."

"I'm not so sure I like the whole spy thing, but you can do anything you want. And I'll even spring for some of the fancy clothes to go along with it."

"Beryl says that the kind of clothes you wear make people look at you in different ways," Rebecca said.

"She's right," Polly said. "What do you think she was trying to portray today?"

"I don't know. That she loves color?"

"Look over there." Polly pointed to where Beryl was standing with Lila Kahane, Lydia Merritt, and Andy Specek. "Tell me who Beryl wore that outfit for?"

Rebecca shook her head.

"She wore it for Lila. Lydia and Andy have seen her in everything under the sun, including those silly shorts she wears in the summer when she's painting in her studio."

"They're the worst," Rebecca said in complete agreement. "She should be ashamed of those."

Polly leaned over, "But I'll bet they're comfortable. However, when she is going to meet someone who already has a preconceived idea of who she is, what does she do?"

"Oh," Rebecca said. "She wore that because she knew Mrs. Kahane wanted to meet a flamboyant artist."

"Exactly. That's what she was trying to tell you. Beryl dressed for her audience."

"But everyone else in town knows Beryl. They don't care what she wears."

"They've seen her in her flamboyant clothes and in her..." The truth was, Beryl rarely dressed sedately. "...less flamboyant outfits."

Rebecca chuckled.

"What I think Beryl was trying to tell you was that you're in charge of how people perceive you. If Beryl dressed in a trim, navy suit with a white blouse and dark pumps, would you think of her as an artist?"

"No," Rebecca looked at Polly like she was nuts.

"But the thing is, Rebecca…" Polly looked straight at her. "…and don't you ever forget this. You're in charge of how people perceive you, but if they get it wrong, that's their problem, not yours." Polly tapped her index finger on Rebecca's chest. "Nobody gets to tell you what's right or wrong for you to wear." Then she smiled. "Except me and Henry, of course."

"So if I wore a slinky dress to school?" Rebecca got a wicked grin on her face.

"I'd lock you in the house until you changed your clothes. You're a smart girl and that would be a dumb choice."

"I know. I was just messing with you. I still think that some of the dress code stuff is stupid, though."

Polly sighed. "So do I, but since there are plenty of people who make bad choices, we get stuck with the rules that stop those bad choices from being made. However," she said with a smile, "junior high and high school are just a short period of your life and you can work within those rules to come up with great outfits."

"She isn't going to be here for my party, is she," Rebecca said.

"Kayla?"

"Yeah."

"It doesn't feel like it. I talked to them again last night, though."

"You did? What did Kayla say?"

"That she misses you. But I actually spoke with Stephanie. We talked about Kayla and school and we talked about keeping them safe."

"I just wish that man would do something stupid so he'd get caught and everything would go back to normal."

Polly nodded. "I get that. We'll just hope this works itself out really soon."

Rebecca stood up. "I'd better go home if I'm going to take a nap. Thanks for everything." She bent to hug Polly. "I love you, y'know."

"I love you, too. Just one more day until your birthday."

"What did you get me?"

"Nice try, goofball. I'll see you at home."

Rebecca skipped to the front door, turned and waved at Beryl, then with the jangle of a bell, she was gone.

~~~

"What are you doing tonight?" Polly asked Sal as she tucked gifts back into boxes, doing her best to make sure the cards were attached.

"Lisa made reservations at a restaurant in Ames." Sal sat back in the booth where she'd taken refuge.

Her mother was still talking with Beryl, and Polly refused to look that way in case Beryl attempted to plead for help. So far, though, Beryl had been polite and nice. The surprising thing was that Lydia and Andy were still involved in the conversation.

"Mark's mom didn't come in until today?"

Sal nodded. "They met about an hour before we came up here. Mom started off right away on the fact that we weren't married. She asked Kathryn if their family would do things that way. Of course this was after she'd peppered Mark with questions last night about why he wasn't being honorable about this." She laughed. "Honorable. Like he's the only one responsible for the choice in this matter. She hasn't asked why I'm not being honorable."

"Are you going to get married?" Polly asked. "You avoid this question all the time. What do you want to do?"

Sal hunched in on herself, turned to glance at her mother and then dropped her head. "I don't know."

"And Mark's okay with that?"

"He has to be."

"What are your reasons for not wanting to get married?"

A tear leaked out of one of Sal's eyes before she brushed it away and hardened her face. "I have a lot of reasons. And now's not the time."

"Okay," Polly said. "I'm sorry. You have to do what you think is right."

"That's not it."
~~~

"You aren't doing what you think is right?"

Sal picked up a piece of tissue paper and smoothed it out on the table, running her hand back and forth across the top of it. She picked it up to brush a crumb off the table and then started smoothing it out again. "I'm so scared, Polly."

"I understand that. This is all really big."

"But what if Mark and I end up like Mom and Dad? Dad hides from her. He refuses to fully retire so he doesn't have to spend time at home. She is gone all the time, doing her own thing, but when she's with him, she constantly tells him what he's doing wrong. He just takes it and turns the television on. He never disagrees with her and never fights back. I don't want to become that harpy with Mark."

"Why do you think you'd start doing that?"

"Surely Mom wasn't like this when they first got married. Why would Dad have married a woman like that? Something changed her. Was it because I came along? Maybe she realized that being a mother changed everything. What if she wanted to do something else with her life but was stuck raising a bratty little girl? They never had any more kids, you know."

"Have you ever asked either of them?" Polly reached out and took the paper from Sal, then folded it down to fit in the gift bag she was holding.

"No. We don't talk about things like that."

Polly chuckled. That was the truth in most of the families she'd known. Fortunately, she'd grown up with Everett Giller and he refused to allow her to get away with hiding her feelings. They'd stayed up until three o'clock in the morning one night after she sulked around the house all day. Every time she tried to get away from him, he found her and sat quietly beside her until she moved on. The only place she'd been safe that night was in the bathroom, and even then, he stood outside the door until she came back to the living room. She'd escaped to her bedroom and he followed her in, pulled up a chair and sat there, reading his book. She couldn't even remember what it had been all about, but Polly had learned that night that it was much easier to just talk to him.

She bent over and picked up the gift from Rebecca. Sal took it out of her hands.

"This is really cool," Sal said. "That little girl shows promise."

Rebecca had done a pencil sketch of Sal working in the nursery, hanging a quilted hot air balloon on the wall. Polly had taken the picture one afternoon, thinking it was a perfect shot and when Rebecca saw it, she agreed. Once it was finished, she'd spent a Sunday afternoon with Henry at the shop picking out wood for a frame and then another afternoon with Polly in Ames picking up glass and hardware to finish it.

"She does," Polly said.

"And how cute was she today," Sal said. "That adorable dress and beret?" She chuckled. "You can tell that Beryl has fun with her. I'm sorry I can't be at her party tomorrow afternoon." She looked around. "Where's my purse?"

A quick glance at the table where she'd been sitting and Sal started to heave herself out of the booth.

"I'll get it," Polly said. "Sit still."

Sal slumped. "Thanks. There's something in it for Rebecca."

Polly collected the purse and then set it on the table in front of Sal, hauling another pile of gifts over to pack up.

"This is a gift certificate for a day out with me. I want to take her to Omaha or Minneapolis to go shopping." Sal looked up at Polly. "Without you, okay?"

"That's fine with me," Polly said with a shrug. "She loves you."

"I might leave the baby with you."

Polly put her hands up. "Oh no you don't. I love you so much you have no idea, but you are not leaving a brand new baby with me for a whole day. Ain't no way. You can call Marie or Jessie or I don't care who, but until that baby of yours can walk and feed itself, I refuse to be responsible."

She stopped when she saw tears in Sal's eyes. "Oh lord, Sal, you know how I am. You can't be upset at me for this," Polly pleaded.

"I can't believe you won't love my baby."

"I'll love your baby like nobody's business," Polly said. "You just can't expect me to take care of it by myself. Please!"

"Mark and I don't have any parents around here to help us. I was hoping that you'd be my surrogate family. And now you're telling me that I have to do this all by myself?"

Sal was working herself up and Polly finally put her hand out. "Stop, honey. Don't do this to yourself today. I'll be there whenever you need me, you know that. I promise."

"Do you?"

Polly took a deep breath. "Of course I do." She picked up a bottle, then looked for the box it had come in before looking back at Sal. When she did, she scowled at Sal's evil grin. "You set me up."

"It was so easy," Sal said through laughter. "You're as bad as Mark when it comes to my tears. I have to keep reminding myself that I can only use this power for good, but then you walk into my web and I can't help myself."

"So you won't make me take your baby a whole day by myself?"

Sal rubbed her growing tummy and smiled. "I am scared to death to be alone with this baby. Why would I expect you to do it?"

"That's awfully sensible. It doesn't sound like you."

Pushing Rebecca's print back at Polly, Sal said, "Stop it. You're being mean."

"I think I deserve to be a little mean. That was quite a performance."

"Yes it was," Sal said, preening. She looked at her watch. "I suppose we should get those ladies moving. I want to rest before we go to Ames. If I don't drag Mom away from Beryl, she'll never let the poor woman go."

"Where did Kathryn and Lisa go?"

"They had some secret hush-hush thing they were going to take care of this afternoon. Kathryn is leaving early tomorrow morning, so apparently it had to happen today."

"Maybe they're going to install a barre in your nursery. You know, in that family, your child is going to learn how to dance at an awfully early age."

Sal chuckled. "That would be okay. Just as long as no one expects me to balance precariously on my tip toes." She finally pulled herself to a standing position. "Especially if I'm pregnant. The other morning, I stood up from the bed and had to catch myself on the bedside table. I nearly pitched forward because my center of balance was so wacky. Most of the time I know where all of my parts are, but that time, not so much." She looked up and her eyes filled with tears again.

"What now?" Polly asked, turning to see what had made Sal emotional.

"He came."

Mark Ogden walked in the front door, as gorgeous as ever, even though he was in an old pair of jeans and a loose fitting plaid shirt, tucked half in and half out of his pants. He strode across the room to Sal, ignoring everyone else and took his cowboy hat off before pulling her into a hug.

Polly stepped back and stared at the two of them. When she looked around, she realized she wasn't alone. Every other eye in the room was watching as Mark tenderly caressed Sal's cheek before kissing her forehead.

"Good afternoon, ladies," he said. "Did you have fun?"

"We had a wonderful time, Mark," Lila Kahane crooned, gliding over to link her arm through his. "Your baby received many nice gifts today. I was just telling Ms. Watson and her friends that I'm looking forward to your little family's first visit to my home so that I can show you off to *my* friends. We'll have another shower for the two of you so that Sal's old friends don't feel like they've missed out on this special moment of her life. Perhaps her father will even have time to spare for the event.

Sal shut her eyes and leaned on Mark.

"Are you tired, dear?" Lila asked.

"Yes mother," Sal said quietly. "If you and Mark could put these things in the car, I'm ready to go home and lie down."

Lila clapped her hands together twice. "Come on everyone, if we each pick up a box, we can do it in one trip."

Mark bit his lip, gave the room a wink and a grin before

releasing Sal. "I think I can handle most everything, Lila. Why don't you take that gift bag and we'll start packing."

Sal looked around to find Camille and Elise and spent a few minutes with them, while Polly grabbed up another stack of gifts and headed for the front door, thanking all of her stars above that she didn't have a mother like that.

CHAPTER SEVENTEEN

"Are you walking or do you want a ride home?" Mark asked, pointing to the darkening sky.

"I'm good," Polly replied. "I should have enough time to get home before the storm hits. Thanks for coming up to help."

He smiled. "I knew that this weekend I'd best plan on being around. Sal and her mother are a pair."

"They've always been at odds," Polly said, "but for the first time, Sal seems more confident and less worried about her mother's criticism." She poked his arm. "I don't know if it's you or the baby, but it's a good place for her to be."

He reached down and took Polly's hand. "Would you talk to her?"

"About what?"

"About marrying me. I don't want to pressure her into doing something that she really doesn't want to do ..." His voice trailed off. "Sorry. I shouldn't do that to you. We'll figure it out."

"No, Mark," Polly said. "We're talking. She's scared and having her mother here isn't helping. She doesn't want to live in a marriage like her parents have. She's certain that something awful happened when she was born that tore her mother's heart out, but Lila won't talk about it. Sal is a smart girl; she'll figure it out."

He chuckled. "I was infatuated with that girl the first time I saw her and couldn't believe she even gave me the time of day. But as I got to know her, she became so much more than just an infatuation. She's exciting and wild, brilliant and ready for anything. She has embraced this pregnancy with every ounce of her being and she loves with a deep, abiding passion. I don't want to live a single day without her and it terrifies me that she'll scare herself away."

"You should say those exact words to her," Polly said. "You made my heart skip a beat and it isn't even about me. Now go on and rescue your fair maiden from the evil queen."

"As you wish," Mark tipped his hand to his hat, bowed slightly, and headed back into the coffee shop.

"Dang," Polly said out loud waving her hand in front of her face. "That boy makes my heart swoon. I'm going to have to have a chat with Henry." She chuckled. "Yeah. That's a bad idea."

Just before she crossed the highway to Sycamore House, Polly's eye caught a glimpse of something gold in a bush up against a fence. She walked over to see what it was and as she got closer, peered at it and realized she was seeing Rebecca's new beret. She shook her head. That girl would lose her head if it weren't attached. Polly picked it up, brushed it off, and crossed into the garden.

The parking lot was filling up with people arriving for the wedding reception, but she recognized Hayden's car right away. Good. She and Henry hadn't talked about inviting him to go with them tonight, but he would love to meet Marie's parents. Then Polly remembered that Henry had spoken about the two of them - Marie and Hayden - getting together for lunch on a regular basis. Of course she did. Marie was probably the one who made the invitation.

She waved to Jeff, who was talking to several people in the hallway, and ran up the steps.

Henry, Heath and Hayden were in the media room, watching a

baseball game. She loved coming home and finding her family just being a family.

"Hi there," she said over the noise of the game. "Good to see you, Hayden."

He stood up and walked over to greet her. "I hope you don't mind me spending the night. Mrs. Sturtz, I mean, Marie, invited me to her house for dinner. It sounds like her parents are really interesting people."

"You know that I want you to feel like this is your home, Hayden. You never have to ask. You're always welcome." She walked with him back to the sofa. "Is Rebecca in her bedroom? She said she was coming home to take a quick nap. I don't think she got much sleep last night."

Henry looked up at her, a frown on his face and shook his head. "I haven't seen her. We've only been here fifteen or twenty minutes, though. She's probably still asleep."

It didn't feel like it had been that long since Rebecca left the coffee shop, but Polly knew she easily lost track of time. "I'll just check on her. The silly girl dropped her beret on the way home. I found it on the ground."

Polly left them to their game and went back across the living room to Rebecca's room. She lightly tapped on the door. "Rebecca? Are you still sleeping? Did you see that Hayden was here, too?"

She waited a moment and when there was no response, she tapped again, a little louder. "Rebecca? I have your beret. Did you even know that you dropped it?"

Pushing the door open, Polly stepped in and over the mess that was on Rebecca's floor. How one little girl could collect so much stuff, Polly had no idea. She walked over to the bed and pulled the blankets back to find that it was empty.

"Henry!" Polly ran out of the room. "She's not here."

They met in the doorway between the living room and dining room. "What do you mean she's not here?" he asked.

"She's not in her room. She was tired and said she wanted to come home, so I let her walk by herself. Oh lord, I shouldn't have done that."

"Stop it," he said. "She walks all over Bellingwood. Maybe she's at the barn with Eliseo or she found Andrew and they're doing something."

"Andrew is with one of his buddies this afternoon since we had so much going on. Where would she have gone?"

"Go downstairs and ask Jeff if he's seen her. I'll call Eliseo. Talk to Rachel and Sylvie in the kitchen." He gave her a quick hug. "It's going to be okay. We'll find her. She probably found something better to do."

Polly headed for the front door. "She wouldn't go anywhere without telling one of us. She knows better than that." She ran down the steps again and rushed over to Jeff. "Excuse me a moment," she said and pulled him away to the office.

"What's going on, Polly?" he asked.

"Have you seen Rebecca? She's not upstairs."

He shook his head, worry etched in his brow. "No, but we should ask Rachel. I was in my office. I could have missed her. Come on."

Rachel and Sylvie were sitting at the back table with three others, wrapping silver into linens.

"Hey ladies," Jeff said. "Have any of you seen Rebecca? She's not where she's supposed to be and Polly's worried."

Sylvie jumped up and crossed the room to them. "Was she at the shower?"

Polly nodded. "She left when things were done and said she was coming home to take a nap. But she's not there." Polly held up the beret. "And I found this across the street, so I know she came this way."

"Maybe she's at the barn."

"Could be," Polly said. "She got a new outfit from Beryl and she could have wanted to show it off, but I don't know why she wouldn't have come to show you first."

"She's not with me," Eliseo said, bursting in the door. "Henry just called. Jason, Kent and Scar started searching the grounds, just in case she fell or hurt herself. I'm heading for the basement."

"Why would she be in the basement?" Polly asked.

Eliseo shrugged. "No stone unturned, okay?"

"I'll check the rooms in the addition," Jeff said.

"I guess I'll look in the garage," Polly said. She felt sick. Everyone that Rebecca knew was either at the shower or here at Sycamore House. She took her phone out as she crossed the threshold into the garage. There were no messages and no calls so she made a quick call herself.

"Hello dear," Marie said.

"I've lost Rebecca. Have you talked to her since the shower?"

"No I haven't. I saw her walking toward home, but that's it. She's not there?"

"We're looking everywhere, but this doesn't make sense. She wouldn't run off."

"She isn't here, but Bill and I will get in the car and come right over." Polly heard something in the background and then Marie said, "We're on our way, dear."

Polly wandered through the garage, picking up boxes to make sure that there was nothing out of place, then rang the doorbell to Doug Randall and Billy Endicott's apartment. Maybe Rebecca had gotten lonely. That didn't make sense either. She never spent time with those two, but anything was possible.

Thundering footsteps on the stairs preceded the door opening and she gave a weak smile to Doug. "Have you seen Rebecca? I can't find her."

"No," he said. "She isn't at your place?"

That question was going to make Polly scream. She wouldn't be out looking if Rebecca was where she was supposed to be. "No. She isn't anywhere she's supposed to be. I'm worried."

"Let me get my shoes on. I'll help you look," he said and turned to go back upstairs. "You go on," he said, turning back to her. "I'll find you."

Polly nodded and stood still when the door closed. She didn't know what to do next. Yes, she did, and swiped another call.

"Polly, you just left the coffee house. What's wrong?" Aaron Merritt said.

"It's Rebecca. She isn't here."

"And she's supposed to be?"

"Damn it, Aaron, I wouldn't be worried if she was where she was supposed to be."

"You're right. I'm sorry."

"No," she said, tears finally breaking through her fear. "I'm sorry. I just know that everyone is going to ask if she's in the apartment and she's not. I found her beret across the street. She was going to walk home from the coffee shop because she wanted a nap before we went to Marie and Bill's tonight. But she's not anywhere. Eliseo hasn't seen her; Jeff hasn't seen her. They're looking all over the grounds right now. She isn't here. Where did she go?"

"We'll find her," Aaron said. "Let me call the office and get things started. Why don't you call Ken up at the police station and alert him so his people can be on the lookout for her."

Polly looked up when Henry opened the door to the garage. He stepped toward her and pulled her into his arms.

"Thanks Aaron. I will. Sorry I snapped."

"It's really okay."

"You called Aaron?" he asked. "I just got off the phone with Mindy at the police station. She's sending someone over."

"Your parents are on their way, too," Polly said. "Eliseo and the boys are searching the property and Doug will be down in a minute to help. Where did she go?"

"I don't know," he said. "But this isn't like her."

They looked up as a car pulled into the driveway and Marie stepped out. "Have you heard anything?" she asked.

Henry shook his head.

Bill opened his car door and stood up. "Come on, Marie. Get back in the car. We're going to drive every street in Bellingwood. When we're done with that, we'll start driving the country roads. We'll find this girl of ours."

Marie ran over to Henry and Polly, then hugged them both together. "We'll find her. You have to have faith."

Doug and Billy had come into the garage while Bill was speaking and Doug patted Polly's shoulder. "We're going out, too.

She has to be somewhere. I called my mom and she said that if you need more help looking, they'll start walking their neighborhood."

"Thanks, bud," Henry said.

"Where are Heath and Hayden?" Polly asked after Doug and Billy left.

"They're already out looking. They were going south past the barn, just in case she went that way for some reason."

"There's no reason," Polly said. "She was coming here."

"I know."

The sheriff's SUV pulled into the driveway, followed closely by Lydia's Jeep. She parked and made it out of her car before Aaron could open his door.

"Oh honey," she said, rushing toward Polly. "Have you heard anything yet?"

Polly wearily shook her head. "Nothing. I don't know what to think. I feel like I'm completely useless. Everyone else is out looking for her and I'm standing here without a clue as to what to do next."

Aaron took Polly's arm. "If she was across the street, maybe your cameras here picked something up. I'm sending Stu to knock on doors and ask people if they saw anything out of the ordinary. Come on inside and let's see if we can catch a glimpse of her."

Polly looked up at Henry. "Again, I'm glad we installed them."

"Me too," he said.

They walked through the kitchen and toward the office where Jeff met them.

"I've been through all of the rooms in the addition and Eliseo checked the basement. She's not here."

"The video feed," Polly said.

He slapped his head. "Why didn't I think of that? Let's see what we can find. Give me a couple of minutes to bring it up. About what time?"

Polly looked at Lydia. "It had to have been around four o'clock or maybe a little after. She didn't want to stay while I helped Sal pack up her gifts. I could hardly blame her. And since she'd spent the night with Jessie last night..." She turned on Henry. "Call Jessie. Maybe she went back over there to get something she forgot."

He nodded and stepped out of the office.

"Anyway," Polly continued, "she wanted to come home and lie down for a while before we went out again tonight. She'd had a big day and was exhausted, so I let her walk home by herself." Polly dropped her head in her hands. "It's only a few blocks."

Lydia put her hand on Polly's shoulder. "Stop that. She walks around town all the time. Today was no different."

"But it was. She's gone," Polly said.

"So about four?" Jeff asked, clicking the keyboard on the main office computer.

"Maybe a little after, maybe a little before," Polly said. "Start at three forty-five."

Jeff pointed to a video feed. "This is the one that aims toward the driveway," he said. "It has the best chance of picking anything up across the street. Most of the cameras are angled toward the building and the property. And beyond the driveway is going to be partially obscured by the trees."

"Thank god they aren't fully leafed out," Polly breathed. "Please let there be something there."

They all watched the video feed. Cars passed back and forth on the highway, some drove into Sycamore House's lot and she watched through the different feeds as they parked, people got out and headed inside.

"There," Aaron said. "Stop it and rewind."

Jeff did just that and Polly felt Henry behind her as they focused on the screen. It was only in black and white, but they distinctly saw Rebecca across the street where Polly had found the beret. A car cut her off and parked. Though they couldn't see details, a person emerged from the passenger side, concealed by the car. When the car drove off, Rebecca was gone.

"She was taken," Polly gasped.

"Oh." Henry dropped into the chair beside her and bent over, his head between his knees.

Polly put her hand on his back and looked up at Aaron. "What do we do?"

"I need a recent picture," he said.

She swiped her phone open and found a picture she'd taken of Rebecca at the shower. "This is as recent as it gets."

"We're going to the police station here in town and we'll get this information out right away. We'll post an Amber Alert and notify everyone that she's been taken. You didn't recognize the car?"

Polly shook her head. "I want to be sick."

Lydia knelt down in front of them and put her hands on Polly's knees. "I know you do, but you have to get through this next part to help them look for Rebecca. It's about her right now. You can fall apart later."

"Will you call Marie?" Polly asked. "Tell them to stop looking and we can't come to dinner tonight." She put her hand up. "I need a minute to completely fall apart. If you don't mind, I'm going into the conference room." She stood up and reached back to take Henry's hand. "Come with me."

He looked up at her, tears streaming down his face, then stood and followed her. As soon as she shut the door, Polly collapsed to the floor and sobbed. "I can't do this. I promised her mother I'd take care of her and I failed. How am I supposed to get through this?"

He sat down beside her and they clung to each other. "I don't know," he choked out.

When Polly finally took a breath, she backed away and looked at him. "I think I'm ready now. Thank you."

"For what? I'm useless. I can't be your strength right now, Polly. I truly don't know how to do this."

She put her hand up to his cheek and brushed away the wet tears. "We have each other and we have friends. They'll do what we can't do. Okay?" Polly stood up and held out her hand. He took it and stood up beside her, his shoulders slumped and his face drawn. He kept his head down as they went back into the office.

"Let me take you to the station," Aaron said. "Jeff's going to keep an eye on things here and Lydia's called Marie. All you two have to do is focus on Rebecca."

Polly and Henry followed Aaron back through the kitchen. Sylvie looked at Polly, questions on her face. Polly shook her head, then walked on through. They climbed into the back seat of Aaron's SUV and sat still as Aaron backed around to pull out onto the highway. They rode in silence and waited for Aaron to open the car door once he parked in front of the police station.

CHAPTER EIGHTEEN

Polly's apartment was filled with friends. Everyone was subdued, even Beryl, who kept walking into the bathroom and then would return, her face more drawn as time passed.

Aaron had brought them back from the police station and tried to assure them that all of the local law enforcement departments were doing whatever they could. Bert Bradford had shown up at the house, just in case someone called with demands.

Polly didn't dare vocalize all of the things that were flying through her mind, though she wouldn't be surprised that everyone else had the same thoughts. If those things were said out loud, she was afraid they'd come true.

While they were at the police station, it hit Polly that the kidnapper could be Stephanie and Kayla's father, which made every single fiber of her being vibrate with fear. If that man hurt Rebecca in any way, his life was forfeit as far as she was concerned. The other thing that she hated to admit was that she didn't want to leave the house and end up on some lonely gravel road, because she was certain that meant she'd be finding Rebecca's body and that was just one thing she couldn't do.

She looked up at a knock on her front door. Lydia rushed to open it and welcomed Sam and Jean Gardner. She spoke quietly to them and Jean walked across the room, hugged Polly and then stepped back and walked over to Marie Sturtz. Polly was shocked that the woman hadn't started talking. Once she started, she couldn't quit.

The door opened again and Andrew flew in, looking around the room, his eyes wild as he searched. Polly was struck by the incongruence of the dance music coming up from the auditorium. They would be completely oblivious to what was happening above them.

"Polly," Andrew cried and people made a path as he ran for her. He leaped the last foot or so and she caught him, then held him close.

"How are you doing, honey?" she asked.

"I don't know. Mom told me what happened and when she couldn't come get me, I finally just ran over here. I can't believe this."

"I know."

"Why aren't we out looking for her?"

"Oh honey," Polly said. "I wish I could, but I wouldn't know where to start. It was one thing for her to be lost in Bellingwood somewhere, but who knows where she was taken." She deflated. "Or why."

Jason came across the room and put his hand on his brother's shoulder. "Come on, Andrew. Let's get you some water."

"I don't want water," Andrew said. "I want Rebecca to be okay and I want her to come home."

"I know," Jason said quietly. "She's going to be fine. That girl is one tough cookie and she can handle herself. Before you know it, she'll call and Polly will go pick her up."

"Can I come with you?" Andrew asked.

"Let her be," Jason said. "Come on. Over here."

It was a struggle, but Jason finally peeled his brother away from Polly, who was too numb to respond any further. She took her phone out of her back pocket again, willing it to ring.

When it did ring, she jumped and swiped the call open without looking at the number.

"Hello? Rebecca?"

"It's me. Stephanie."

"Hello Stephanie. I'm sorry. Rebecca's been kidnapped and I don't have anything in me right now. Are you okay?"

Polly heard Stephanie's intake of breath. "He has her. I just checked my other voice mail and he took Rebecca."

"Oh god," Polly cried and sagged.

Bill Sturtz was the one who grabbed her around the waist and led her to a sofa. He sat down with her and she tried to hold back tears.

"What did he say?" Polly asked.

"He said that if I called him and promised to bring Kayla back to him, he wouldn't hurt Rebecca. Polly, we're leaving right now, but I don't know what to do."

"We aren't making that trade," Polly said, though it nearly killed her to be so gallant. "Have you called him?"

"I just picked up the voice mail. I have until nine o'clock to tell him what I'm going to do."

Polly leaned back to see the clock on the dining room wall. If they were leaving from Omaha, Stephanie and Kayla could be in Bellingwood just around nine o'clock.

"Don't call him until the last minute," Polly said. Her relief that he promised not to hurt Rebecca began to break through the haze in her mind. "I'll ask Aaron to be here when you arrive. This gives us some time to find them. Even if you do make that call, we certainly don't want you to have to see him."

"I won't let him hurt Rebecca," Stephanie said. "Even if I have to go back to him myself, he won't hurt those girls. No way."

"We won't let that happen either, Stephanie. I promise." Polly looked up at Bert and was grateful she was thinking clearly again. "Can you give me your password for the phone number? I want the police to hear those messages now. Especially this last one."

"Sure," Stephanie said and rattled off four numbers. Then Polly remembered. The code was Rebecca's birthday. She took a deep, dragging breath and repeated them to Bill. He nodded, then pulled a card out of his shirt pocket and waited while Marie found a pen for him.

"Be careful coming back, Stephanie. Don't hurry. This is all going to work out."

"I know it will," Stephanie said. "I'll make sure it does. Okay, Kayla is here now. I'm already in the car. We'll call you when we get to Bellingwood."

"I tell you what, Stephanie. We'll move a truck out of the garage. You pull in there, so no one knows that your car is here, okay?"

"Thanks, Polly."

Polly hung up and then took the card and pen from Bill. She wrote Stephanie's phone number on it and handed it up to Bert.

"Stephanie's father has been leaving her voice mails. That's her number and her pin. He left one this afternoon telling her that he'd taken Rebecca, but wouldn't hurt her if Stephanie brought Kayla back to him. They're on their way to Bellingwood right now. Maybe you can get something from his messages?"

"I'll call this in," Bert said. "You did good."

Polly looked around. "Where's Henry?" she asked his father.

"The crowd was too much for him. He said the dogs needed a walk and left with them about twenty minutes ago."

"I need to find him." Polly turned to Marie. "He's really messed up about this. I don't know how to help him."

"He feels the same way, dear," Marie said, taking Polly's hand. "You two just need to keep talking to each other."

"I'm worried about Heath and Hayden."

Marie nodded. "I'll talk to the boys. You go find your husband."

"But what about everybody who's here?"

Lydia stepped in and sat down on the table in front of Polly. "We're all here for your family. You don't need to be here for us. Go on. Find your husband and take care of each other. I'll call you if I hear anything from Aaron."

Polly stood up and headed for the front door, turned to look around the room. Finding all of their stares uncomfortable, she opened the door and bolted down the steps. She quickly crossed to the addition and ducked inside, taking refuge in the dark and quiet hallway. Then she called her husband.

"Hi Polly. I'm sorry I left."

"It's okay. I left too. Where are you?"

"In the barn with Eliseo."

"Do you care if I come down?"

"As long as you don't bring a crowd."

"Your mom and Lydia have that under control."

Polly darted out the door and ran down the sidewalk to the gates, opened them, and headed for the barn. She took a deep breath when she opened the barn door. It had only been three years since these horses had come into her life, but just the scent of them was enough to steady her nerves. Passing Daisy's stall, she opened the door into Demi's and slipped inside.

"Do you mind if I take a minute with you?" she asked him.

He nosed her hands, looking for a treat.

"That's the way it is? I'm falling apart and you want something from me?" She reached up and stroked his shoulder, then leaned against it. "You are so strong." Polly stepped back. "I remember the first time I saw you in that farmer's pen. Your coat was a mess and honey, you could barely lift your head. I hope you never remember those awful days." She smiled and touched his chin. "And then there were all of those days when I had no idea what I was doing. But you just let me learn. You didn't judge or criticize me. Nothing. And that's the way it is with my kids. I feel like I'm always tossed into the middle of the fire, then I have to learn something new so I can get out. But I don't know how to handle this. I can't fix it. I can't feed her good food or brush her coat or do anything." Polly leaned on him again. "I can't even tell her I love her and it's going to be okay. I've never been so scared in my life."

"Polly?" Henry came into view.

"Hi. I'm just getting some strength," she said.

He bowed his head. "I'm sorry I ran out on you."

"Don't be. There were too many people up there. Andrew just showed up. He's completely freaked out."

Henry ran his hand through his hair. "I can't stand the waiting. We should be doing something."

"Stephanie called."

"Oh god," he said. "It *is* him." Henry started to retch and Polly rushed to his side.

"No. It's okay," she said.

It was too late. Henry ran for the front door of the barn and she heard him throwing up outside. Polly sank to a bench and started crying again. This was more than she could handle. She couldn't worry about her daughter *and* her husband.

"He'll be okay," Eliseo said, coming up to stand in front of her. "He just needs to take it all in."

"I keep trying, Eliseo, but I don't know how to do this."

"The first month after I was burned, I said those same words every time I was alert enough to focus on my body. I heard doctors talking about how I should have died and they couldn't believe I was still here. And then they weaned me off the drugs that kept me knocked out. I wanted to scream because of the pain I was in, but I couldn't find my voice. I couldn't even scream. I had no idea how I was ever going to come back from that. The buddies who made it out without injury felt guilty, so they quit coming to see me. I was alone and didn't think I could do it."

He smiled again, his eyes showing Polly how much he loved her. "But every day, a young man stopped by my bed for just a few minutes. He turned my hand so that my palm was up and he could touch my skin. And he closed his eyes for a minute. I knew he was praying. Then he smiled at me and told me that I had the strength to get through anything. I never spoke to him; I never found out his name. He was gone by the time I was mobile and starting physical therapy. But I want to tell you that you have the strength to get through this. Both of you do."

Polly looked up to see Henry standing in the doorway.

Eliseo continued. "You have friends up in your apartment that are praying for you and for Rebecca. You have the strength to get through anything." He gently squeezed Polly's shoulder and walked to the back of the barn, disappearing into the feed room.

Henry came over and sat down beside her. "I'm so sorry. I've never felt like such a weak human being in my life. What did Stephanie say?"

"He does have Rebecca. He called and left a voice mail on her phone. But he told Stephanie he wouldn't do anything to Rebecca if she consented to bring Kayla back to him."

"We can't do that," Henry said, pounding his fist on his thigh. "We can't let her do that."

"We won't," Polly said. "Stephanie is supposed to call him tonight at nine o'clock to tell him what she plans to do. That gives us some time. And once she makes the phone call, that gives us even more time. And if they set up a place to meet, that gives us something more."

Henry looked at the watch on his wrist. "I can wait until nine o'clock. What did people say when you left?"

"Lydia told me not to worry about them. She and your mom will take care of everyone upstairs. We don't have to go back tonight if you don't want to."

"I don't want to," he said. "Can we just stay here?"

"Sure." Polly leaned up to kiss him and he backed away.

"Not yet. Let me clean my mouth." He stood. "Eliseo, do you have gum or something?"

The door to the feed room opened, its light shining into the barn's alley. Obiwan, Han, Kirk and Khan all dashed out, running for Polly. Obiwan jumped up on the bench, taking the spot where Henry had been sitting and pushed his head into her body.

"I know, bud, I know," she said. "It's going to be a long night."

He whined and lay down beside her, his head and front paw on her lap. Han wagged his tail in happiness and when she scratched his ears, he settled on the floor in front of her. She petted Khan and Kirk and then ran back to the feed room to find Eliseo.

"Where are the donkeys?" she called out.

"Do you want them in here?" Eliseo asked, stepping into the alley. "I shut their door so they'd stay out in the pasture while you two were here."

"Ask Henry," she replied. "I'm fine with having as many animals around as I can."

Henry came back, holding a Diet Dew. "Want it?" he asked, then held up a Coke that had already been opened. "Eliseo's got everything we need down here."

"It's probably not a good idea to get completely drunk and pass out, is it," she said.

"Not tonight."

She reached for the Dew and popped it open, the fizz and citrus scent a safe, comfortable sensation.

"I never thought that having kids would be so difficult," Henry said. "Until Rebecca and Heath came into my life, I never felt like this." He took Polly's hand and looked desperate as he spoke. "I want to kill this man, Polly. I want to hold him down and choke him until I see the life leave his eyes. I've never felt that way about anything or anyone before. Ever. And if he does hurt her, I don't know how you'll keep me out of jail for what I plan to do to him."

"I know," she said.

"We can't have any more kids in our lives."

Polly frowned. "What?"

"I can't do this."

"Are you serious?"

His shoulders drooped. "Probably not. I'm not handling these emotions very well, am I?"

"Neither of us are. Don't you think we'll be better when Rebecca is home?"

Henry reached across her lap and stroked Obiwan's head. "How am I going to let her walk outside by herself ever again? How will I let her go off to college? How will I let her..." He stopped. "I want to fold her up in bubble wrap and lock her in her room."

"The thing is, Henry, we can't stop her."

"I know. It's what I want to do, though."

"All we can do is teach her how to be strong and confident so she can take care of herself. I don't want our daughter to think that she has to rely on you or any other man to keep her safe."

"Kind of like you?"

Polly gave him a crooked smile. "If this man's balls aren't kicked clear up to his teeth at the first opportunity she has, I'll be very surprised."

"Do you think she'd do that?"

"In a heartbeat," Polly said. "We've talked a lot about how girls are taught to be nice and not fight back when they're being attacked. That's wrong. If someone tries to hurt you, don't worry about hurting them in order to protect yourself. I've shown her how to poke at eyes, rip at nostrils, grab or kick at nuts." Polly smiled. "You men have a lot of tender parts and they're fair game when abuse is involved."

He took a deep breath. "I hope she remembers everything you taught her."

"She's a smart girl, Henry. She'll be watching for any chance to get away and find safety. If it requires her to hurt him, she'll do it. If she has to take a beating to get out of trouble, she'll take it. We talked about how a person recovers from those types of things. She won't like it. She didn't like it when she took that punch at school, but she lived through it and now it's just a memory. As long as he doesn't touch her, Rebecca will be fine."

"He'd better not." Henry shuddered at his words.

"Stephanie thought that he'd wait for her to get here with Kayla. And speaking of that, we need to move one of the trucks out of the garage so she can pull in and hide her car."

"I can go do that. I'll bring my truck down here," Henry said. He reached out and pulled her close to him. "As much as I don't know how to do this," he whispered. "I would be lost without you. I don't know how you do it."

"Do what?"

"You take strength from everyone around you and then you give it back ten-fold. I saw you drawing it from Demi and that blew my mind."

"He's a big horse," Polly said with her arms around Henry's neck. "He has a lot to share."

CHAPTER NINETEEN

Overcome with emotion, Henry and Polly finally said goodbye to Eliseo and walked up to Sycamore House, hand in hand, the dogs running by their sides. They went around back so Henry could move his truck. Polly went on in and up the back steps with the dogs. He'd be a few minutes since he was parking it down at the barn. Many of the people that had come to stay with her had gone on home. She'd responded to texts, telling her that they were loved.

When she walked into the media room, Hayden jumped up from the sofa where he was sitting with Heath, Jason and Andrew. He pulled her into a tight hug, but couldn't find the words to say anything. Polly smiled at him, put her hand on Heath's shoulder and walked on through to the living room.

Bert Bradford had been joined by Stu Decker and Aaron Merritt. Bill and Marie Sturtz were talking quietly with Lydia, but everyone else had gone home. Polly was thankful for some quiet in her household. They didn't need everyone here while the rest of the night unfolded.

Aaron stood and pulled her into his arms. "I'm so sorry, honey.

We have everyone on the lookout. I wish we could have gotten more on that car."

"I know," she said. "Thanks for coming back." Polly glanced over her shoulder at the clock. "They should be here pretty soon. What is Stephanie supposed to say to him?"

Lydia handed Stephanie's phone to Polly. "Jeff brought this up so she could call him from a familiar number."

"Thanks." Polly turned back to Aaron. "I don't want her or Kayla put in harm's way over this. Rebecca would hate that."

"I'll talk to her," Aaron said and gestured for an unfamiliar woman to join them. "This is Lenore Hart. She's a psychologist and a negotiator in situations like this. I want her to spend a few minutes with Stephanie and Kayla, to measure how they're handling this. If she thinks they can be strong, we'll recommend that Stephanie agree to meet him and we'll be right there to protect her."

Polly nodded at the woman who had come up to stand beside Aaron. She was medium everything. Medium height, medium length-medium brown hair. Just medium. She looked nice enough, pleasant even, but she would easily get lost in a crowd. In fact, Polly hadn't noticed her in the living room until Aaron called her up.

"You don't think he's stupid enough to just tell them to meet him somewhere and then actually be there, do you?" Polly asked.

Ms. Hart shrugged. "He's in unfamiliar territory, and he's been on the hunt for these girls for a week at least. All he's thought about is getting to Kayla and punishing Stephanie. That's his focus. He's been frustrated by the fact that they weren't immediately accessible to him. In looking at his background, the man isn't extremely intelligent, so I don't expect him to come up with an elaborate, convoluted plan to sneak the girls away from us. In all likelihood, he'll bully his way through this. He probably has at least one weapon - a knife and maybe a gun. He will threaten Rebecca's life. Will she remain strong if he does?"

"She sure will."

Polly heard Henry's footsteps behind her. "This is my husband,

Henry Sturtz. Henry, this is a negotiator with the Sheriff's Department. She says that Stephanie should agree to meet him."

He heaved a sigh of relief. "Thank you. I know it isn't fair, but I just want my daughter home."

"It's okay, Henry," Aaron said, taking Henry's hand. "We all do. But we will keep the Armstrong girls safe, too."

"He killed their mother," Henry said. "And then he escaped from prison in order to track them down. Keeping them all safe just can't be that easy."

Aaron smiled as he released Henry's hand. "I've spoken with the warden and state police in Ohio as they've tried to figure out just how he managed to escape. The man took advantage of a hole in their security that rarely happens. Everything had to come together just right and one night it did. The power cut out for a few minutes due to a storm coming through. A delivery truck was right in the middle of crossing through a gate. Before the generator could start up and the gate could manually be closed, several prisoners were gone into the darkness. He made it out, and while the others were captured, he'd known exactly where he was headed."

"To Iowa," Henry said.

"We'll get him," Aaron said.

Obiwan and Han skittered across the floor, heading for the back door.

"They heard the garage door," Polly said, and followed the dogs. She got to the top of the back steps when she heard a quiet knock on the door at the bottom and ran down to open it.

"We shut the door, is that okay?" Stephanie asked.

"I hoped you would. Come here. I've missed you," Polly said and pulled both girls into a hug. She shut the door behind them and pointed for them to go upstairs first, even though they'd be greeted by the two dogs.

Kayla sat down on the top step and pulled Obiwan into her arms, hugging him. "I've missed you guys. Did you miss me?"

"Get up, Kayla," Stephanie said, tugging at her sister's arm. "You're in the way. Go on into the apartment."

Kayla stood up, brushed her bottom off and headed for the media room.

"I'm so sorry for all this trouble, Polly," Stephanie said. "Kayla really has no idea what's going on. I told her that Dad kidnapped Rebecca, but she doesn't know what he wants. All she knows is that we're here to help get her friend back."

"You don't have to apologize for any of this," Polly said. "It isn't your fault."

"If I hadn't left, Mom would still be alive and Rebecca would be here."

"And you'd have to put up with continual abuse as well as watching your sister go through the same thing."

"It's just that..."

"It's just nothing," Polly interrupted. "Aaron is here and wants to talk to you. They're going to recommend that you agree to meet your father."

"I was afraid of that," Stephanie said. She sat on the edge of Henry's desk, bracing her hands on her thighs, as if it were an effort for her to hold herself upright. "It's the right thing to do, but it scares me to death. I never wanted to see that man again. I thought I was done with him."

"Come on in," Polly said. "Do you two need something to eat or drink?"

"I can't eat a thing. My stomach feels like it could revolt at any minute." Stephanie looked through the doorway. "Are there a lot of people here?"

"There were, but most everyone has gone home. It's just Lydia and Henry's parents. Andrew and Jason are here and then some other law enforcement."

"Okay. That's good."

"Jeff's downstairs. Do you want him to come up?"

It was the first light Polly had seen in Stephanie's eyes, but then it faded. "He's probably busy with the reception."

"Honey, you're more important than a reception to him." Polly took out her phone and sent a quick text. "He'll probably be at the front door before you get to the living room."

When they went into the media room, Polly smiled at the sight of Kayla seated between Heath and Andrew. She was telling them what had happened during the week and asking questions about all of the events in Bellingwood.

"Can I help with anything?" Hayden asked.

"She hasn't eaten supper," Polly responded. "If she's hungry or thirsty, maybe you could take care of that."

"Thanks. I will."

Polly took Stephanie's arm and walked with her into the living room, then released her and got to the front door before Jeff knocked. He shook his head when she opened it.

"I was just getting ready to knock," he said.

"I knew you'd be here. Come on in."

Jeff strode over to Stephanie and gathered her in his arms. "Don't you ever leave me like this again," he said. "I have been so scared and I'm so pissed at you and I missed you so much and..." He took her upper arms and held her at arm's length. "Don't ever do that to me. You're too important. We can take care of anything."

"I hope we can take care of this," she said. "I'm sorry for running out. I know you had a lot of work around here."

"It's not about the work. It's about you and me. We're a team. We needed each other this week and you were gone." He pulled her close again. "Have I made you feel guilty yet?"

"A little bit," she acknowledged.

"It's after nine o'clock," Aaron said, interrupting. He handed Stephanie her old phone with cords hanging out of one end of it. "Make the call. We'll be able to listen and record it, but the only thing he'll hear is your voice." He plugged the cords into a box that was sitting on the table, with more cords and headsets weaving in and out of it. Polly hadn't noticed any of that earlier, either. She hated to admit how out of it she was.

Aaron, Lenore Hart, and Stephanie, who kept Jeff close, stood in a huddle for a few moments, talking quietly. Polly sat down beside Henry and took his hand. His mother had his other hand clasped tightly in her own lap.

"It's going to work out," Polly said.

Henry squeezed her hand. "You almost have me believing," he said.

She leaned around him and said, "I'm so sorry we messed up your parent's dinner tonight. How long are they going to be in town?"

Marie smiled and shook her head. "No one was thinking about dinner. They'll be here for a few more days. Mom and I were planning to drag our husbands down to Des Moines tomorrow morning for a Mother's Day extravaganza. She chuckled. "They won't think it's that exciting, but they'll go along to make us happy." Tears filled her eyes. "Of course, we aren't leaving Bellingwood until your little girl is home and safe."

"It's okay, Mom," Henry said.

Aaron pointed to one of the chairs and Stephanie sat down. She put the headset on that he handed to her and adjusted it. They checked volume and she made a test call to Aaron's phone. When they were certain that everything was in place, he nodded.

Stephanie closed her eyes, took a deep breath and pressed the button to re-dial the call that had come in earlier.

Polly put both hands on the back of her head and rubbed her scalp, worry and fear driving themselves to the forefront of her mind again. She looked around the room. Stu had stepped into the dining room and spoke quietly to the kids while Bert, with another headset on, stood back from Stephanie.

Polly looked up at Aaron and he gave a quick nod. She didn't know whether to be grateful or upset that she wasn't listening to the phone call, but chose grateful.

Jeff knelt in front of Stephanie and put his hands on hers when she set the phone down. "You've got this," he whispered.

"Hello?" Stephanie said.

Polly let go of the breath she'd been holding. Some part of her had been worried that he wouldn't answer the phone.

"I know. I'm sorry." She paused and listened. "You're right. I've never been on time. No, you can't expect much from me. I told you I'm sorry."

Polly's heart broke as Stephanie's voice grew more and more childlike. "Please, daddy. I said I'm sorry."

Glancing at Lenore Hart, Polly set her jaw. This wasn't going well. Stephanie didn't have the strength to face down her father.

Stephanie dropped her head. "I'm sorry."

Pause.

"Please let me show you how sorry I am. Just like I used to."

Aaron's lip turned up in a snarl.

"Where do you want me to come?" Stephanie asked.

Pause.

"And the little girl is still okay? Can I talk to her?"

Aaron, Stephanie, Bert and Lenore all cringed and Henry nearly leapt up, but Aaron put his hand out and gave a slow nod, then mouthed, "She's fine."

"Tonight? What time?" Stephanie asked. She listened and said. "I'll be there. I promise. Will you let her go now?"

Pause.

"I know it's not about her. But I don't want you to get in any more trouble."

Pause.

"Of course I'm alone. Kayla's in the other room, but I'm all by myself. No one knows where I am."

Pause.

"I'll see you soon, daddy." Stephanie shuddered and gulped. "I love you, too."

She swiped the call closed and threw the phone at Jeff. "That bastard. That asshole." She stood up, flung the headset off and paced toward the front door. "Thinks he can try to make me feel guilty. Like hell." She spun on Aaron. "I don't care what happens tonight. If he puts up a fight, shoot him. Don't let him get away with this. He either needs to die or else rot in a cold, dark cell for the rest of his life."

Polly sat back. She wasn't expecting that. All of the baby girl stuff was gone. Stephanie was quite an actress. The thought flashed through her mind that she should start up a community theater with her friends as actresses. She pushed it away.

"You did very well," Lenore said. "You even had me believing you were cowed by him."

"How stupid is he?" Stephanie asked. "Does he really think I'm going to show up and turn Kayla over to him and play his little games again?" She turned on Jeff this time. "I'm asking a question. How stupid is this man?"

"Pretty stupid," Jeff said. "And for that, I'm grateful."

Aaron stepped in front of Stephanie, stopping her. "Me too. Now, you have an hour before meeting him. We'll have our people in place long before either of you get there."

"What happened with Rebecca?" Henry asked.

"He slapped her and then she must have kicked him, because he yowled." Aaron said. "She might be a little worse for wear, but she sounds very much like Polly in a bad situation. I recognized that voice yelling. And she said that she was okay."

Tears fell from Henry's eyes and he took Polly's hands again. "She's okay."

"I know," she said, barely able to believe it.

"She's okay?" Hayden asked from the dining room. Stu stepped aside so the kids could all join them.

Polly looked at Aaron, letting him take the lead. "Yes she is. She's mad, but she said she was fine. He wouldn't let her talk to Stephanie, but that didn't stop her."

"Is she coming home tonight?" Andrew asked.

"We hope so." Aaron beckoned to Kayla. "Come here, honey."

"What's wrong?"

He shook his head. "Nothing. Stand here beside Ms. Hart."

Polly watched Lenore Hart transform herself to match Kayla's height. She slumped her shoulders, just like Kayla and she looked at Kayla's arms, then matched how the girl held her hands. "I can do this," Lenore said. "Can I borrow some of your clothes?"

"What are you doing?" Kayla asked.

"I'm going to be you. We'll put a hoodie on me, a pair of your pants and a sweatshirt. Maybe I can borrow your glasses, too?"

Polly turned to Henry, who was as shocked as she was by what they were seeing.

"Are your suitcases in the car downstairs?" Jeff asked.

"I'll go with you. It's so packed, you'll never find anything," Stephanie said. She looked back at Lenore. "I can't believe you're doing this."

The woman smiled. "I do it a lot." She turned toward Polly. "Years and years of acting while I got those psych degrees. My thesis was about transformation of personality in theatrical presentations. The world's a stage, you know."

Jeff preceded Stephanie back into the living room, bearing three heavy suitcases. "I assume they'll be staying with one of us tonight," he said.

"Come with me, Stephanie," Lenore said. "Help me turn into a facsimile of your sister."

They went into the kids' bathroom and Polly stood up. "Where are they going to meet him?" she asked.

"No," Aaron said, shaking his head. "I'm not telling you. This isn't yours to fix tonight."

Polly took his arm and led him back into the kitchen.

He stopped and said, "I'm not telling you."

"I know," she whispered. "But I have to ask you. Do you believe that Stephanie's father was responsible for that girl's death earlier this week?"

He dropped his head and shook it in the negative. "No. I believe it's something else entirely."

She wasn't expecting that answer. "What does that mean?"

"It means I don't want to get into it with you tonight. We need to focus on bringing Rebecca home."

"What do you mean you don't want to get into it with me? Why would you get into anything with me about that?"

"Not tonight, Polly."

"You're making me nervous, Aaron. Does her death have something to do with me?"

"I hope not." He turned to go back out into the living room.

Polly caught his arm. "You know I'm going to worry about this. I won't sleep because of what you just said."

"Then I didn't say anything. What I am certain of is that

Stephanie's father never met that girl and had nothing to do with her death. It's a completely separate issue. Can't you just take that as good news?"

"It is good news. I haven't wanted to voice my fears about that out loud, because I didn't want it to be a possibility. If he was willing to kill her, he'd be willing to kill Rebecca."

"Well, that's not a concern. The only thing we're concerned with tonight is keeping all of these girls safe."

"And Lenore Hart can do that?"

"She's highly trained."

"Where did she come from? I've never seen her in your office before."

"She came in from Ohio. Part of a specialized team there."

Polly smiled. "Kind of like Hawaii Five-O?"

"She's just a specialist with the state police. But she's highly motivated to get this man back. We're lucky to have her working with us."

"It always surprises me that you don't worry about mixing it up with other law enforcement agencies. It always seems like such a battle on television shows."

"I've been around a long time, Polly. If we do things all by ourselves, we might get all of the accolades, but we also take all of the heat when something goes wrong. If we work as a team, we get more information, more cooperation and more good ideas. I don't care how many wins I have in my personal column, but I do care that our people are kept safe."

"Thanks for bringing her in, then," Polly said.

"Like I had a choice," Aaron replied with a laugh. "Let's go see how they've done."

They went back into the living room and Polly sat down by Henry, then pulled him close. "He won't tell me where they're going. Said we need to stay here," she whispered.

He patted her knee. "Makes sense. Can you believe this?"

"No. Not at all." Polly looked up at Aaron, trying to process what he'd inadvertently said to her about the dead woman. How would it have anything to do with her?

Stephanie came out from the bathroom first and stopped at the door, waiting for Lenore to emerge.

"Wow," Andrew said. "She looks like a kid."

Lenore came out with the hoodie pulled forward over her face. Polly didn't know what they'd added to her wardrobe to flesh out her body since Kayla was heavier than Lenore. She swung her body with a lilt that mimicked Kayla's and managed to hold herself tight like Kayla did, as if she were afraid someone might startle her at any minute. Kayla's glasses helped to finish the face, but Lenore had also managed to purse her lips just as Kayla usually did when she was concentrating. The transformation was remarkable.

"Is that me?" Kayla asked.

Andrew looked back and forth between the two. "It really looks like you from a distance. In the dark nobody could tell the difference. That's so cool."

Checking his phone, Aaron stepped forward. "My people are in place. It's time to go."

Stephanie hugged Jeff, then came over to Henry and Polly. "We'll get her back. I promise. I'm so sorry that this happened."

"No need to apologize, Stephanie," Henry said. "Thank you for doing this, though."

"How can I not?"

Aaron took her arm and led her back through the house to the back steps, the garage and her car.

More waiting, but at least something was finally being done.

CHAPTER TWENTY

Roaming around aimlessly was making everyone else nervous, so Polly finally went out to the kitchen. She fumbled around in the cupboards, looking for anything to do.

"Can I help?" Hayden asked from behind her.

She jumped.

"Sorry," he said. "I'm so sorry. I thought you heard me."

"It's okay." She gave him a shaky smile. "I'm not paying attention." Polly put the can of black beans back on the shelf. "I just need something to do."

Hayden slipped past her and took eggs and butter out of the refrigerator, then said, "What about simple chocolate chip? You can never have too many of those around."

She rubbed her hand across his back. "That sounds good. You warm up the butter and I'll measure out the sugars." Polly reached in front of him and turned the oven on.

In minutes the mixer spun as it creamed the butter and sugar together. Polly leaned against the peninsula. She closed her eyes and tried to settle the jittery feeling that began when Stephanie agreed to meet her father.

Hayden coughed and she opened her eyes. "Do you want to do this?" he asked, holding the measuring cup filled with flour.

"Yeah. Thanks." She gently shook it in and laughed at a memory of Rebecca sending flour everywhere when she poured it right over the beaters. "Bring her home," Polly whispered.

Hayden took the empty measuring cup from her and replaced it with the opened bag of chocolate chips which she poured in, sighing as the mixer beat against them, the familiar sound comforting.

"Do you realize that we all know she's going to be fine because you're here?" he asked, taking her cookie sheets out of the cupboard.

"What do you mean?"

"If you were out looking for her, I'd be worried about you finding a body, but since you're allowing everyone else to handle this, the rest of us know that she's alive and perfectly fine." He stepped in front of her, turned the mixer off, and tipped the head back.

Polly looked at him, her mouth curving into a slow smile. "As much as I hate to say that out loud, it's true, you know." She lowered her voice. "But I always worry that there is just going to be that one time when it doesn't work."

"Don't even think that way. It's your thing. We count on it." He opened a drawer and handed her the scoop she used. "You know that some of us do actually rely on that, don't you?"

"What do you mean?" Polly took a spoon out and reached into the bowl for a bite of cookie mix. There was really nothing better.

"As long as we have our eyes on you, everybody we know and love is safe."

She rapped his arm with the back of her spoon. "Stop that."

"Okay, I'm exaggerating. But you smiled."

They dropped cookies onto two cookie sheets and he put the first in the oven and turned on the timer. "Now what?" he asked.

"Yeah, that didn't take quite as long as I'd hoped," she said.

He bent over and took out a glass cake pan. "Wanna help me make tomorrow morning's casserole?"

"Isn't that supposed to be a surprise?" Polly asked.

"Nah, not this part."

"You mean there's more?"

He winked at her and opened the refrigerator again, handing her two more sticks of butter and a second container of eggs. "It's Mother's Day. Heath and I haven't had a chance to do this in years." He went back in after sausage, green peppers and onions. Putting those on a cutting board, he reached over and drew her into a hug. "You have no idea how much we appreciate you."

"I wasn't expecting anything," Polly said.

"That's why it's fun. You wanna crack the eggs?" He put a large mixing bowl in front of her.

Polly opened twelve eggs into the bowl and, after finding the whisk, whipped them together.

"Did Marie talk to you and Henry?" Hayden asked.

"About what?"

"About me and Heath working on the house."

Polly remembered the conversation with Henry, but it felt like such a long time ago. This week had really been tough. She hadn't spent much time at all in the interior of the Bell House. Was it really just last Monday that she'd fallen down into that room?

"Polly?"

"Sorry," she said. "Yeah. Marie talked to us. It's a good idea, but unless you two want to camp all summer, I think you should live here. We have rooms available in the addition or you can sleep in Heath's room."

"Maybe we stay here until water and electricity are fixed in part of the house."

She grinned and took the chopped vegetables from him. "Kitchen first?"

"Of course."

"I still can't believe you enjoy cooking so much. Did your mother teach you?"

"It was actually Dad. Mom didn't like to cook. She did it when she had to and she really liked to bake, but Dad was the creative one in the kitchen. He made all sorts of things. One of these days

I'll make his double crust breakfast pizza for you. One piece and you're stuffed." He gave her a wistful smile. "One time a bunch of us ended up at the house after a game. Dad said he'd make breakfast and started building this monstrosity. He challenged the guys, telling them that no one could eat more than two pieces. They were absolutely miserable trying to get through that third piece of pizza."

"Really?"

"It was his homemade pizza dough on the top and the bottom of the pizza. He filled the insides with *so* much. Mom and I just watched it happen. No one ever went hungry at our house."

The oven timer rang and Hayden took the cookies out while Polly bent over and brought out the cooling racks. He slid the next cookie sheet into the oven and reset the timer.

"Can I have a warm cookie?" Andrew asked, coming over to the kitchen. He slid a stool out and sat down on it. Polly realized that he wasn't jumping up to sit any longer. The boy was growing like a weed. He'd be as tall as Jason soon.

"Sure," she said. "Jason? Heath? Come on over. We have cookies."

The two boys stopped playing their video game and came over to join them. Kayla was in the living room and Polly pointed that way for Jason to go get her.

"Hayden," she said, pointing at the refrigerator. "Could you get the milk out?"

He nodded, took it out and after handing it to her, opened the cupboard for glasses.

"Are you going to get Rebecca a phone now?" Andrew asked, taking the glass she handed to him. "Mom said I can't have one until she does because it wouldn't be fair, but Jason got his when he turned thirteen and I did that weeks ago."

Polly hadn't intended for Rebecca to have a phone until high school, but this changed everything. It infuriated her that she was about to react to a crisis, but there was no way she wanted Rebecca to ever be out of touch with her again. She hated having outside forces interfere with the things she believed to be right.

"I need to talk to Henry and your mom," Polly said. "But you're right. It isn't the worst idea in light of what happened today."

Henry stepped into the dining room. "A phone?" he asked.

Polly nodded up at him.

"I'm all for it. Especially when she..." He stopped and looked at the boys in front of him. "Nope. I won't ruin the surprise."

Andrew jumped right on it. "What surprise? Her birthday present?"

"That's right and you aren't talking us into telling you what it is," Polly said. She slipped the rest of the cookies off onto the cooling rack and moved around Hayden to leave the kitchen. "Can you handle this?" she asked, handing him the spatula.

"No problem." He passed it to Heath. "You're in charge of the cookies."

Polly took Henry's arm and walked him toward his office. "Do I change my mind now about a cell phone?"

"It's not a bad idea." He bit his lower lip. "I want her to always be able to reach us."

"Me too. Andrew says Sylvie wouldn't let him have one because I wouldn't let Rebecca. I should probably talk to her before we say anything." Polly glanced over her shoulder at the kids hanging out in the kitchen. "Hayden asked about living at the house this summer. You need to settle the numbers with him so he isn't worried about getting a summer job."

Henry nodded. "Not tonight, though, okay?"

"I know. Not tonight. But at least talk to him before he heads back to school on Monday. He's only got a week left. He's been patient enough."

Henry frowned. "I've already talked to him about working for me. That's settled. He knows I'll take care of him."

"Then he was probably just asking whether or not we'd let him and Heath live over there while they worked on the place." Polly reached out to touch him and he pulled away.

"No." Henry said. "It's too dangerous. They can sleep here."

She looked into his eyes and saw that his fear was hurtling toward anger. "Okay. No worries. They stay here."

Henry looked at his watch and then up to the clock on the wall. "How long is this going to take?"

"I don't know."

Both of them jumped at a knock on their front door. Henry took Polly's hand and ran to the living room, only to sag when Sylvie came in. He turned away and walked into their bedroom; Polly watching with worry.

"How are you doing?" Sylvie asked.

"Worried. Jittery. Freaked out. Pick a description like that," Polly said.

She looked around. "I thought there would be more people here."

"They went home. We aren't much company."

"That's not what we're here for." Sylvie took Polly's arm. "Henry?"

"I don't know. I'm worried about him. Is everything over downstairs?"

"All closed down. Eliseo was putting the last of the tables away when I came up. He's pretty worried about you all."

"Tell him to come on up and wait with us. He's family. He should be here."

While Sylvie composed the text, Polly said, "Henry and I are getting Rebecca a phone now. Neither of us want her to be without one. Andrew said you were making him wait because I wouldn't let her have one."

Sylvie chuckled. "The last thing I wanted to do was stir up more trouble with you and Rebecca about that and Andrew doesn't care." She leaned to see into the kitchen. "Jason really wanted one. He was so ready to grow up."

"Do you have a free afternoon this week?" Polly asked. "Maybe the four of us could go to Boone. We'll get phones, go to the bookstore and do dinner."

"The two of them picking out phones together? That will be entertaining."

Henry came out, walked past Polly and into the dining room. "Obiwan. Han. Let's go outside," he snapped.

The two dogs ran to his side and he headed for the back door. Polly turned to his mother, who stood up and came over to join them.

"He's not handling this very well, is he," Marie said.

"I suppose he's handling it better than some," Polly said. "But this isn't like him. I don't know what to do."

Marie took Polly and Sylvie's arms and led them into the dining room, then pointed at two chairs. "Sit. Let me get you something to drink."

Lydia had followed them out and looked at the activity in the kitchen. "Cookies? That's a good idea." She wandered over to the peninsula and sidled up between Jason and Kayla. "Got some for an old lady?"

"You aren't old," Kayla said. "You're pretty."

"Thank you, sweetie," Lydia said. "Hayden, be a dear and hand me a plate. I need to rescue some of these cookies before y'all eat them up."

Han bounded through the rooms, followed closely by Obiwan. They stopped in front of Polly and she reached down to give them each a snuggle. "Where's Henry?" she asked, then looked up as she heard his footsteps.

"Have you heard anything yet?" he demanded.

Polly stepped back at the fury in his tone and in his face. "Not yet."

"I can't just sit here and wait for her to be returned to us. We have to do something."

The decibel level in his voice grew with every word, causing everyone in the apartment to stop what they were doing and stare at him.

"Stop staring at me," he roared. "We should be doing something. This monster has my daughter and you all expect me to sit here and wait for someone else to rescue her. How am I supposed to do that?"

He stormed back through the media room into his office and when his feet hit the back stairs, Polly shot a panicked look to Marie and ran after him. She caught up to him as he put his hand on the door leading into the garage and hesitantly reached out to touch his shoulder.

"What?" he snapped, turning on her.

"Henry..."

Before she could say anything more, he brushed her hand away and pulled the door open, walking out into the darkness of the garage. "Don't try to make this better," he growled.

With light coming from the store room, she stepped around her truck and stood in front of him. "Okay. It's not better, but you're making it worse."

"I don't care. I can't bear it when everyone I love faces appalling horrors. The rest of you expect me to sit passively while a storm rages within me."

She reached out for him and he stepped back. "I can't," he said. "It's too much."

"But Henry, you have to."

He stopped and peered at her. "What?"

"You have to be our rock. Look at the family you have around you. I find dead bodies and get myself into situations any sane person would run from. It's not like I want to be there, but that's what happens. Heath lost his parents, lived with a cruel aunt and uncle, tried to become a hoodlum and had to watch as a friend murdered two others. He feared for his life through all of that. Rebecca's mother died last year and she was only twelve. She is as gregarious and creative as anyone I've ever met and she loves with passion that I can't believe. With all that the three of us bring to this family, what is the one thing it needs?"

Henry reached for the hood of her truck and used it to hold himself up. "This isn't fair."

"Of course it's not." Polly stepped into his space and when he didn't pull away, put her arms around his waist and drew him close.

He released the truck and wrapped himself around her. "Sometimes it's too much."

"But only for a moment," she said. "We all know that you aren't passive. Nobody would accuse you of that. But we do know that you're strong and the depth of your love for us knows no bounds. That's why this family works. No matter what happens, you will love us and take care of us."

"It's a lot of responsibility."

Polly tilted her head up and brushed her nose across his chin, then waited for him to kiss her. He brought his hand up to the back of her head and put his lips on hers, crushing them with the intensity of that raging storm that frightened him so badly. Polly had never known him to be like this. The heart-melting, knee wobbling kisses that she anticipated paled in comparison, and she responded with all that she had.

When they separated, he looked at her, brought his thumb to her cheek and brushed away tears. "I made you cry?"

Since she was incapable of forming words, Polly kissed him again and they held each other.

"I'm sorry I got loud," he finally said.

"No one is upset about that."

He chuckled. "Really?"

"Okay, I was a little upset. But everyone understands and it's one of those things that makes me love you even more. You don't get angry very often, but when you do, it's important."

"Mom is going to have my head."

"No," Polly said with a smile. "She's raised two children. She knows what it's like to worry when you have no control over a situation. Do you want to go back upstairs or stay here?"

"How many more do you think will have left the apartment this time?" he asked.

"I'm afraid those who are left are staying the duration."

Henry took her hand and they walked to the back door. "I can't stand this waiting. My mind creates scenarios and images that are unspeakable."

"That's why I made cookies, why Hayden is making tomorrow's breakfast and why the kids play video games," Polly said. "Everyone finds their own way to blur their thoughts."

He took his hand off the door handle and led her out of the garage to the back yard. "I can't do it. I just can't do it. I can't sit quietly while my family stares at me, worried about how I'll react if something awful has happened to Rebecca."

"Then we walk," she said.

"Is it fair that we left the kids upstairs?"

Polly squeezed his fingers. "They have other people to take care of them right now. Don't worry."

Henry heaved an immense sigh and guided her down the lane toward the corner garden. They sat on the bench, listened to the bubbling of water, while Polly leaned against his shoulder. All she had to do was breathe.

Her phone rang and Polly jumped to her feet, taking it from her back pocket.

"It's Aaron," she whispered, swiping the call open.

CHAPTER TWENTY-ONE

"Calm," Henry said before she answered it. "It's going to be okay."

Polly looked at him and nodded. "Aaron?" she asked tentatively. "Do you have her?"

"Yes. Stu is taking her over to the office. Could you come down?"

Polly nodded to Henry, beckoned to him, and they walked out of the garden. "We're on our way. Is she okay?"

"She's not hurt badly, but she's pretty shaken up. It's been a rough night."

"What happened?" Polly asked.

"I'm sorry, Polly," he replied. "I need to take care of things here. We'll talk later. Come get your girl."

Polly slid her phone into her pocket and gave a little skip. "He says she's okay, Henry. We just have to go get her."

They arrived at his truck and Polly looked up at her apartment. "We should tell them that she's okay."

"I don't want to make her wait," he protested.

"I'll run up, grab a sweater for her and tell them we're heading out. They need to know."

He put his hands on the front of his truck and bent his head. "Go ahead. I just need to say a few things here."

"By yourself?"

"Yeah. I'm fine. Go on."

Polly ran in and up the steps, then in to the apartment. "She's okay. Aaron has her," she yelled.

Kayla jumped down from her stool, another cookie in her hand. "Is Stephanie okay?"

"I'm sure she is, honey," Polly said, realizing she hadn't even thought to ask.

Polly was surrounded by people and questions about Henry and Rebecca and Stephanie. "Stop," she said. "I need to go get her. Henry's waiting in the truck and I wanted to tell you, then grab a sweater for her."

"Do you want us to wait here?" Marie asked.

"That's fine," Polly replied. "If you don't want to wait, you'll see her at her party tomorrow."

Lydia touched Polly's arm. "You're still having it?"

"Absolutely. This time it will be a 'Welcome Home - Happy Birthday' thing."

When Polly came out of Rebecca's bedroom, she walked into a mild argument between Andrew and his mother.

"He wants to go with you," Sylvie said. "I told him we could wait here until you all get home."

"I want to go too," Kayla said.

Polly's mind swirled with the questions about what Henry would think, what Rebecca needed and how much she could handle. She glanced at Heath and Hayden; brothers who wanted nothing more than to be part of this family.

"Why don't you all stay here for now. I don't think we'll be that late. If it looks like it's going to take a long time, I'll text you." She looked at Sylvie. "And everyone can go home until tomorrow."

Sylvie put her hand on Andrew's shoulder and grabbed up Kayla's hand. "That's a good idea. Come on kids, let Polly go."

Polly darted over to Heath and gave him a quick hug. "I know you're worried," she whispered. "She's okay. We'll be back soon."

He gave her a small smile as she ran for the back steps and out to Henry's truck. He'd already turned it around, so as soon as she jumped in and belted up, they were off.

"Andrew and Kayla wanted to come with us," she said.

"I'm glad they didn't."

"I thought about it for a split second, but then I looked at Heath and there was just no way we were going to get everyone in the truck. If it isn't too late, they'll still be there when we get home."

"I couldn't have taken Andrew's chattering all the way down," Henry said. "Love that boy, but he doesn't know when to turn it off."

Polly smiled. "He's a good kid and I know this scared him."

"Can you blame him?" Henry asked. "He's known you longer than Rebecca and you've done some scary things. If people didn't know better, they'd think she was yours by birth with all the scrapes she gets herself into."

He turned into Boone and Polly looked at the homes as they drove past. People were doing what they did every Saturday night: lights turned off as they went to bed, televisions were playing, a couple was sitting on their front porch. Life was normal for them and they had no idea what had been going on in a little girl's life this evening. She remembered having the same thoughts when she'd gotten the call that Everett had died. No one else knew that inside, a girl who had just lost her last connection with home was silently screaming.

Polly remembered walking past a local bar. Young people were outside, while smoking cigarettes, laughing and talking. One young man was tapping out a beat on the brick wall of the building with a pair of drumsticks he'd produced as if by magic. They were living their lives and Polly felt like she was losing hers. If the world was so connected, how was it that she felt so alone at times?

"You're thinking awfully loud over there," Henry said, putting his hand on the console, palm up.

She took it in hers and gave it a squeeze. "Just thinking about how all of these people have no idea what's going on with us tonight. They're just doing their thing with no thought to the fact that a little girl was kidnapped and held hostage."

"I wouldn't want to know about all of the awful things that happen in some of those homes every night," Henry said. He turned right on Mamie Eisenhower Avenue.

He drove into the parking lot of the sheriff's office and they went inside. Polly was nearly sick to her stomach with excitement at seeing her daughter. Just as they were about to give their names to the front receptionist, Stu Decker walked through.

"There you are," he said. "She's been asking for you."

"Where's Stephanie?" Polly asked.

Stu took a deep breath. "Aaron didn't tell you?"

Polly looked at him in panic. "What didn't Aaron tell me? Is she okay? Did her father hurt her?"

"They've taken her to the hospital," Stu said. "Things didn't go quite as easily as Aaron planned. There was a fight."

"With Stephanie?" Polly stopped in front of Stu before he opened a door. "Tell me what's going on."

He nodded toward the room. "Rebecca will probably tell you everything. We don't have any word yet on Stephanie's condition. They were taking her into surgery..." He looked up at a clock on the wall. "About now. Let Rebecca tell you her story and if you have any more questions, I'll be close by. Okay?"

Polly glanced at Henry. This evening was never going to end. "We have to get Kayla down here," she said.

"Why don't we find out what's going on and then I'll call Mom or Hayden or somebody. But I want to see my girl."

Stu opened the door and Rebecca burst up out of a chair and leapt into Polly's arms. "I'm sorry!" she cried.

Polly held her and then Rebecca looked up at Henry. "I love you guys. I didn't know if I'd ever see you again."

He put his arms out and she threw herself at him, sobbing. Henry bent down, tucked his arm under her knees and cradled her in his arms as he walked to the sofa. Rebecca cried into his shoulder while Polly rubbed the girl's back.

Rebecca choked out a few more sobs and then sat up, collected herself and stood, rearranging her dress. "Sorry about that," she said. "I'm not a little girl."

"Yes you are, honey," Polly said. "At least to us you are. Can you tell us what happened tonight?"

"I don't even know where to start," Rebecca said. "I thought that after I told Mr. Decker everything I'd have it all straight in my head, but it's gone back to being a jumble. Did he tell you if Stephanie is okay? Nobody will say anything to me. I keep asking and asking."

"He said she's going into surgery. That's all we know," Henry said.

"Is someone bringing Kayla down?" Rebecca asked. "She should be at the hospital when Stephanie wakes up."

Polly and Henry exchanged a look and he stood up. "I'll call home." He held his index finger out. "But no talking until I'm back."

Rebecca flung herself at Polly again. "All I could think was that I hadn't hardly seen you at all these last few days and I was so sorry."

"It's all okay," Polly said. "Whether we're near or far, I know you love me. You know that too, right? Your whole family loves you. All the time. Even if we get mad and say rotten things to each other, it never changes how much love there is. Do you know that?"

"Kinda," Rebecca said. She pulled back. "Yes. I know that. I worked so hard to try to figure out how to get away from that man." She drew her eyes together and pursed her lips. "He was evil, Polly. His face was mean and he said bad things. I can't believe he's Kayla's dad. She's nothing like him."

Henry came back in. "Aaron already talked to Lydia and it sounds like everyone is meeting at the hospital. We should go over there." He waited for Rebecca to stand beside him. "Hayden and Heath can't wait to see you."

"Hayden?" Rebecca asked. Then her eyes grew big. "He came home because of..." She glanced at Polly. "I forgot all about that. We're still doing it, aren't we?"

"I already know about him making breakfast," Polly said.

Henry and Rebecca looked at each other and nodded.

"What?" Polly asked.

"Breakfast casserole. You got it. Happy Mother's Day," Henry said. "We're free to go. Come on."

When they got into the truck, Polly handed Rebecca her sweater and the beret she'd found earlier.

"I knew you'd find that," Rebecca said. When he got out of the car to grab me, I threw it."

"You did that for a clue?" Polly asked. "That was smart."

"I wanted you to know I had come that way." Rebecca sat forward. "I knew you'd think I had just gone somewhere else if you didn't find me at home."

"Good for you. What did he say to get you in his car?"

Rebecca shook her head. "No. I would never get in a stranger's car. I thought he was just going to ask me for directions, but then he slid over and jumped out and grabbed me. He had a really ugly knife and told me he would be glad to cut me all the way up my belly if I screamed or made a scene."

Henry gripped the steering wheel, the veins on his hands popping up.

"Then what happened?" Polly asked, as calmly and quietly as she could.

"We came down here to Boone. He was staying in a hotel and told me that if I was quiet, he wouldn't hurt me. I didn't know what else to do. I thought it would be smart to just figure out all of my options and as long as he wasn't hurting me, I had time to find a way to escape."

"That's awfully pragmatic," Polly said.

"I told myself to think like you would."

Henry gave Polly a sideways glance and a quick shake of his head. She wasn't sure whether he was upset at that comment or proud. For the moment, she was going to just be proud.

He pulled into the parking lot at the hospital and they went inside and inquired about Stephanie Armstrong. Once they received directions, Rebecca stopped in front of a vending machine. "Do you have any money?" she asked. "I haven't had anything to eat since Sal's shower."

Henry patted his pocket and sighed. "What do you want?" he asked. "I'll go pick something up." He looked at Polly. "I'm hungry too, I guess."

"None of us had anything to eat except those cookies I made," Polly said. "Are you sure you want to go out?"

"I'll pick up plenty. You go on," he said. Henry drew Rebecca into another hug. "I've been so worried about you today. I'm glad you're back. You'll have to forgive me if I never let you leave the house alone again."

"He's kidding, right?" Rebecca asked, taking Polly's hand as they walked toward the waiting room.

Polly chuckled. "I'm not sure. He was more upset today than I've ever seen him."

She pushed through the door and Jeff looked up. "Polly, you're here. I figured you'd take Rebecca straight home."

"I don't want to leave Stephanie," Rebecca said. "Not until I know she's okay." She turned to Polly. "It was her that saved me tonight. She was amazing."

Jeff nodded. "She *was* amazing. I was so proud of her."

"What happened?" Polly asked.

He glanced at Rebecca.

"We haven't had time yet," she said.

"You go, then."

"I'm going to have to keep telling this story until I get it straight," Rebecca said. "It's still a jumble."

She sat down across from them and leaned forward, her hands on her knees. "We left the hotel after he finally talked to Stephanie. I knew that was going to be my last chance to get away from him. He hadn't done anything to me yet, but he kept talking about how pretty I was and how much he couldn't wait to be able to see his Kayla again." She grimaced. "Before we got to the hotel, he stopped and picked up something brown in a bottle. He got pretty drunk. I thought maybe that would help me when I wanted to get away. Mom used to have some boyfriends that got drunk." She took a breath. "Anyway, he got really mad when he kept having to leave messages on Stephanie's phone. I didn't know how to tell him that she had left town. He kind of knew that she wasn't around, but then he quit making sense about it. When I heard him tell her that she had to call by nine o'clock, I started to get worried, though."

"I'll bet you did," Polly said.

"I was never so glad to hear that phone ring. He'd tied me to the bed." Rebecca sneered. "Using my own new scarf. He did some weird loop-di-loo with my hands and then he tied it around my neck so I couldn't move. I was pretty freaked out."

Polly forced herself to breathe.

"When Stephanie called, he sat down on the bed beside me and I thought it was all over." Tears squirted out of Rebecca's eyes, but she put her hands up to stop Polly from moving toward her. "I'm fine. He didn't do anything. In fact, he lay down and put his hand on my leg and then," she looked up, "he fell asleep. I couldn't believe it. He totally passed out right there. I knew what time we were supposed to meet Stephanie, so I kicked him and woke him up."

Rebecca looked at Polly. "I couldn't reach his balls." She clasped her hand over her mouth and grinned. "Sorry. But I couldn't, even though I wanted to. I just kicked him in the leg. He didn't even notice. He asked me what time it was and when I told him, he untied me from the bed, but tied my hands behind my back and took me out to the car again."

Jeff reached over and took Polly's hand. It felt good just to have someone else with her while she heard this. Polly's mind reeled as she tried to figure out a good way to tell all of this to Henry so he didn't fall apart. Emphasizing Rebecca's strength would be a start.

"We drove to the park," Rebecca said, "and he stopped right where he said he would."

"He was driving drunk?"

Rebecca shrugged. "It wasn't that far and he did okay." She scowled at Polly. "And really? After all this, you're worried about him being drunk in the car?"

"Whatever. Go on. But this is the last time I want to hear about you in a car with a drunk driver. Got it?"

Rebecca looked at Jeff with mock frustration. "Will you talk to her, please?"

He smiled. "Go on."

"I turned around to watch for the cars and when I saw one pull in, I didn't know whether I hoped it was Stephanie and Kayla or not. I didn't want Kayla to go through that." Rebecca furrowed her brow. "There weren't any lights on in the park. I didn't realize that until now, so I couldn't tell that it wasn't Kayla. They parked a ways away from us and Stephanie got out. Her dad opened his door and then opened my door. I was in the back seat right behind him. He pulled me out by my hair and he did it so fast, I fell down." She put her hands on her knees and Polly realized they'd been bandaged. "He pulled me back up and I had to figure out how to get my feet under me so I didn't do that again. He was pissed and yanked me around."

Polly turned to Jeff. "Were you there? Did you see all of this happening?"

He blew air out through his nose. "Yes. We were back in a covered shelter. And Aaron had all of the lights inside the park turned off so this guy couldn't see anyone."

"That was it," Rebecca said. "Stephanie parked so she had to come around her car. Kayla was in the back seat behind her and she got out of the car, too. He was so gross, Polly. He kept telling them that he loved his girls and they were the only people in the world who understood him and the only reason he let their mother live so long was because she took care of them and made them ready for him. He didn't like old ladies, just pretty young girls who could be trained to make him happy."

"Oh ick," Polly said. "I'm so sorry you had to hear that."

"That wasn't the worst of it, trust me." Rebecca shook her head. "All I could think was how bad it was that Stephanie had to grow up like that and she'd better not let Kayla ever have to go through it. I was going to do anything I could to make sure that never happened. I didn't know that it wasn't Kayla right away. They came around the car and walked toward us. He was dragging me." Rebecca rubbed the back of her head. "It really hurt but I knew you wouldn't cry or scream about it. You told me that those kinds of hurts don't last long and I kept trying to remember that."

"Oh, honey."

"No," Rebecca said. "You were right. It helped me keep focused. I just had to ignore it and wait for the right moment."

"You shouldn't have had to wait for any right moment. It shouldn't have happened at all," Henry said from behind her.

Polly looked up in shock. She hadn't heard him come in either.

"I brought a crowd." He pushed the door back open and people came flooding into the room.

One by one and in small groups, they all rushed to Rebecca to hug her and tell her how worried they were.

Heath picked Rebecca up so her feet dangled and buried his face in her shoulder. From her vantage point, Polly saw tears streaming down his face. He didn't say a word, just held onto Rebecca as he cried. His brother put his hand on Heath's shoulder, rubbing it back and forth.

Andrew and Kayla held back. When Rebecca was finished hugging Heath, she turned and looked for them and ran to Kayla. "I've missed you all week long," she said. "You can't ever go away like that again. Not ever."

"I missed you, too," Kayla said. "Are you okay? Did he hurt you?"

Rebecca shook her head. "I'm okay."

"What about Stephanie? No one will tell me anything. What happened?"

Jeff stood up and walked across the room. "Come with me, Kayla. I'll tell you what happened with your sister. You should be very proud of her." He turned and nodded at Polly, then walked the girl out of the room.

Rebecca stood awkwardly beside Andrew, unsure as to what to say or do.

"I'm glad you're okay," he finally said. "I was scared something bad would happen."

"You didn't know that I'd take care of myself?" she asked and gave a sly grin to Polly.

"No?" His worried face brought laughs from everyone.

"It's okay, son," Henry said, putting his hand on Andrew's back. "She's going to be a lifetime of trouble for men who love her. I can tell that right now. Just like Polly."

Andrew looked back and forth between Rebecca and Henry. "That can't be true. She can't be like Polly. I can't take it."

Henry guided him to the chair next to where Rebecca had been sitting. "I'm with you. Come on. I have plenty of sandwiches. Have a burger while Rebecca finishes telling us her story."

CHAPTER TWENTY-TWO

"Hmmm..." Rebecca said, dragging out the word. She looked around the room to make sure everyone was paying attention to her. "Where was I? Oh yeah. He had me by my hair and was dragging me across the parking lot."

Andrew put his burger into his lap and braced his hands on the arms of his chair before turning to stare at Rebecca. Since no one else had been party to the earlier details of her story, shock rippled through the room.

"But he wasn't done with me yet," she said quietly. "He pulled me up so I was standing in front of him and then all of a sudden he had that big knife in his hands again. He held it right here." She touched her neck. "Then he told Stephanie that he didn't want her and he didn't want me. All he wanted was Kayla. That she hadn't been spoiled by the bitch who raised her and he hoped Stephanie hadn't been telling her a bunch of lies. He told Kayla to come to him, but he wasn't letting me go until she got in the car."

Rebecca looked around. "I couldn't even tell that wasn't Kayla. That woman looked just like her. But he made some nasty comment about how she'd let herself go, just like the bitch he married. He was going to fix that, though. If he had to starve her until she was little again, he'd do it. Stephanie didn't say a word and Kayla started across the parking lot to us."

Rebecca took a deep breath and put the burger she'd been given back in Andrew's lap, as if the thought of food suddenly repulsed her. "Something gave it away then. I don't know what he saw, because it was really dark in that parking lot." She drew in a halting breath. "He tensed up and that lady saw something too. He was going to kill me. He yelled at her to stop and she threw her hoodie back and had a gun in her hand, yelling at him. He yelled that he was going to kill me and he screamed at Stephanie. He called her a bitch and a traitor and said that it was her fault and she'd have to explain why I was dead."

Polly felt her stomach lurch and grabbed the hand of the person next to her, while watching Rebecca's face turn red. She glanced up and saw that it was Heath. He gripped her hand back with so much strength, she finally pulled away and then put her hand back on top of his. Henry was standing behind Rebecca and reached out to touch her shoulder, making her jump. She looked up and relaxed, then nodded.

"That's when Stephanie screeched like a maniac," Rebecca said. "She rushed her dad. I don't know what she thought she was going to do, but he dropped me to the ground and went right for her. I..." Rebecca looked at Polly. "What's the word? I was on the ground and tried to get away. Scrambled?"

"Scrabbled," Polly said.

"Yeah. That's it. I knew I had to get out of there, but I couldn't take my eyes off what was happening. He rushed back at Stephanie and..." Rebecca began to shake, her voice quavering. Andrew dropped what he had in his hands and put his arm around her, then with his other hand, took hers to calm her. Henry's hand was still on her shoulder, but he bent forward and laid his head on top of hers.

"He stuck the knife right in Stephanie's stomach. There was so much blood everywhere. The lady, I think her name is Miss Hart. Anyway, she shot him."

"Oh, Rebecca," Polly said. She went down on her knees and crossed over to Rebecca, then held on to her waist. "I'm so sorry."

"He let go of the knife and fell down. The lady kicked the knife away. It came over toward me and I just stared at it. Then all of a sudden there were a million people around me and I started crying when Sheriff Merritt picked me up just like I was a little girl. I didn't think I was going to cry, but I did. One of the other deputies untied my hands." Rebecca touched Polly's arm. "I told him I didn't want to see that scarf again. Is that okay?"

Polly chuckled through her tears. "They can burn it or do whatever they want to it. I'll never let it back in the house again. I promise."

"I saw Jeff with Stephanie. I couldn't believe he was there and you weren't." Rebecca tilted her head back to Henry. "Aaron told me he wouldn't let you guys come. Were you really scared?"

"You have no idea, baby," Polly said. "We were out of our minds."

"It's a good thing we didn't know what was happening," Henry said.

Hayden, who had taken the seat on the other side of Rebecca, stood up, gesturing for Henry to take it instead. Polly was glad Henry didn't protest. He came around and sat down beside Rebecca, putting his arm around her so she was completely encompassed.

"I've never been so upset in my entire life," he said.

"Can Kayla stay with us tonight?" Rebecca asked.

"If she wants to." Polly turned to Marie, who got up and stepped out of the room, coming back in a few moments later with Kayla and Jeff.

Kayla was pale and her face pinched and tight. She came around the chairs and stood in front of Rebecca. "I'm really sorry he did that to you. Jeff told me what happened."

"Stephanie is a hero," Rebecca said. "And I'm sorry your dad is dead."

"I'm not." Kayla clenched her jaw and her fists. Her eyes flashed with fury. "He deserved to die after what he did to you and then to Stephanie. I hate him so much. I just wish he would have died a long time ago."

"Don't say that," Rebecca said, taking her hand back from Andrew. She reached over and took Kayla's hand. "He's your dad. He was really messed up, but you don't want to hate him."

"Don't you?"

Rebecca shook her head. "No. He scared me, but if I hate him, Mom always said that was on me. It eats me up instead of him. He's dead and doesn't care. Mom always told me that I shouldn't let hate and anger take over my life, especially when the other person doesn't even know I'm mad."

"I still hate him."

"Okay," Rebecca said. "You can tonight. But tomorrow you gotta be over it, okay?"

Polly took Kayla's other hand. "We'll give you until Monday if you need it," she said with a smile.

Rebecca maneuvered herself around Polly and slowly let Andrew and Henry's arms drift away as she stood to hug Kayla. "You're back in time for my birthday party. You can stay with me tonight, okay? I kept Silver with me all week because I missed you so much. He's waiting for you."

"Jeff said I could stay with him," Kayla said softly. "He thought you guys might want to be just a family tonight."

Rebecca spread her hands out. "Look at all of these people. This is our family. But you can stay with him. It's okay."

"You wouldn't care? He said we'd wait here until Stephanie was out of surgery and then we'd sleep in late tomorrow before coming back here and then up to your party."

"You can do whatever you like," Polly said, standing up. She backed up to sit down beside Heath and took his hand again.

The door to the waiting room opened and a young man in scrubs beckoned to Jeff, who stepped out. The room went silent. A few minutes later he returned.

"She's going to be fine. It wasn't as bad as they feared. No organs were touched by the knife. In fact, he said that it was fairly superficial, given the size of the knife. They did a CT scan to make sure they hadn't missed anything, then stitched her up. She'll have a nice scar on her belly and she's got some scrapes and bruises on her arms and a bump on her head where she hit the pavement. They're keeping her tonight at least and as long as she takes it easy, she might be able to go home tomorrow."

He gestured for Kayla to join him. "They've assigned her a room and we're going up to be there when she arrives. You can all go home, I guess."

Polly grabbed Henry's hand as she stood and walked over to Jeff. "Tell her that she can have anything she needs to make this easier for her. We're so grateful for what she did tonight."

"I don't think she would have done it any other way," Jeff said. "She had to confront this man."

Kayla reached up to hug Polly. "I can't believe it's over. We get to go home again." She turned to Jeff. "Do you think I can go to school on Monday?"

"I'm sure of it," he said. "Let's go wait for your sister."

As she watched them walk down the empty hallway, Polly took a deep breath and forced her muscles to go slack, trying to relax. "I don't know what to feel right now," she said.

"Me either." Henry replied.

"You take your family home," Bill Sturtz said, standing up. "You don't need to be worrying about any of the rest of us tonight. We're just glad this little girl is safe and out of harm's way. Tomorrow we'll have a birthday party and celebrate all thirteen years of her life. Right, folks?"

A murmur of assent went through the room as people gathered their things.

Andrew stepped in front of Rebecca and gave her an awkward hug, looking around to make sure no one would chastise him. "I'm glad you're okay. I can't wait for things to get back to normal."

"Me either," she said, then leaned forward and kissed his lips.

Both of the kids hurriedly looked at Polly and Henry to see if there would be any repercussions. Polly just grinned up at her husband.

He sighed deeply and shook his head. "I have no control, do I?"

Andrew's face flushed bright red and he nearly leapt out of his skin when his mother put her hand on his shoulder.

"Come on, Andrew. You have a lot to think about tonight. Maybe some warm milk so you can go to sleep."

"I can't believe you got a kiss before me," Jason said.

Andrew looked at him with a sly grin and then quickly looked away. He shyly waved goodbye to Rebecca as they left.

"Boys, do you want to ride with me?" Eliseo asked Hayden and Heath. "Or go back with Henry and Polly."

"They go with us," Henry said. He stepped forward to take Eliseo's hand. "Thanks for bringing them down. And thanks for being there tonight."

Lydia took Polly into a hug. "I love you," she whispered. "I'm so glad your family is okay. They are as important to me as my own. Aaron and I will be at Rebecca's party tomorrow. I'm thankful this all turned out so well."

"Thanks, Lydia." As she did every time Lydia hugged her, tears filled Polly's eyes. For as much as they were friends, this woman was the mother she'd been missing in the last few years since Mary's death. When she needed to be taken care of, Lydia was always there.

"We'll see you all tomorrow," Marie said. "If you need anything, just call."

"I'm sorry dinner didn't work out tonight," Polly said.

Marie scowled. "Who was thinking about dinner? You have your girl back and that's all that matters." She hugged Polly, then bent down to hug Rebecca and then stopped in front of her son. "I'm proud of you, you know."

"Because I turned into a feckless fool?"

"That's exactly right," she said, patting his hand. "That, and the fact that you found ways to get through the worst life could hand you and you hung in there. Fear causes people to react in a million different ways and sometimes we don't know what we'll do. Being angry and frustrated doesn't make you any less. Managing through it and being here; that's what makes a mother proud." She reached up and hugged his neck.

"Ditto," Bill said, clapping his son on the back. "We're proud of you."

When all that was left in the waiting room was their family, Henry took Polly's hand. "I'm both wrung out and wired up. I don't know whether to run a marathon or drop in a heap."

"I'm starving," Rebecca said, picking up an unopened bag. "Can I eat one of these?"

"You can eat whatever you want," he replied. "Let's pick up our leftovers so we don't leave a mess."

Heath and Hayden swooped around the room; tossed trash into receptacles and gathered the last few burgers into a bag.

"People weren't all that hungry, I guess," Polly said. "What do you want to do with this?"

Hayden chuckled and draped his arm around his brother's shoulders. "We'll manage it. I promise."

~~~

Henry took hold of Polly's hand when they got in the truck. He looked up into the rear view mirror and then gestured with his head for her to turn and see.

Rebecca was tucked under Heath's arm, her eyes closed while leaning against him, and Hayden had her hand in his lap. She looked peaceful enough, safe between the two boys.

"Polly?" Rebecca asked.

"Yes, honey."

"Am I supposed to be upset because I saw someone die tonight?"

"Maybe a little bit. Why do you ask?"

"Because every time a policeman kills someone, they have to see a psychologist before going back to work."

"Do you want to talk to someone about what happened tonight?"

"Should I?"

Polly glanced at Henry and was surprised to see a small smile on his face. He lifted his eyebrows.
~~~

"What do you think?" Polly asked.

Hayden chuckled. "You sound like a therapist. Maybe she doesn't need anybody else."

"I think you should," Heath said quietly.

Rebecca opened her eyes and looked up at him. "But I don't want to be a drama queen about this." She heard what she had just said and sat up, then put her arms around him. "That came out wrong. You aren't at all. It's just that it feels like I'm always getting into something. Andrew already thinks I'm high maintenance."

"Those are two separate things, honey," Polly said.

"But worse things happen to you and you don't talk to anybody."

"She talks to me," Henry said. "All the time. She never shuts up. It's always talk, talk, talk, talk, talk with this one."

Polly swatted at him. "No I don't. Part of it, Rebecca, is that you've had a pretty extreme year. Your mother died, you were adopted by us and now this. You've had a lot to process and it's all been very personal."

"You've had an extreme year, too," Rebecca said.

"I'm thirty-something," Polly said with a cough. "Not twelve."

"Almost thirteen. Can you believe that Kayla is back for my party? I hope she can come. I hope Stephanie comes home tomorrow. Is it bad that I want them to come to my party when this awful thing just happened to them?" Rebecca pursed her lips in concentration. "Maybe I shouldn't have the party tomorrow. It might be too much for them after their dad died and Stephanie got hurt." She sat forward. "Do you think we should wait until next week?"

"Can you wait?" Polly asked with a smile.

Hayden let loose a laugh.

"Stop laughing," Rebecca said. "If I'm being selfish by having a party, then somebody should tell me that. Maybe we can just have our own family birthday party and then have the big one next weekend." She looked up at him coyly. "I wouldn't want to miss the great present you're giving me. Right?"

"Right," he said. Hayden tapped his brother's shoulder. "We

left it at my apartment. I told you that you were supposed to remind me. Darn."

"Maybe she can wait until next weekend's big party," Heath replied. "It's not that big of a deal anyway. Just a case of grape juice boxes." He clapped his hand over his mouth. "Oops, I wasn't supposed to tell. Sorry."

"You're kidding, right?" Rebecca asked.

Heath and Hayden both shrugged their shoulders.

Rebecca put her hands on both of their knees and gripped, making them groan. "You're kidding. Right? Polly, make them tell me they're kidding."

"I have no idea what they're doing for your birthday," Polly said. "As far as I know, it's grape juice boxes."

"Henry?" Rebecca asked.

"Grape juice sounds about right to me," he said. He pulled into the convenience mart on the highway. "I feel the need for ice cream treats before we get home. Grape popsicle for you, Rebecca?"

She crossed her arms and huffed. "You all are mean." Rebecca looked up at Polly while keeping her head down and winked. "I want a fudgy, nutty bar with colorful sprinkles on it. And if you don't get that for me, I'm going to cry."

"A what?" Hayden asked.

"You heard me. I want a peanut butter, chocolate shake with banana topping."

Henry shook his head and got out of the truck. "Anybody else have a special request or shall I just get what I always get?"

Polly waved him off and sat back in her seat. This had already been a long evening and by the time they were home, it would just be the beginning of an even longer night. Rebecca was wound up and the boys didn't look as if they'd be going to sleep soon.

"Maybe a little Star Wars when we get home," she said.

"It's kind of your go-to stress reliever, isn't it?" Rebecca asked.

"Either that or a good book." She turned back around. "Was the house a mess when you left?" she asked Hayden.

"Not too bad. Lydia and Marie did their best."

"I'll take care of the dogs," Heath said.

"Thanks, honey. That would be great." Polly tried to relax again. "I'm looking forward to sweat pants and bare feet."

"Me too," Rebecca said. "I ripped this dress when I fell. Do you think Beryl would be mad if I never wore it again?"

Polly chuckled. "I think Beryl would be glad to burn it for you."

Henry opened the truck door and handed a bag to Polly. "It's a good thing they have gotten used to my buying habits. I never have to worry if they're out of stock. We can eat ice cream all night long."

"This is what he does when he tries to fix our emotions," Polly said, holding up a heavy bag. "Thanks, sweetie." She didn't want to remind him that the freezer was already stocked after last night's party. He had to do what he had to do.

"I'm glad tomorrow is Sunday," he said. "There's no way I could go to work after today."

"Tomorrow will be a good day," Polly said. "We're all together now."

CHAPTER TWENTY-THREE

Silence greeted Polly when she woke up. There were no dogs, and the cats were on the cat tree, lolling in the morning sunshine. She had no idea what time it was.

They'd stayed up late last night talking about everything, from Rebecca's adventure to Hayden's worries over finals week; from the dreams she had for the Bell House to teasing Heath about all of the girls who were interested in him. Henry had finally sent everyone to bed a little before one o'clock and when Polly's head hit the pillow, she'd gone out like a light.

"Where is everyone?" she asked the cats, who studiously ignored her. Polly got out of bed and threw on a robe, then tiptoed out into the living room to see if anyone else was up yet. All of the bedroom doors were open and there were still no dogs to be found. "All right," she said. "What's the joke?" She looked around for a note, but found nothing. "Fine then. I'm going back to bed." She walked back to her room, sat down on the edge of the bed and picked up her phone.

It was only eight o'clock. Where had they gone? But ah ha. There was a message waiting from Henry.

"Happy Mother's Day, Polly. Take a shower and get dressed for the day. We have a surprise for you, but you have to find us. Let me know when you're ready to go!"

She chuckled and shook her head. There would be no breakfast in bed for her. Leave it to her family to make an adventure out of Mother's Day. The truth was, though, she'd barely thought about it. She'd been so focused on Sal's shower yesterday and Rebecca's birthday party today, there hadn't been any time to wonder whether or not her family would do something beyond breakfast.

As Polly stood in the shower, she realized how strange it felt to be thinking about this being a day she'd celebrate. That reminded her she needed to be prepared for Father's Day. After Henry's last year, he deserved a huge celebration. The poor man had been thrust into fatherhood with a vengeance.

Once she was dressed, she sent a text saying, *"Ready!"*

"Your morning starts at the barn. Eliseo is ready for you. Go ahead and drive down, though. You'll need wheels."

Polly smiled. No better place to start today than with her animals. It made her tear up a little when she thought about it. The very first things she'd mothered back to health were those big horses. She'd be glad to give them a hug this morning. She ran down the back steps to her truck and then drove around to the barn. She parked, got out and went through the gates, then opened the barn door. She laughed out loud when she saw Eliseo standing in the alley of the barn with all four horses decked out with garlands of flowers on their heads.

"What is this?" she asked.

"They wanted to tell you Happy Mother's Day," he said. "We're glad you found them and gave them a home." Eliseo stepped forward and handed her a card. "I'm glad you found me and gave me a home, too, Polly." He took the garland from Demi's head and placed it over hers, allowing it to fall around her neck.

"Oh Eliseo," Polly said, tears springing from her eyes. "Thank you." She hugged him and then snuggled each of the horses.

He gave a small whistle which brought in Tom and Huck. Eliseo handed her a little bag of carrots which she shared with the donkeys, after which she received a head butt from Tom and a nuzzle from Huck.

"This is amazing," she whispered.

"You can't stay," Eliseo said. "Open the card and your next set of directions is in there." He stepped forward and gave her another hug. "Thanks for believing in us."

Polly opened the card and smiled back at him as she read it.

A three by five index card was tucked inside and written on it were the words, *"Your next stop is just down the road. At Sycamore Inn, your talents, they glowed. Grey has the next piece of your journey."*

This was going to be a rough morning if this continued. Polly waved to Eliseo and went back to her truck. It was only a short trip to Sycamore Inn and she pulled in under the canopy.

When she went inside, Grey looked up from the computer and smiled. "Good morning, Polly. Your family is on a mission to tell you that you are loved."

"I guess so. What do they have for me here?"

He came out from behind the counter to greet her and handed her another card, then pulled her in for a hug. "This is from me," he said, presenting her with a small wrapped box. "Thank you for believing in me, even when you had no idea who I was. I'd lost myself and yet you saw something in me. I don't have a mother to celebrate with today, but I'm grateful for your caring."

"Oh Grey," she said. "This wasn't necessary. You've done so much here."

"Hush," he replied. "We don't often get an opportunity to tell you thank you. Accept it, please."

"May I open it now?"

He gave a slight bow. "Of course."

Polly tore the wrapping and opened the small jewelry box to find a small silver paw print charm on a chain. "This is adorable," she said. "Thank you so much." She handed him the chain. "Would you?"

"I'd be honored."

She bent at the knees so he could fasten the necklace and then lift the garland over it.

"While the card is from me, the directions for your next stop are in there as well," he said. "Have a wonderful morning and Happy Mother's Day."

Dazed, Polly walked out of the hotel lobby to her truck. She quickly turned to wave goodbye, but Grey had already opened the door to his apartment and slipped inside. She read his sweet note and then took out the next three by five card.

"You are almost home. Just one more quick stop where Camille will have your coffee ready for you. Don't delay. You don't want it to get cold."

"Thank goodness for coffee," Polly said and drove toward the downtown area and Sweet Beans Coffee Shop. She parked in front and reached up to take the flowers off, but then thought that she didn't need to do that. It was Mother's Day, the first time she'd ever had an opportunity to celebrate, and she was going to enjoy it. She jumped out and went inside.

The coffee shop was busier than she expected on Mother's Day morning, but Camille waved at her and waggled a coffee cup from behind the counter.

"Good morning, Polly," Camille said. "It sounds as if you're having an adventure."

"I guess I am," Polly said. "But I've been promised coffee. Is that mine?"

"Only if you follow me." Camille beckoned for Polly to follow her back to the kitchen.

"Happy Mother's Day," a chorus rang out. Sylvie, Jason and Andrew, Jessie, Molly, and Elise smiled at Polly.

Sylvie stepped forward. "We're not your family, but you've helped us all find a future to be excited about, so we wanted to be a little part of your day." She pressed a bundle of crazy daisies into Polly's hands as they hugged. "There's a little something in the middle of this," Sylvie whispered. "You can open it later."

Jessie picked her daughter up and stepped forward so Molly could wrap her arms around Polly's neck and kiss her. "When I was at my lowest, you didn't let me fall down, but showed me how to stand up. I still can't believe how lucky I am to be part of your big family." Jessie smiled at her daughter. "Give Polly her present, honey."

Molly opened her little hands to expose another small box.

"What's this?" Polly asked.

"A flower," Molly said proudly, making the room laugh.

"You can open it later," Jessie said. "It will go with your necklace."

"Pretty flowers," Molly said, reaching for Polly's garland.

Jessie grabbed her daughter's hand and stepped back.

"It's my turn," Elise said. "I came back to Bellingwood because it was the first place I'd ever been where someone didn't care whether or not I was just myself. You showed me what courage looked like and it changed my life." She darted at Polly, gave her a quick hug and then handed her another small box. "Open it later. It will make sense."

"I don't know what to say," Polly said.

"We aren't done," Jason responded. "This is from me. I was supposed to come up with a reason why you were so important to me, but I can't think of a reason why you aren't." He glanced at his mother, then said, "I love you, Polly."

That destroyed her and she wept. "Thank you, Jason," she managed to say.

"This will remind you of me," he said and handed her yet another box. "And yeah. You can open it later."

Andrew stepped in front of his brother. Polly hadn't seen them stand together in a long time and was startled to see how tall Andrew was getting. He was still lanky and looked nothing like his brother, but he was growing like crazy.

"I won't make you cry," he said. "And I didn't wrap this box, so you can see what it is." He snapped the box open to expose a charm in the form of a book. "It's always been about books with us," Andrew said. "And I hope that never stops."

As Polly stepped forward to hug him, he muttered, "Neither does the hugging stuff, apparently."

She pulled him into a hug and he whispered in her ear. "I love you, too. Thanks."

Sylvie stepped forward. "Your family is waiting for you. After you pick up your coffee from Camille, head over to your new house. We'll see you this afternoon at Rebecca's party."

"I'm at such a loss," Polly said. "I love you guys. I didn't do any of this on purpose. You are the ones who filled up my life." Tears ran down her cheeks. "And now I don't know how I'm going to drive. You made me cry."

"Go on," Sylvie said. "Get a napkin from Camille, too.

Polly looked at Jessie and Molly, then Elise and Sylvie's boys. Her family was immense. "Okay," she said. "I'm going. Thank you so much for sharing this with me."

Camille met her in the hallway with a small bag for her to drop the boxes into and a tall cup of coffee. "Have fun," she said.

"Are you going to see your mother today?" Polly asked.

"They're coming over this afternoon," Camille said with a nod. "Mama says she wants to fill my little house up with family today. I'm not sure what she's thinking, but since it's Mother's Day, I won't argue."

"Have a good time with them," Polly said. "And thank you."

She got back into her truck and looked at the treasures in front of her, then backed out and headed for the Bell House. Henry had gone to a lot of trouble this morning and she wasn't sure what else he might come up with.

Polly pulled in beside Henry's truck and looked around, surprised to not see anyone. When she got out of her truck, she grinned at the arrow made from rocks on the driveway. It pointed to the back yard. She reached back into the truck for her coffee and the bag of boxes, hoping she'd have an opportunity to open them yet this morning. She looked at the bundle of daisies and snatched those up, too. You could never go wrong with flowers.

"Hello!" she called out as she crossed the breezeway.

"There you are," Rebecca said, running to greet her. "Have you had a good morning?"

"It was wonderful. Were you in on the planning?"

"A little. Henry did all of this, though. Come on. You have to see." Rebecca tugged on Polly's arm.

"I'm coming. I'm coming. Happy thirteenth birthday, sweet girl. How are you doing this morning?"

"Okay," Rebecca said. "I'm glad it's over and I'm glad Kayla and Stephanie are back and I'm glad Stephanie is doing okay. I talked to Jeff and Kayla this morning. They're going to the hospital to see if she can go home with them. Hopefully they'll be out in time for my party. But Jeff said he'd make sure Kayla got there at least."

"That's good. Now where are we..." Polly looked up and gasped. "Oh my."

"Do you like it?" Rebecca asked.

"I love it."

Hayden and Heath stood up from a small table in a gazebo, each holding a leash attached to a dog. Obiwan and Han wagged like crazy when they saw Polly.

Henry stepped out from the side of the house to offer Polly his arm. "What do you think?" he asked.

"It's gorgeous. What have you done?"

He chuckled. "We made you a gazebo. This back corner is the perfect place for it. The big old trees offer a lot of shade and I thought we might put a garden in out here."

"You made this? You haven't had time. I thought you were working on the front porch."

"We're working on that, too. We can have both, don't you think? This isn't completely finished yet," Henry said, "but we got it close enough for today. We had help from a lot of people yesterday morning. It was almost like a barn-raising."

Polly looked at him with a frown. This wasn't what he was supposed to be doing yesterday. He'd told her that he was working on Rebecca's present.

"Come on in," Henry said with a smile. "We have breakfast and a few more gifts for you."

She bent over and snuggled Obiwan and then stood to give Hayden a hug. "Thank you for your work on this. It's gorgeous."

He held out a chair for her to sit in and Rebecca pulled up a seat between Heath and Hayden.

"We're having my party here this afternoon," Rebecca

announced. "We changed all the plans this week when Henry decided to build the gazebo."

"You what?" Polly looked at Henry.

"Rather than decorating the auditorium, she wanted her friends to come to her new house."

"The lawn looks terrible," Polly said.

Rebecca shook her head. "I don't care. It's pretty back here and I want them to see the big hole in the ground and tell them about the tunnel and show off the gazebo. Isn't it perfect?"

"That's easier on me," Polly said. "Whatever makes your day great."

"Since it's Mother's Day and my birthday, I thought it should be easy on both of us," Rebecca said. "You aren't upset, are you?"

"Not at all," Polly said. "Even with the scrubby lawn, this is nice." She grinned. "And think about how beautiful it will be next year."

Henry reached over and rubbed Polly's arm. "I'm glad you like it."

"I love this. What a wonderful surprise. Thank you." Polly looked at Hayden and then at Heath. "Thank you guys for working on this for me. It means so much."

"We kept the casserole hot," Henry said. "When Camille called to tell me you'd left the coffee shop, I brought it out."

Heath opened the familiar Sweet Beans box beside him. "We picked up some of Sylvie's muffins, too."

Polly shut her eyes and took in a deep breath. When she opened them, she smiled. "It's a perfect morning. You are all amazing."

"Rebecca had the idea for the gifts from your friends," Henry said. He reached over and took the garland from around Polly's neck. "There should be something on here. Eliseo texted me that he hadn't had time to tell you it was there." He felt around it and then stopped. "Right here. Take that."

Polly put her fingers where he had shown her and had to break a stem to retrieve the small horse charm. "It's a theme, isn't it," she said.

Hayden, Heath and Rebecca all pushed boxes across the table to her.

"We were supposed to come up with something that connected you to each of us," Rebecca said. "Open them."

"How long have you been working on this?" Polly asked.

Henry chuckled. "Rebecca had the idea at Christmas and she's been working it since then. Don't be surprised if some of your other friends show up with small boxes this afternoon. Everybody wanted to get in on it, but didn't have time to see you before breakfast." He took out a long box and put it in front of her.

"While Grey gave you the necklace, we wanted you to be able to wear all of them together."

"Is that a...?" Polly started, stopping when she found herself choking up.

"It's the bracelet." He looked around the table. "We should eat while the food is hot. Hayden, would you serve us up?"

Polly couldn't take her eyes off the gifts in front of her and finally opened the package from Henry in between bites of the sausage and hash brown casserole that Hayden had made the night before.

"Oh, honey," she said, then leaned over to kiss Henry. Not only had he given her the bracelet, but at the very end was a cloisonné heart in full color. All of the other charms so far had been pewter. "Thank you."

"Mine next," Rebecca said.

Polly deliberately picked up Hayden's box. "This one?"

"No," Rebecca said. "But go ahead. I can wait." She heaved a dramatic sigh.

"We don't have a lot of history yet," Hayden said, "but the thing I remember most is that you wanted me here for your family's holidays."

"Our family," Polly corrected and opened the box. "A Christmas tree. That's perfect." She leaned over and gave him a quick kiss on the cheek and then sat back, looking at the charm. The table had gone silent and she looked around.

Everyone was staring at Hayden, so she turned back to look at him and was surprised to see tears in his eyes. "Did I do something wrong?" she asked.

"It's nothing," he said, wiping his eyes with a napkin.

"Did I upset you?"

"Not at all. It's just been so long since anyone kissed me like that. It brought back a lot of memories."

"I love you, Hayden," she said. "And I should kiss you like that more often. Yes?"

"Okay."

Polly gave a wicked grin to Rebecca and picked the box up that Heath had given to her.

"You're mean," Rebecca said.

"Uh huh. That's me. Mean Mommy. Let's see what this is." Polly opened the box and then clutched it to her heart. "A pickup truck," she said.

"Do you remember the first time you let me drive your truck?" Heath asked quietly. "That was a big deal to me. And then you and Henry trusted me with your old truck. Thank you both for taking me in. I hope I never disappoint you."

Henry was sitting beside Heath and reached across to put his hand on the boy's back, rubbing it lightly. "We love you, Heath, and we're glad you are part of our family."

"Thank you, sir," Heath said.

Polly picked the bag up that she'd brought from the coffee shop. "I have some unopened boxes in here. They told me I could open them later. I think now is later, don't you?"

"Come. On," Rebecca whined. "You can't do this to me."

"I know that Jessie and Molly gave me a flower and Andrew gave me a book. I don't know what came from Sylvie or Jason or Elise. My curiosity is killing me."

"Please open mine," Rebecca said.

"Okay. Since you begged." Polly picked up the box from Rebecca and removed the top. She sat in silence as she looked at it, then turned the box so everyone could see the tiny globe charm within.

"You give me the world," Rebecca said. "And the thing is, I

never had to worry about whether or not I was going to be lost. You were always just there. Mom told me that you and Henry would make sure I had everything I needed and I trusted you with that. Every single day you tell me that I can become whatever I want to be and I believe it." She jumped out of her seat and ran around Hayden to hug Polly.

They held on to each other while Polly breathed in the familiar scent of Rebecca's shampoo. She'd come much too close to losing this precious girl and just the thought of that brought fresh tears to Polly's eyes.

"I love you so much," Polly said quietly. "It's so hard to be thankful that you live with me when I know what you had to go through to get here, but I'm glad you are here."

"Me too. Mom kept telling me that it was going to be okay. All I had to do was trust."

Rebecca let Polly go and went behind her to put her arms around Henry. "I love you, too."

"I love you, sweetie," Henry said.

"Now we should probably stop with the silly emotional stuff," Rebecca said. "We need to be in a party frame of mind by this afternoon. No more of this teary junk. Everybody is happy and doing good. Right?" She trailed her fingers along Heath's back as she walked behind him and back to her seat. "Right?" she asked him pointedly.

"Right," he said.

"What were the other charms you got this morning?" Rebecca asked.

Polly took the little box out from the bunch of daisies, then handed the flowers to Henry. "These are going to need water. Don't let me forget." She opened it to find a chef's hat charm. "Perfect," she said with a smile. "I think this one's from Jason." Polly grinned at the charm of cowboy boots. From Elise, she got a lion charm and was thankful that Elise had given her a clue before she'd opened it. "This is a fun gift," Polly said to Rebecca. "You had a great idea. Thanks for organizing it."

"Everybody wanted to once I gave them the idea," Rebecca

said. "Since it was really your first Mother's Day with a family, I thought it should be special."

"It really is. I can't imagine having a better family than this." Polly reached out and took Hayden's hand. "What a great bunch of kids to be a mom to. Thank you for giving me this day."

CHAPTER TWENTY-FOUR

When Polly finally pushed back from the table, Henry held out his hand. "Come with me."

She'd eaten too much and really wanted nothing more than to go home and curl up with her dogs until this afternoon's party. Henry and Rebecca assured her that they had everything under control. People were bringing lawn chairs and card tables. Now that she didn't have to worry about there being any extra holes in the back yard, those chairs and tables were safe anywhere. Sylvie and her boys were bringing the cupcakes and Rachel had already made up sandwiches. For a thirteenth birthday party, things couldn't have been easier.

After last night's trauma, she and Sylvie were on the same page regarding cell phones for Andrew and Rebecca. Polly had created a gift certificate for each of them. It was an additional birthday gift this year, but she was going to do it anyway; might as well score a few extra points.

"Where are we going?" she asked as he tugged on her arm to drag her up.

"You'll see. Come on."

She followed him across the back yard to the room she'd fallen into earlier this week. It was hard to believe that it had been less than a week since that happened. It felt like months had passed between then and now.

"Go ahead. Climb down," he said, putting his hand on the ladder.

Polly looked at him with a frown. "What are we doing?"

"Go on. You'll see in a few minutes."

Polly climbed down the ladder and Rebecca came right behind her. Hayden was the next down and then Henry. A few moments later, Heath stood at the top of the ladder, holding four LED lanterns.

"Go ahead and toss them one by one," Henry said. "We'll catch them." Then he put his hand up. "No wait. Don't let any of them get near Polly. It will either conk her on the head and knock her out or will just fall to the ground and break."

"Hey!" she yelled, then laughed and put her hands up in defeat. "You're right."

Heath tossed them over the edge to Hayden and Henry, one to Rebecca and then climbed down while holding the last one.

"Don't I get one?" Polly asked. "And what are we doing with these?"

"You can have mine," Henry said. "Go into the tunnel."

She stood in the entrance and turned to look inside it, holding out the lantern Henry had given her. "Are you sure?"

"It's perfectly safe."

"I don't want it to be perfectly safe," she complained. "I want there to be a *little* adventure."

"We left an adventure for you," Henry said. "I promise. Now go ahead."

Polly had to crouch, but held her lantern out and went forward. "How far does this go?"

"About fifty feet," Henry said. "The end is obvious. Just keep going."

She looked at the walls of the tunnel surrounding her and tried not to think about the fact that she was in a tightly enclosed space with no idea of what was ahead. She hated being claustrophobic and refused to think about the fact that there were four people behind her who would have to lie down and be trampled if she wanted out in a hurry.

"It's okay," Rebecca said quietly. "You're okay."

"How did you know I wasn't?" Polly asked.

"You started breathing faster. Just a little bit farther."

"Have you been down here already?"

"I'm not telling," Rebecca said with a laugh. "But we left the best for you."

"What does that even mean?"

"You're almost there. Keep going."

"How do you know that? It feels like I've walked for blocks and blocks. What if I missed it?"

Rebecca reached forward and touched Polly's arm, making Polly jump. "What?"

"Look at the wall there," Rebecca said. "See the hole?"

"Does that mean dirt is going to come flowing in on me?"

"No. Henry is going to put lamps in here so we can see later on. He numbered them from the end. This one says 'two.'"

"Why didn't you tell me that earlier?" Polly asked. "I could have been keeping track."

"We weren't thinking," Henry said from far behind her. "I always forget that this happens to you."

The tunnel grew wider and curved to Polly's left before opening into an even wider space in front of a wooden door.

"Have you opened this?" Polly asked. "What's behind it?"

"This is your adventure," Henry said, making his way through the kids. "I don't know what it's going to take to open the door, but I'm ready for anything."

Polly put her hand on the doorway, then rapped on it with her knuckles. It sounded hollow, which gave her hope. "How do you know it wasn't closed up with cement or bricks behind it? What if there's nothing on the other side?"

"This is where the kids from the university came in handy," Henry said. "They measured the house and the tunnel and know where it should come out. There's an extra room in the basement that's been closed up for all these years. Unless you're looking for it, you'd never know the space was there. I wouldn't let them go in. This was your surprise." He chuckled. "I'm under strict orders to call them tomorrow and invite them back. The suspense is nearly killing them."

"Did you try just turning the handle?" Polly asked, putting her hand on the old metal door handle. She turned it and when the door didn't open, shook the handle. The door moved a little, but refused to open.

"That's why I wasn't too worried about concrete or bricks," he said. "The door isn't attached to anything solid on the other side. We just have to figure out how to unlock it."

"I don't suppose you have an old key on you, do you?"

"Well," he said.

'You're making it too easy. You could have just opened it and gone in."

"But we didn't," Rebecca said.

"You really have a key?" Polly asked.

"I talked to an old locksmith in Des Moines and told him what we had." Henry said. "He told me to just drill the thing and break the lock."

Polly furrowed her brow. "Break it?"

"We can replace the lock, honey." He handed her a long key. "Unless you want to try to open it with this first."

She grabbed the key from him and inserted it into the lock and twisted it. "That didn't work."

"Try again. Jiggle it around in there. Mr. Gardner thought this key should match this door. He has a million of these things."

Polly knelt down, handed her lamp up to Henry and then tugged on it to move it around in order to get better light on the lock. "Do you really have a drill?"

"I can get it if necessary," he said. "Try again. Slowly this time."

She inserted the key again and pushed it just a little deeper into the lock, then slowly turned it until she felt pressure. Polly took a deep breath and pushed the key through its revolution and stopped as she heard the lock snick open.

"I think I did it." She looked up into the expectant faces of her family and turned the handle again, pushing the door forward. At the last minute, it occurred to Polly to worry about stale air, but what came out of the room smelled no worse than the old basement of the house.

"Well?" Hayden asked.

"I'm terrified of finding more bodies," she said. "Maybe one of you should go first."

Henry pushed the door all the way open and held up the lamp. "Go on in. We're here for backup. This is your discovery."

Polly grabbed Rebecca's arm and lifted it so the lamp would shine in front of them. "You're coming with me."

"Haven't I had enough trauma this weekend?" Rebecca asked, a lilt in her voice.

"Not yet. Come on." Polly tugged on her and the two of them stepped into the room, followed by Henry, Hayden and Heath. "This looks like an office of some sort," Polly said. She hardly knew where to look first.

They had entered at the center point of a room that was about six feet wide and ten feet long. There was no perceptible door in any of the other walls, but someone had to have accessed this room at some point in the past. Heath had moved to the south end of the room and held his lamp so that she could see a large roll top desk with a chair pushed up in front of it. On either side were pedestals, each holding an oil lantern. The desk's tambour had been rolled closed and she wanted to know what was in it, but there was so much to take in.

At the other end of the room were more shelves like those that had been in the underground room with the kegs.

"Are those bottles full?" she asked.

Hayden walked over and held his lamp up so she could see. "Not all of them. They're all labeled like they're ready to go, but only a couple of them are full." He reached to the back and took out a bottle filled with a dark amber liquid. "This has been aged a while," he said with a laugh.

"How many full bottles?" Henry asked, walking over to join him.

"It looks like just three," Hayden said. "Unless you can see something I'm missing here."

The long wall in front of Polly and Rebecca was covered with wooden pegboards of various sizes. "What in the world?" Polly asked, pulling Rebecca with her so she could look at them more closely. At the top of each board was a name; mostly last names, but some with an initial preceding them. "Whitney, Bradford, Carter..." She looked down at Rebecca. "Do you suppose that's a relative of Beryl's?"

"What are these?" Rebecca asked.

"I'll bet these are the tally marks for gallons of whiskey these people brought in for sale," Henry said. "If we're talking about illegal sales here."

"It's the craziest way to keep a record, though," Polly said.

Hayden ran his fingers through the holes on one of the boards. "Not really, if you think about it. It's better than keeping paper records that could be used against them. It's odd enough that if someone came into this room, they wouldn't know what it was. For all they knew it could be game scores of some kind." He pointed at the wall above the desk. "Darts, for instance. And who knows, maybe we're completely wrong and they are dart scores."

"Have you got that desk open yet?" Polly asked Heath.

"It's locked. All of the drawers are locked," he said. "I felt around underneath to see if I could find a hiding place for a key, but it's not here."

The rest of the room was filled with crates and more barrels. Polly bent down to lift a lid off a crate at her feet. "Look at this," she said, pulling out a china plate. "Why would they have packed the china in here? And who shut this room up, by the way? And where's the door to the basement?"

Henry had been working on something over at the shelving unit and came back to hand her a flat piece of metal. "Try this on the desk."

"What do you mean?"

He showed her a search he had done on his phone. "It says you should be able to open a desk drawer with this. Push it in all the way to the back, jiggle it up and down a little and turn it clockwise. Just like you did with the key on the main door."

"You're funny," Polly said with a laugh. "Are you looking for the doorway?"

"We'll look around. Come on, Hayden. Pat these walls. There has to be an opening here somewhere."

Polly took the piece of metal he'd given to her over to the desk. "Do you want to try it?" she asked Heath.

"Could I?"

She laughed. "As long as lock-picking doesn't become something you plan to put on your resume."

"Thanks." He took it from her and then turned back. "And I won't. I promise."

She watched him work the lock on the top of the desk and in just a few minutes, he finally pushed the tambour up an inch.

"Got it. But it doesn't want to go very easy."

"It probably warped over the years," Henry said. "Just keep it straight and continue to work at it."

"How about I do this and you try to unlock more of those drawers," Polly said. She stood at the center front of the desk and put her hands out to either edge of the tambour, working it upward. It was slow going, but about the time Heath announced that he had gotten the last drawer unlocked, she finally pushed the roll top open as far as it was going to go. Polly sank down into the chair. "That's disappointing."

"What?" Henry asked.

"There's not much in here. Some old pens and an ink well. I have an empty tin and a bowl with more of those pegs. And here's a weird little bell." Polly rang it a couple of times. "It still works." She looked down at Heath, who was sitting on the floor. "Did you find anything?"

"There might have been some papers in these drawers, but I can't read anything on them. They must have gotten wet. And there were mice in here, too," he said, wrinkling his nose.

"Dang it. I was hoping for more information."

He grinned up at her and reached into the bottom drawer. "Well, there's this." He handed her an old metal box.

"It's locked," she said with a frustrated laugh.

"But I have a key." He handed that up to her. "It was sitting on top of the box."

Polly stuck the key in the box, turned it and opened it. "Bring your lamp up here," she said to him. "We have papers."

"What is it?" Rebecca asked, running over to join them.

"It's filled with Franklin Bell's personal papers," Polly said, almost reverently. "Here's his will." She passed that to Rebecca. "And here is the note from the bank when he built this place." Polly took out a small notebook and handed that to Heath. "Look in there and see what it is." She took out three photographs and recognized Hiram Bell from pictures she'd seen when Beryl was going through her family's things. But in one of them he stood with a young boy. She assumed it was his son, Franklin. There was another picture of him with a rather severe looking woman who was holding a baby.

"They didn't take happy pictures in those days." She showed it to Rebecca.

"That woman looks mean."

"She was probably very nice, but they didn't smile very often for photographs."

"There's not much in here," Rebecca said. "He didn't have any family, but it says that if he died, all of his money was to go to pay off the hotel and then there's some guy named ..." Rebecca peered at the writing on the page. "It looks like Reginald Adams inherited the estate."

"That name was on the abstract we pulled," Polly said. "And I've seen the Adams name before." She took out her phone and scanned through the notes program until she landed on one of Beryl's historical photographs. "Here. There was a Leonard Adams who founded the Bellingwood National Bank with Hiram Bell and some others."

Heath put the little notebook in front of Polly on the desk, his fingers holding two pages open. "I think they had a fight," he said. "This says that Reg wanted to stop selling whiskey. He was worried about the government."

"The revenue-ers," Henry said with a grin.

"And Franklin didn't want to?" Polly asked.

"They had a fist fight." Heath laughed. "He mentions the fountain upstairs in the lobby. That Reg pushed him into it in front of a big crowd of people. His father was there when it happened and he was embarrassed for them. There were bankers from all over the Midwest here at the time for a convention."

Hayden and Henry had stopped searching for the door as they listened to Polly, Heath and Rebecca discuss their findings.

"What else?" Hayden asked.

Heath started reading. *"I've asked Reg to meet me here in the office to discuss this as gentlemen. If we must shut down our still, I will accept that, but too many people in the county require sales of the whiskey they cook in order to pay their bills. Father knows what it is that I am doing and wholeheartedly approves, but Reg's mother has been going to that church down in Boone and believes whiskey will send a soul to hell. Old Mister Adams still has a lot of power in town, even though the bank board forced him to retire. He's instructed Reg to shut me down at any cost. I wonder what the cost will be."*

"That's the end of it," Heath said.

"You don't think that ..." Rebecca started. She stopped and looked around. "Especially if his mother was really religious. He wouldn't become a killer, would he?"

"Let's keep looking around the room," Henry said. "Open up more of these crates. I want to find that doorway out of here."

Polly put the papers back into the lockbox and left the key in the lock. This had been exciting, but suddenly she felt the loss of someone who had once owned this building and from the looks of it had tried to do what he could to help people during a rough time in America's history. She took a deep breath and pulled the top off another crate. It was more china. She, Heath, and Rebecca worked on opening crates, finding glassware and china, until Rebecca stood up.

"Ummm, guys?" Rebecca said.

"What did you find?" Polly asked.

Rebecca pointed into the crate. "I'm not touching that."

Polly walked over and looked into the crate as the others joined her. "Henry, she found the gun, I'll bet."

"Aaron will want to see this," Henry said. "It would be interesting if they find that it's the gun used to kill whoever was in that room. Heath, do you want to drag this crate over to the door of the tunnel?"

Heath started dragging it away and Henry beckoned to Polly.

"We're going to have to break through."

"I can't believe there's no door," she said.

"There used to be. Look here." He pointed at dark marks on the wall. "Those are old hinge marks."

"What's on the other side of this?"

"I can't tell you off the top of my head," he said. "My guess would be that it's the furnace." He tilted his head and lifted his eyebrows. "That would make sense if it was done by dear Reginald. He closed the room off, put a new furnace in and no one would have ever known this was here. Franklin was killed far enough away from the house for the smell to be contained and he went on as if nothing had changed. Didn't you say that everyone believed Franklin just took off?"

"Yeah," Polly said. "That would have been an easy story for him to tell. When he never came back, Reginald claimed the estate. I wonder if he has any descendants still living in the area."

"They'll be hard to find," Henry said. He looked around. "Are you okay with leaving this as it is and we'll cut in from the other side when I have better tools and more workers?"

"That's fine," Polly said. "Thank you for this adventure today." She hugged him. "And thanks for not letting those university kids take it away from me. This was a fun way to end my Mother's Day celebration."

"Maybe we should go get the dogs and head home for a while," he said.

Hayden nodded. "I need a few hours of study time."

"I forgot," Polly said. "I'm sorry. We should have gotten you home earlier."

He laughed. "I wouldn't have missed this for the world. My first final isn't until Tuesday afternoon, but I want to ace it."

"We'll just leave that right there," Henry said, pointing to the crate with the gun sitting in it. "I'll bring Aaron down this afternoon when he's here for the party. Are you ready to go, Polly?"

"How many numbers until I'm out of the tunnel?" she asked.

"When you get to number ten, you're almost there."

"Then let's go."

CHAPTER TWENTY-FIVE

It was unbelievable how exhausted everyone was. The stress of Rebecca's kidnapping, the late night, and the excitement of the morning showed on everyone's faces.

"Who's up for a nap?" Polly asked as they climbed up the steps."

"I'm too excited," Rebecca said. "I could stay awake for days. It's my birthday now!"

"It's been your birthday all day, sweetie, but thanks for sharing the morning with me." Polly put her hand on Rebecca's back as they walked into the dining room.

Hayden smiled. "I really need to study. But I'll be quiet."

"Come on, my sweet teenager," Polly said, taking Rebecca's hand. "Lie down for just a few minutes. You've had a huge weekend so far and yawning while you're thanking people for gifts is really bad form."

"Can I take Obiwan in with me?"

Polly pulled Rebecca in for a hug and kissed her forehead. "You can have as many animals as you'd like. Thank you for organizing my awesome gifts. You make me feel like a real mom."

"You are a real mom," Rebecca said. "You just started different." She glanced around. "What if Heath and I played a game. We could play chess or something and be really quiet."

Heath's face was drawn with fatigue. Polly wondered if he'd slept at all last night. He'd hovered over Rebecca from the moment they returned home, not letting her out of sight for a moment."

"He's going to lie down," Polly said. She looked at the clock on the wall. "We have three hours before the party. Stay in your rooms for an hour. I don't care if you read, I just want you to rest."

Heath glanced into Rebecca's bedroom and then back at the girl he was trying so hard to take care of.

"She'll have the dogs, Heath," Polly said gently. "She's safe. We're all right here."

He nodded and went into his room.

"Go on, Rebecca," Polly said, giving her daughter a push forward.

Rebecca heaved a huge sigh and patted her leg for the dogs to follow her. Polly was absolutely positive that if anyone other than Rebecca tried to enter her bedroom, they would either trip on something and break their neck, or kick something and raise such a ruckus the whole world would know.

"I need a nap," Polly said to Henry. "I'm pooped."

They went into their room and she sat down on the edge of her bed and slipped her shoes off. "So what's up with the gazebo?" she asked.

"What do you mean?" Henry stretched out on top of the covers, turned to face her and patted the bed.

"I mean, I thought you were working on a little shed so Rebecca could have a studio."

"Oh, that," he said with a grin. "The boys and I talked about it and we have a much better idea. Instead of an actual shed which she couldn't use right now anyway because we don't live over there…" He looked at Polly. "We're giving her plans."

"Plans. What does that mean?"

He turned back over and grabbed his phone, then brought up

an image of a small building.

"Okay," she said. "It's a building."

"It's the building we're going to erect over that hole in the ground." Henry swiped through a couple of pictures. "We'll put a stairway here and she can store all of her supplies in the lower level, leaving the upper level completely open for her to work. When there's bad weather, she can use the tunnel to access the studio."

"This is so sweet," Polly said. "Do you think we're spoiling her?"

He chuckled. "Of course we are. But this was mostly the boys' idea. Once I get the lower rooms finished and sealed, they'll put the framework up and build it out. Dad and I will keep an eye on the project, but we'll only get involved if they have questions or need help." He tapped the phone. "Heath did the drawings at school. He said his engineering teacher gave him some pointers, but he figured it out on his own."

Polly tucked up close to Henry and rested her head on his arm. "I can't believe you didn't tell me."

"It would have ruined your surprise this morning and that was the last thing any of us wanted to do. We like surprising you."

"That was a pretty nice surprise." She yawned. "And even better that I don't have to do a lot of preparation for this afternoon. I can't believe you got everyone to do the work for me."

"They're just bringing lawn chairs and a few card tables. It's Mother's Day. You should get a pass."

Polly took two deep breaths and forced her shoulders to relax, then worked her way through the muscles down her body until she started to drift off to sleep. Henry startled her as he pulled his arm out from underneath her, but she turned over and snuggled back into him.

"I love you," she said.

"I love you too."

~~~
~~~

Having a catering company in your house made party planning a snap. Polly and Rachel set food containers out on two tables Eliseo and Henry had brought from Sycamore House while Doug and Billy set up the drink coolers on another table, just outside of the gazebo. It was enough for Polly that food would probably be spilled on the floor of her new building; she wanted to avoid sugary, colorful drinks staining the floor. Heath, Hayden, and Rebecca were setting up the croquet set in the side yard. For as much as they laughed when Polly wanted to play it, the kids all chose to pull it out when they had a group of friends over.

She looked up at the sound of voices and recognized a few girls from Rebecca's class.

"Rebecca, you have friends here," Polly called out, pointing at the other side of the house.

Rebecca ran over and grabbed the two girls by the hands, pulling them back to where she'd been helping Heath and Hayden.

"She looks really happy after what happened to her last night," Rachel said.

Polly nodded in agreement. "I don't know if it hasn't hit her or if she is really just that resilient. But for today, I'm just going to let her be happy and relaxed. She's with people who love her and make her feel safe. That's all that matters right now. It might be different tomorrow and if it is, I'll deal with it."

"You know everyone is going to be talking about it today, right?"

"I hadn't thought about it," Polly said with a laugh. "But you're right." She shook her head. "It will make for a long evening if I have to answer the same questions over and over."

Rachel looked over at her and grinned. "You could just tell them you'll send an email blast out tomorrow with all the pertinent details."

"You're rotten." Polly sighed. "But it sounds like a great idea."

Two more kids came in, saw where the others were and ran across the yard.

"Hello, Hello," Beryl called out as she crossed into the back yard. "I brought my posse." She turned back to the front of the house and yelled, "Posse, hurry up. You're making me look bad."

She stopped in front of the steps up to the gazebo. "Isn't this fancy. Henry will do just about anything to get you into the sack."

"Beryl!" Polly scolded. "Where did you get that idea?"

Beryl laughed out loud as she looked at the faces of the young people standing there. "Can't let these youngsters think they're the only ones who like..." She craned her neck forward. "Sex," she said in a loud whisper.

Doug shook his head and Billy gave Rachel a pinched look.

"You can't be starting the party this way," Polly said, walking forward. "Be good."

Beryl rolled her eyes. "You never let me have any fun. Boys, would you go help Aaron? He's bringing in tables and chairs."

The two boys ran away from the gazebo with looks of relief.

"They're so easy," Beryl said. She handed a package to Polly. "Here it is. Where shall we put it?"

"I brought Rebecca's easel," Polly said. We'll just put it up here for now. Let everyone wonder what it is." She took the painting-shaped package and propped it up on the easel at the back of the gazebo. Beryl had taken one of Polly's photographs of the two of them sketching the walnut trees on Beryl's land from last January and turned it into a painting to hang on Rebecca's bedroom wall.

"What do you think of my Mother's Day present?" Polly asked Beryl, turning back around to see Lydia and Andy crossing the yard, both of their mouths gaping open.

"Is this it?" Lydia asked. "It's gorgeous. You are such a lucky girl. I could never get Aaron to build anything like this."

Andy looked at Len, who was coming up behind them with an armload of lawn chairs.

"Your back yard looks out over the cemetery," he said.

"So does Polly's," Andy quipped. "You don't see her complaining about it." She took two of the chairs from him and set them up. "For that matter, you don't see me complaining about it either."

"Your yard isn't quite as big." he said.

"Okay, I'll give you that," she replied. "But wouldn't it be nice to sit outside in a swing under a gazebo?"

Len shook his head. "It's a cemetery."

She laughed at him as she came up the steps to Polly and Beryl. "He complains about it every time I try to do something in the back yard. I think he's afraid that I'm going to dig a hole and push him in someday."

Lydia flipped out a table cloth and spread it across her table. "Do you have those clips, honey?" she asked.

Aaron pulled a handful out of his pocket and handed them to her, then walked away as Lydia clipped the cloth to the table, smoothing out nonexistent wrinkles.

"Did you girls do it yet?" she asked.

Beryl scowled. "We were waiting for you. Get your tidy butt up here and hurry. We don't want to embarrass Polly in front of a crowd."

Lydia put her hand on the railing and smiled down at the steps. "This is a very nice addition to the yard. You're going to enjoy it."

"I hope we all do," Polly said. "I can see a few of our parties happening back here."

"Not without bug spray." Beryl brushed a bug away from her face. "Okay. Your little girlie-girl told us what was happening for Mother's Day for you and we wanted in on it. So here is mine." She held her hand out with a small box.

At the same time, Lydia and Andy presented theirs.

"You shouldn't have done this," Polly said.

"We had to," Lydia replied, stepping in to give her a quick hug. "It's your first Mother's Day as a mom and it's fun to celebrate with you. Go ahead, open them."

Polly smiled. "You are embarrassing me, you know." She opened the box from Beryl and took out a painter's palette. "I love it. Of course it's you. Thank you." She reached up and gave Beryl a quick kiss on the cheek, then opened the second box from Andy and started howling with laughter. "Are you kidding me?" she asked, holding up a gravestone charm.

"I thought that since we shared the cemetery now, it was the perfect reminder of our friendship." Andy grinned and pointed. "Whenever you can't sleep, just signal me and we'll meet in the middle and share a glass of wine. How's that?"

Polly laughed. "You've been hanging around Beryl too much, but I love it. It's awesome." She opened the last box in her hands and took it out, then looked at Lydia. "What is it?"

"It's a teardrop," Lydia said. "A simple teardrop. For all those times you need a mother of your own so you can weep and be safe."

"Oh," Polly said, tears rushing to her eyes. "Look, you did it again. Thank you for this. These are so perfect."

"Did you bring the rest so we can see them?" Beryl asked.

"No," Polly said. "That was dumb of me. Everything is still at home. I'll work on the bracelet and show you later this week. You can't believe how wonderful people were about choosing the charms. Each one is so unique."

"You have a lot of unique friends," Lydia said.

Andy nodded. "You engage with everybody in such different ways, too. That's pretty terrific."

"Thank you again," Polly said, looking up and out. "There's Sylvie and the boys. I should help her get the cupcakes set up."

The ladies backed up so Polly could step past them and run down the steps to Sylvie. "Let me help carry this stuff."

"The boys have more," Sylvie said. "I'm sorry we're so late. I meant to get here a half hour ago."

"That's okay. This is a relaxed party. No need to be in a rush."

"Thanks. But still, the afternoon went longer than I planned."

"What did you do?"

Sylvie smiled as she followed Polly up the steps into the gazebo. "This is beautiful. Andrew and Jason told me about Henry's plan. They were over here helping yesterday morning. I'm glad you know about it now. They were nearly ready to burst." She put a large Sweet Beans box down in an empty spot on the table. "They did a great Mother's Day for me. After church, they asked if we could go to Ames for lunch. Come to find out,

Jason had called for reservations. The boys had saved up for the dinner and after that they wanted to take me to the Reiman Gardens." She smiled at her audience. "And get this. They actually told me that they wanted to walk around a beautiful quiet place with me because we never get to spend a lot of time together these days. How was I supposed to say no to that? So, we're a little late and even if I say I'm sorry, I'm really not. It was a perfect day."

She started setting out the cupcakes, which had been decorated with little painter palettes and easels. "I think Rebecca had a hand in the day, though," she said. "Andrew let it slip that she told him they needed to step it up with me."

"That girl is quite the little schemer," Beryl said. "If we aren't careful, she's going to have all of us being nice to each other."

"Wouldn't that be wonderful," Lydia said. "Have you heard anything from Kayla and Stephanie today?"

Polly shook her head. "Not yet. The day has just run away from me. Kayla kind of promised to try to be here for the party, so we'll see. It all depends on whether or not Stephanie gets out of the hospital."

"Thank God she wasn't hurt any worse than she was," Lydia said. "Oh look, there she is."

"I'll be back," Polly said and went back down the steps, crossing over to Jeff and Kayla. "There you are. I was just wondering if you were going to come."

Kayla looked exhausted, but she smiled and held out a little box to Polly. "This is for you and I'm going to have to give Rebecca her present later. It's stuck in the car somewhere and I couldn't find it."

"Rebecca will just be glad you're here," Polly said and gave Kayla a hug. "Thank you for this. Can I open it?"

"It's from me and Steph," Kayla said. "She said that I'm supposed to tell you that even though it's a bud, we blossomed because of you." She looked up at Jeff. "Was that right?"

"That was perfect," he said, putting his hand on her back. "Rebecca and some of your friends are over there. She'll be glad to see you."

"Thank you so much, Kayla. Can I hug you again?" Polly asked.

Kayla reached up and put her arms around Polly's neck and the two held on for a moment. "I'll be back later," Kayla said and ran off.

"How's Stephanie?" Polly asked Jeff as they walked across to the gazebo.

"She'll be fine, but they're keeping her another day." He put his hand on Polly's arm to stop her. "Can I ask a couple of things of you?"

"Of course. What can I do?"

"Sheriff Merritt said they'd bring her car up to Bellingwood for us. Can they park it at Sycamore House?"

"Absolutely," Polly said. "That's easy. Is there anything I need to get out of it to keep safe?" She shook her head. "No. We'll just park it in the garage until she can drive it. That's no big deal. What else?"

"Would you have room for Kayla for a few days this week? I hate to ask, but I'm probably taking Stephanie back to my place while she recuperates. I want to keep an eye on her and I want her to feel safe."

Polly pursed her lips. "Of course we'll keep Kayla, but Jeff, why would you not put Stephanie in one of the rooms in the addition? Her sister can stay with her, you can take care of her during the day and if she's in bad enough shape to need Evelyn Morrow, we can ask if she's free to help in the evenings. That way if Stephanie wants to be around people, she can be, rather than hidden away in your apartment clear over in Ames."

"I didn't want to ask."

"You're a moron," Polly said with a laugh. "After all of the people I've put in those rooms, when it comes to one of our own, why would you think I'd do anything different?"

"What if I take her back to my place tomorrow night and then when I come to work on Tuesday, I'll bring her and she can stay from then on. I want to make sure she's okay just getting out of the hospital. Please?"

"You two do whatever you want to do," Polly said. "But of

course I'll keep Kayla with us until Stephanie feels good enough to have her around. Are you going back to the hospital this evening?"

He nodded. "I told her that I'd bring Kayla up to the party and arrange for her car to get to Bellingwood. All of Kayla's clothes for school are in the car or already up in your apartment, so at least she can go tomorrow."

"That's great." Polly took a deep breath. "It's going to take some doing for her to catch up on her school work, especially since there are so few days left in the school year. We'll have to push."

"I'd be glad to talk to her teachers. Tell them what happened," Jeff said.

"They probably know already. Don't worry. I'll help get her through this. Rebecca and Andrew will make sure she's in good shape."

"Speaking of Rebecca," Jeff said. "This is for you." He slipped a package into her hand. "And this is for her. I'm going to wish her happy birthday and then get out of here, okay?"

"Thanks, Jeff. Take care of our girl and let me know if you need anything else." Polly squeezed his hand and let go as he walked across the yard.

Rebecca looked up to see him coming toward her and ran to him with her arms wide open. He caught her up and hugged her as they spoke for a few minutes, then he released her and watched her run back to the croquet game. Kayla and two of the other girls were standing off to the side, talking to each other and giggling behind their hands. Polly looked around for the source of their laughter and realized that Doug and Billy, Hayden, Heath and Jason were moving croquet balls when Rebecca turned her back.

Polly headed back for the gazebo until she heard her name being called and turned to see Sal and Mark come in with Joss and Nate and their twins. Marie and Bill Sturtz followed them soon after with Marie's parents as well as Jessie and Molly Locke. Three more kids Rebecca's age came into the yard and ran over to where the other kids were playing.

"Are you okay?"

She turned into Henry's arms at the sound of his voice behind her. "I think I'm a little overwhelmed. This family thing gets bigger and bigger all the time. How am I supposed to keep it all under control?"

He laughed. "Maybe the chaos is a good thing." Then he reached beyond her to shake Nate's hand. "Hey buddy, how are you?" he asked, drawing Nate and then Mark Ogden away and over to the drinks.

Sal hugged Polly. "How are you doing?"

"I'm good," Polly said, leaning down to pick Cooper up. She hefted him onto her hip. "Look at her," she said, nodding toward Rebecca with her friends. "She's having a great day after an awful night. That's all I can ask." She looked around. "Where's your mother? I thought you weren't coming to the party."

"I left her at home. We were done with each other," Sal said. "We took her out for lunch. She criticized everything. I gave her a crystal vase and she told me that I'd have to ship it to her because the airlines break everything. I finally told her to take a nap because we were going out for the afternoon."

"Well," Polly said. "I guess that's that. So when's she coming back to Bellingwood?"

"Not gonna happen," Sal said.

"Good luck with that," Joss interjected. "She'll beg to come see your baby."

Sal rubbed her belly. "I'm going to teach him, her, it to vomit all over Mom's beautiful blouses and anything else she might wear that's expensive." She looked down at the ground where Polly had set the boxes when she picked Cooper up. "I have one of those for you," she said.

"You didn't have to," Polly said. "This is embarrassing."

"I do too," Joss said, bending down to pick the two boxes up. "But since you're holding my little boy, I'll wait to give it to you.

Sal swatted at Polly's hand. "Don't you dare be embarrassed. It's exactly what should have happened. There wasn't much cost involved and it gave your friends a chance to tell you how important you are. Be nice."

"Are you yelling at me?" Polly asked, bouncing Cooper as he laughed and played with her necklace.

"I don't get to do that very often, so I'm taking the opportunity when I can." Sal pointed at the gazebo. "That's really nice. Are you going to invite us over for parties this summer?"

"All the time. Come on," Polly said. "Let's get close to some of those women who love holding little boys and girls." She poked her finger in Cooper's tummy, making him laugh. "You like all of these pretty ladies, don't you, you little flirt."

CHAPTER TWENTY-SIX

No one else was left but Kayla, Rebecca and Polly. Henry, Heath, and Hayden had packed the last of the tables into the truck and gone home.

"This house is really cool," Kayla said, walking to the entrance of the gazebo. "Especially that tunnel. I can't believe you get to use it whenever you want to."

"I never expected any of these presents," Rebecca said. "Mom would say that you're spoiling me."

"We get to do that," Polly replied with a smile. "The boys are so excited to be able to build the studio for you this summer."

"It's like a dream come true." Rebecca jumped up from her seat and ran to hug Polly. "And a trip to Taos with Beryl? I never expected anything like that."

"Between her travel miles and the two of you staying with Tallie, it made the trip quite reasonable," Polly said. "You'll have a wonderful time with those two artists. I hope you learn tons."

"Beryl said we're going to paint something every day and take lots of pictures so we can paint more when we come back." Rebecca turned to Kayla. "I wish you could come."

"Me too." Kayla said quietly, then she perked up. "But Stephanie said we're moving into a real apartment when she gets out of the hospital. I'm going to be busy decorating my room." She blinked her eyes. "Maybe you can paint something for me when you're there and I can hang it over my bed."

"I will!" Rebecca said. She bounced on her feet. "I've never flown in a plane before. Beryl says you see the clouds from the top instead of the bottom. Is that true?"

Polly nodded. "It sure is."

"Will I see mountains from the plane?"

"I suppose so," Polly said with a smile. "And you'll drive through them on your way up to Taos, so you'll see plenty."

Rebecca dropped back down into her chair. "I didn't think about that. Is Beryl driving from the airport up to Tallie's house? We'll be lost for sure."

Polly laughed out loud. "No. I've already spoken with Tallie. She'll be at the airport to pick you two up. We won't let Beryl loose in a vehicle any time soon."

"Good," Rebecca said with a sigh of relief. She turned to Kayla. "Otherwise, I might end up in some little town off the beaten path and never find my way home."

"You have to come home. I'll miss you." Kayla pointed at Rebecca's hand. "And Andrew will miss you too. Can I see that again?"

Rebecca pulled the ring off her middle finger and handed it to Kayla.

"This is just so cool. Is he going to write notes to you?" Kayla spun the top of the adorable secret decoder ring that Andrew had found. It wasn't quite as gaudy as those Polly remembered from her childhood; this was stainless steel and quite simple. Henry had raised his eyebrows at a ring, but when he saw what it was, they lowered just a bit. Not completely, but he tried not to panic.

"He said that he would," Rebecca said. "Maybe whole letters when I'm gone."

"But there won't be enough time for mail to get to you," Kayla protested.

"He can send texts to me." Rebecca grinned at Polly. "Thank you for letting me get a phone. I really promise to be responsible."

"I know you will, honey." Polly shivered and rubbed her hands on her arms. "It's starting to get chilly. Shall we head home?"

"We can leave," Rebecca said, "but I'm not ready to go home yet."

"Where should we go?"

"Down to the hospital to see Stephanie? I haven't seen her today and really should say thank you. She saved my life last night."

"It's getting late," Polly said. "Visiting hours are over and she needs her rest so she can come home."

"Stephanie was worried that you guys would fire her for leaving like we did," Kayla said.

Polly shook her head. "No way. Jeff has been lost without her. I don't ever want to live through a week like that again. He complained every single time he saw me. And besides, I know something that you don't know yet." She winked at Kayla as she stood and folded her chair up. "Let's put these in the garage. We're supposed to have storms this week and I don't want them to blow away."

"What do you know?" Kayla asked as they walked to the truck.

"Maybe I shouldn't tell you and let her surprise you with it." Polly and Jeff had already discussed Stephanie's raise and new title, as well as the fact that they were cleaning Polly's office out for her. He texted Polly that he had told Stephanie this afternoon and she should go ahead and let Kayla know. Kayla had been worried about how they could afford a new apartment and could use a little boost.

"That's not fair," Kayla said.

Rebecca stopped in front of Polly and turned around. "Did anyone ever tell you that you're mean?"

"Who, me?" Polly asked, laughing. She opened up the door into the garage and took the girls' chairs from them, stacking things along the inside wall. "Mean? Go on, hop in the truck. We'll go riding around for a few minutes before we go home. Let's see what's happening downtown." She watched the girls run to her truck and climb in the back seat. That was one thing she liked about having Andrew with them; at least one always wanted to sit up front with her.

"When we get home tonight, Kayla, you and Rebecca need to find your school clothes. You're staying with us for a couple of nights."

"And then to Jeff's house?"

"No," Polly said. "I think you might stay in the addition while Stephanie gets better. That way she has people around her all day long and you guys are close at night. She can also go to work when she feels better."

"I get to stay with you," Kayla said, jumping up and down in the seat.

"Put your belts on, girls," Polly said. She waited until she saw them both snap their belts into place before backing out of the driveway. Polly still found it hard to believe that someday her family would live here. It was so far away, but events like today's made it seem more probable.

"You still haven't told me the surprise," Kayla said. "I haven't forgotten."

"No, I guess you haven't. What would you say if I told you that we were giving Stephanie my office?"

Kayla grinned, while Rebecca frowned. "Why won't you keep your office, Polly?"

"Because things are changing at Sycamore House. Stephanie is going to be Jeff's assistant. Her new title will be Assistant Manager. We're going to hire a receptionist to answer phones."

"Will she make more money?" Kayla asked and then looked ashamed. "I'm sorry. I shouldn't ask that."

"But you should. Yes, she will."

"So it won't be so expensive for us to live in a better place? Stephanie said we were going to be able to just barely get by and we'd have to cut back on some things in order to swing it."

"Hopefully this will help."

"It will be great," Kayla said. "And we won't have to live in the trailer park anymore and I can have friends come over and see where we live. It will be awesome."

Rebecca sat forward. "I can't believe you aren't going to have an office, Polly."

"I'll share Henry's for now," Polly said. "When we move out, Jeff and I are talking about moving all of the main offices upstairs to the apartment. Sylvie and Rachel can have an office for their catering and if we hire other people as we grow, there will still be plenty of office space."

"Wow," Rebecca said, sitting back again. "That's weird to think about. Things are really changing, aren't they?"

"They always do, honey. Remember, change is good." Polly turned a corner and drove past the coffee shop. "Where do you want to go tonight?"

"Everything's closed, isn't it," Rebecca said.

Polly nodded. "It's Sunday night. People are home getting ready for the week."

"I'm just not ready to be done with the day. Can we drive to Ames? It's not even eight o'clock yet."

"This is me spoiling you," Polly said, pulling into a parking space. "Just a second. I'm calling Henry to tell him we're going to be late getting home."

"Yay!" Rebecca and Kayla said together, high-fiving each other.

Polly swiped the call open.

"Hey there, sweet stuff, what'cha doin'?" Henry asked.

"Spoiling our daughter. She's not ready for the day to be over so we're going to drive to Ames."

"You're doing what?"

"Driving to Ames. I know. I'm a pushover, but..."

He interrupted her. "It's okay. You don't have to explain. How late will you be out?"

"We're just driving down there. Maybe we'll go through McDonalds and get a little ice cream cone or something."

The girls repeated their "Yay" and high five in the backseat.

"Apparently that's a good idea," he said. "Let me know if you'll be later than nine thirty."

"Everything quiet there?"

"Hayden's working in my office and Heath is at the dining room table. I'm in bed watching television."

"Okay, that's cool."

"Did you hear me?" he asked.

"Uhhh, yeah."

"I'm in bed. All by myself. Alone. Without you."

Polly chuckled. "Oh that. Do you think you can stay awake long enough for me to get home tonight?"

"If I can't, you have my permission to wake me up."

"I love you, Henry Sturtz."

"I love you too. Take care of our girl and I'll see you later."

Polly put her phone down and turned to the back seat. "It's a go. And for the record, if I hear that you fell asleep in school tomorrow, it's not my fault."

"Of course not," Rebecca said. "It never is." She laughed a little maniacally. Polly knew she was wound up. It was probably good to try to drain some of this energy before she settled down for the night.

Polly backed out and headed down the highway toward Boone. She soon tuned out of the conversations Rebecca and Kayla were having. They'd had an entire week without each other and it seemed that Kayla had missed out on just so many important happenings at school. Just north of Boone, Polly turned east on the road that would take her across to Highway 17. This road was so familiar to her now. Only a few miles and she'd turn south again. It always fascinated her to drive past homes at night, seeing lights glowing inside. She wondered at the stories behind those walls. They couldn't all be good, but at the same time, they couldn't all be bad.

She stopped at the sign and waited for a grain truck to go past before turning onto the highway.

"How are you girls doing?" she asked. "Still awake?"

"Not funny," Rebecca retorted. "I don't know if I'm ever going to sleep tonight."

"You do have a pile of gifts to go through at home." Polly shook her head and chuckled. "And that's on top of the pile of stuff you have all over your floor. If I'd known Kayla was spending a few nights, I would have made you clean."

"But it's my birthday," Rebecca whined.

"Yeah, yeah, yeah. It's still a dump."

"I could clean it up," Kayla said. "I like to do that."

"I tell you what, Kayla. If you can get that room cleaned up and organized, there would be money in it for you."

"Hey, I'd clean it for money," Rebecca said.

Polly laughed. "No you wouldn't."

"Do you mean it?" Kayla asked.

Rebecca huffed. "Of course she does. I don't care if you clean."

"Really? You'd let me? Will you let me clean out your locker at school, too?"

"I suppose," Rebecca said. "I have to get everything out of there before the end of the school year. We might as well start this week."

"What does your locker look like, Kayla?" Polly asked.

"Her locker is always clean," Rebecca replied. "Everything is in its place. She has pretty things hanging inside the door and it's all organized."

Polly stopped to wait for a train to cross in front of them. She looked down the line and didn't see any hope of it being a short train, so she threw the truck in park and sat back, watching the rail cars go by. That got boring so she glanced to her right into the parking lot of the big Co-op, wondering if the grain truck had turned in. She didn't see it, but wasn't surprised. The place was so big, it absorbed trucks.

"What do you suppose that is?" she asked, pointing into the lot.

"I don't know," Rebecca said, peering out at it. "Probably a dead body."

"No way," Kayla said. "She wouldn't."

"Wanna bet?" Rebecca asked, putting out her hand. "If it's a dead body, you have to ..."

Polly put her hand up to stop Rebecca from going any further. "No. Kayla doesn't have to do anything." She looked behind her to make sure that no cars were approaching, backed up, then pulled into the parking lot and drove over to the dark pile that she'd seen. "You two stay here. I just want to make sure it's nothing."

"It's gonna be something," Rebecca said. "I just know it."

Polly got out of her truck and walked over to the pile and bent over. "Damn it," she said under her breath. "Just damn it, damn it, damn it. We did not need this tonight." She reached down and touched the young man's neck, feeling for a pulse. The scrapes on his face looked fresh and she shook her head, then stepped back and pulled out her phone, swiping a familiar call open.

"Polly?" Aaron asked. "Why aren't you home with your family?"

"Because I'm at the Co-Op on Highway 17. You need to send your team. I did it again."

"I'm sorry, Polly. Are you alone?"

"No. Rebecca and Kayla are in the truck. We were going to Ames for one last hurrah before calling it a day."

"Male or female?" he asked.

"It's a young man. His face is all scraped up. Do you think this has anything to do with that girl I found last week?"

"I don't know," Aaron said. He sighed. "I just don't know. I'd hoped you had enough to deal with for one week. I'm so sorry. Go sit with your girls and we'll be there soon."

"Thanks Aaron. You know you can never retire, right? Who would I call?"

"They might vote me out of office one of these days, Polly. You never know."

"I'm not too worried. Will I see you here?"

"Not tonight. But Stu will be there soon. Take care."

Polly ended the call and walked slowly back to the truck. She got in and pulled the door shut, then leaned back. "You were right, Rebecca."

"I knew it! I just knew it."

"It's a dead person?" Kayla asked.

"Yes. I called the sheriff and he's sending his people. We have to wait."

"We're not getting ice cream tonight, are we?" Rebecca asked.

"We still have plenty in the freezer at home." Polly dropped her head forward. "I'm sorry girls, but when we're done here, I just want to go home."

Kayla reached up and patted Polly's shoulder. "That's okay. We understand. We already talked about it. Rebecca said that this is hard on you." She kept patting Polly's shoulder. "Since I've never really seen a dead body, I don't know what it feels like, but I guess it must feel pretty awful."

"I just need to process it," Polly said. "I'll be okay by tomorrow." She reached her hand back and patted Rebecca's knee. "I'm sorry this happened on your birthday."

"I'm never going to forget my thirteenth birthday," Rebecca said. "There were so many things that happened this weekend I can't even believe it."

"Some of it has been bad, though," Kayla said. "Like my dad kidnapping you and then stabbing Stephanie." The truck went silent and then Kayla continued. "And he's dead now. That's weird, right? That he's dead? Should I be more upset?"

"How do you feel about it?" Polly asked. This was the second time that someone had asked her if the fact that they didn't have powerful feelings over this man's death was weird. Maybe they'd been exposed to her pragmatic behavior too much and took it in stride. Both of the girls had lived through traumatic changes and she was thankful they had each other.

"I don't feel anything. He was a bad man and he hurt my mom and Stephanie. He was never a dad like Henry is. He came home drunk all the time and we had to be really quiet so he wouldn't know we were there. I'm only twelve and don't have a mom or dad anymore."

"You have Stephanie, though," Rebecca said. "She's like a mom."

"Yeah, I guess. I'm really sorry that he did that to you, though."

"It's not your fault," Polly said.

"It feels like it is, though," Kayla replied. "He was *my* dad and the reason he took Rebecca was so that he could find me."

"And hurt you," Rebecca interrupted. "He wanted to hurt you. Even if he hadn't kidnapped me, I would have done anything to not let him hurt you."

Polly smiled in the darkness of the truck.

"There they are," Kayla said, pointing.

The train had long since passed and the lights of the emergency vehicles flashed as they approached from Boone.

Polly put her hand on the truck door. "Hopefully we won't be here too long once they arrive."

"Because they know where you live," Rebecca said. "And it's not like you have any information on who did it."

"Not yet I don't." Polly opened the door and jumped down from her truck as Stu Decker pulled in beside her. She waited for him to get out of his car. "Were you guys slow tonight? Not enough business?" she asked.

"Is that what this is about?" he asked, crossing to shake her hand. "If we don't have enough going on, you head out to look for a body?"

She grimaced. "I swear. This is exhausting."

"You've already had a long weekend." Stu waved two other deputies over to the young man's body and they watched as the rest of the emergency vehicles drove in. "You didn't see anything?"

"I was just waiting for a train to cross," Polly said. "When I saw what I thought was a pile of something, Rebecca commented that it might be a dead body. I was already backing up to come in and look."

"You might as well take the girls on home, then." He turned and waved to the truck. "We've got it from here. All you did was drive in and walk over?"

She shrugged. "That was it."

"Okay. If we have any more questions, we'll call tomorrow. Tonight we'll try to figure out where he came from."

"Thanks, Stu," Polly said, touching his back. "I appreciate you coming out."

He laughed. "I don't know what would happen if we didn't."

"You know what I mean."

He nodded and she walked away and back to the truck."

"Ready to go home now?" she asked.

"Are you?" Rebecca asked.

"I think so. I could use a doggie hug."

CHAPTER TWENTY-SEVEN

"Good heavens." Polly opened the garage door and laughed as she pulled in beside Stephanie's car. There might be more boxes and pieces of furniture here now than when she had emptied her father's storage unit.

In between his finals this week, Hayden had emptied his apartment and packed everything in here and then he, Heath, Henry and Jeff had emptied Stephanie and Kayla's trailer. Polly, Kayla and Rebecca spent the evening last night cleaning the trailer. There were nearly two weeks left on the lease, but there was no reason to drag any of this out.

On top of all that, Polly talked Andrew, Rebecca and Kayla into helping her box up all of her things from the office. It felt strange to no longer think of that as her office, but change was on the agenda. As she looked at all of the boxes and furniture in front of her truck, it wasn't so much change as it was hurry-up-and-wait. Until she moved into an office at the Bell House, she didn't need any of the decorations and knick-knacks. Star Wars characters could just wait. Files that she needed to access on a regular basis had been moved into Henry's office. He made a crack about giving up half of his file drawers, but he'd rearranged things anyway.

Stephanie and Kayla had moved into the downstairs rooms of the addition. It was funny to watch Stephanie and Jeff. He wanted to be a mother hen and she wanted him to leave her alone. The girl had found a backbone in the middle of all that had happened. Polly wondered if part of it wasn't the promotion she'd been given.

When Jeff had tried to take Stephanie to his apartment Monday night after leaving the hospital, she put her foot down. She was willing to accept the room at Sycamore House, but she wanted privacy again. Two nights in the hospital with people walking in on her every moment was plenty. She'd let Kayla spend another night with Rebecca, but after that, the two of them were going to figure life out on their own.

Hayden had one more final and he was finished. They would attend his graduation this weekend and have yet another party. Polly was about ready to be finished with parties. But this one would be small. They were moving Henry's grill over to the house and grill burgers and brats for their friends. Polly had asked about inviting his aunt and uncle. He'd made the call, but they weren't interested in participating. He shrugged it off, but she knew that it had hurt. It was still difficult for her to understand how indifferent those two could be to their brother's sons. That was probably one reason he wanted this to be low key.

The door from Doug and Billy's apartment flew open and Doug burst out with his two dogs. He stopped and looked at her, still sitting in her truck, then made the motion for her to roll her window down. Instead, she got out.

"What are you doing down here?" he asked.

"Just thinking about things." Polly pointed at piles in front of them. "All of the changes that are happening."

"Did you hear about Billy and Rachel?"

She flattened her eyes and pursed her lips. "No."

"Yeah. They set a date."

"When?"

"Halloween weekend."

"This year? What day is Halloween?"

"It's a Monday, but they're going to use all of the decorations from your big party and have their reception on Sunday. They already talked to Jeff."

"That's a really good idea, but wow? What do you think about this?"

He shrugged. "I don't know." Doug stopped himself. "That's not what I mean. I think it's great that they're going to get married, but we haven't figured out who's going to move out yet. They told me I could stay here, but I have to get another roommate. I don't want to live up in that big place by myself."

"I'm sure it will work out," she said. "Wow. They're finally getting married. She didn't say a word last weekend when we were setting things up for Rebecca's birthday party."

Doug chuckled. "They had a big fight on Monday because he was waffling on a date." He dropped his voice. "If you ask me, I think she has baby fever. There were a lot of babies and pregnant people and little kids at Rebecca's party."

Polly tried to count in her head. It hadn't seemed like a lot. "And how does Billy feel about that?"

"After they got over their fight, she had to go work and he told me he felt ill. He's totally not ready to be a dad."

Polly nodded. "Hopefully he'll have some time between now and when that happens to get used to it."

"I'll make a really cool uncle, though," Doug said.

"And Billy's good with setting a date?"

Doug rolled his eyes. "If it were up to him, he'd keep things the same and never change them. He's such a boob. I tried to tell him that he and I can't live together forever, but he thinks that if he just doesn't talk about it, Rachel will forget. I finally told her that she was going to have to push him into this. His mom told her the same thing."

"He's going to drive her nuts for the rest of her life," Polly said.

"Yep. Lucky for her I'm around to help keep him in line, right?"

"Sure."

Doug headed for the back yard. "If you think of someone who would make a great roommate, let me know, okay?"

"On it." Ever since Doug had mentioned he was going to need a roommate, Polly's mind had been racing through all of the people she knew, eliminating them one by one and then considering others. She put her hand on the door to go inside and glanced back at Doug chasing his dogs. More change in store.

She'd barely made it inside when her phone rang. What would Lydia be calling about?

"Hello there," Polly said.

"I had to tell someone. Aaron's taking me on a cruise!"

"What? He never takes vacations. What am I going to do..." Polly refused to say the words. This wasn't about her. "How did you talk him into this?"

"I didn't have to. Jill and Steve were planning an Alaskan cruise and Steve's being transferred so they can't go. Jill called us this morning and Aaron actually agreed to go. Can you believe it?"

Polly stood stock still in front of Andrew's old nook. It had filled up with supplies this last year since he'd found a place in his own room at home for his books and treasures.

"Are you there?" Lydia asked.

"I'm in shock."

"We leave in two weeks. It's perfect timing, isn't it?"

"Sure?"

"Well, Beryl will be in New Mexico and so I won't worry about being away from her. Then we'll be back before all of the excitement starts for the Sesquicentennial celebration. Won't it be perfect?"

"You're leaving in two weeks for an Alaskan cruise. And Aaron is going." Polly was still shocked. Good heavens, she hoped she didn't find another body while he was gone.

"I know. Okay, I can't talk, I have a million things to do to get ready, but I had to tell you. I have to tell everyone. I love you, dear."

"I love you too."

Polly dropped her hand with the phone and shook her head.

Good for them. Good for Jill and Steve. Lydia forgot to tell her where they'd be transferring to, but it would come up again.

She went upstairs and looked around at the chaos that had erupted in the apartment this week. Rebecca's gifts were still lying around, even though they had told her over and over to put them away. Kayla was steadily working on Rebecca's bedroom, but at the same time, they were bringing home more junk from the girl's locker. Hayden had brought things upstairs that he would need for now. Polly knew better than anyone that little by little, more of his stuff would creep up from the garage, as it should.

When she got to the living room, she sat down and moved things around on the coffee table. Rebecca had been working here each night, writing thank you notes for her birthday gifts. Cards, envelopes, pens and stamps were everywhere. And so was Polly's charm bracelet. Rebecca had gathered all of the boxes, opened them and put it together one evening when she begged to be released from writing more notes.

Polly ran her fingers across the charms. Each of these people had taken the time to think about their relationship to Polly. From Sal she'd gotten a coffee mug and from Joss there were two charms – a set of twin babies and she'd found a classic car. Henry told her it was a '62 Impala – Nate's car. Jeff had given her a calendar. She chuckled. It was perfect.

Polly placed it on her wrist and fumbled to close it, finally getting the clasp to do what she wanted. She leaned back on the sofa and stroked Obiwan's head. "Where is everyone?"

At least now she could track Rebecca down. They'd gone to Boone after school on Tuesday to get cell phones for Andrew and Rebecca. Kayla had made the trip with them, but Stephanie insisted she had to wait for her birthday before getting a phone. It was only a couple of months away, so Kayla hadn't been too heartbroken, but she'd paid close attention when her friends were making choices.

Rebecca had been beside herself and started downloading free apps before they got in the truck to come home.

"Where are you?" Polly texted to Rebecca.

In a split second, she received a reply. *"Check it out. You can find me now. How cool is that?"*

Polly laughed. *"It's cool. But where are you?"*

"Sorry. We're in Stephanie's room. She's showing Kayla pictures of the apartment they're going to rent."

"She found one already?"

"Yeah. It's really nice. It's in Andrew's old building. On the top floor."

That would be perfect for them. Jessie and Molly lived in the same building. It was close to everything. The girls would have a great time. *"When do they move in?"*

"June first if everything works out. She's close to Jessie! We can babysit all the time."

"Sounds awesome. Did you take the dogs out?"

Polly had to wait a few seconds for a reply. *"Oops. No. Sorry. Andrew's on his way there."*

"What have you been doing all afternoon?" They didn't have much homework, but Polly knew there were a couple of big projects still due. *"Did you get homework done?"*

Rebecca sent back a sad face.

"Tell Stephanie goodbye and come home. You know the rules."

The front door burst open and Andrew rushed in. "We're sorry. I'll take them out right now. Come on, Obiwan and Han. Let's go outside." He ran on through to the back door with the dogs rushing to beat him there.

Polly shook her head at the commotion and sat down on the sofa. It took longer than she expected, but Rebecca finally came in the door.

"I'm sorry, I'm sorry," Rebecca said. "We got busy with stuff and time got away from us."

"What kind of stuff?" Polly asked. "You certainly weren't putting your things away."

"I found this great game on the phone and we were..." Rebecca finally looked at Polly. "That was stupid of me. I shouldn't have said anything."

Polly chuckled. It was so hard for Rebecca to lie about things, even when it got her into trouble. She put her hand out. "Phone, please."

"But I won't do it anymore," Rebecca said, holding the phone behind her back.

"We talked about this. Responsibilities come first. You aren't losing it forever. Just tonight. You can have it back tomorrow."

"But that is forever. I can't text Andrew tonight."

"I'm guessing that if his mother knew what happened today, he wouldn't have his phone either. No worries."

Rebecca frowned. "You can't tell her."

"Oh, I think you'd be surprised what I can do. Phone, please."

"This isn't fair. I just got it."

"And you'll get it again tomorrow. But for now, you have work to do."

Rebecca slammed the phone into Polly's outstretched hand, then winced when she realized what she'd done. "Sorry."

"Uh huh. Go on out to the dining room and get started."

"Please don't get Andrew in trouble, okay? It was my fault."

Polly nodded. Tattling on kids wasn't her thing. She waved her fingers at the dining room and set Rebecca's phone on the coffee table in front of her. Stupid little girl. She laughed at the frustration Rebecca was going to continually face in her quest to become an adult. Polly distinctly remembered learning lessons over and over again. One night her father had sat down with her and asked why she didn't just do what she knew was right to do. That might have been one of the nights she'd stayed out too late without calling him.

"It doesn't have to be this hard, Polly," he'd said. "My rules aren't difficult to remember. Figure them out and life gets much easier."

They ended up having that conversation a couple of times before she finally realized that none of her friends were going to laugh at her for making a quick call to her dad to let him know where she was and when she'd be home. But with every new issue, it had always taken Polly a couple of stabs at independent thought before she realized that it was easier to follow his rules.

She chuckled at the memory. Her adolescent brain insisted that he was just making rules to drive her crazy.

"I get it now," she said. "You wanted so much for me. But I do believe the one I'm raising is more independent than I ever was. Serves me right? Probably."

The dogs' nails clicking on the floor made her look up and she caught Obiwan as he leapt into her lap. "I missed you too," she said. "You were gone so very long."

Andrew walked into the living room behind the dogs. "They ran all over the place. Sorry about being late."

"You're fine. But you need to get busy on your homework."

He looked back at the table. "I don't have much time before Mom picks me up."

"Because you wasted it playing games?" Polly asked.

He looked at the floor.

"Maybe you should put in some extra effort while you have time. Okay?"

"Okay." His shoulders drooped and he dragged his feet as he went back into the dining room to sit with Rebecca.

Polly laughed again and kissed her dog. "They're so much fun to mess with."

Both dogs took off at a dead run for the back door again and Polly stood up. It was a little early for Henry to be home, but he'd been around more this week. He still wasn't over Rebecca's kidnapping. Every night he sat down with her and asked questions about her day. It didn't take much to draw her out; she was a gregarious little girl. They'd talked about what had happened last Saturday night. Both Polly and Henry wanted to make sure that Rebecca had plenty of opportunities to talk about what she'd felt and how she was feeling now. That would slowly lessen over time, but Rebecca wasn't interested in talking to a therapist and Grey told them the best thing to do was let her talk about it when she needed to as long as she wasn't obsessing over it. So far, things were normal. Then again, Rebecca had dealt with quite a bit in her young life and she was pretty good at taking things in stride. Sarah Heater had raised a strong child.

"Hello there," Henry said, coming in to the living room. He pulled her in for a hug and a kiss. "Good day?"

"It was," Polly said. "You?"

"I'm home early and I didn't punch anyone, so yeah. It was a good day."

Polly took a deep breath. "I don't want to cook tonight. Can we go out to eat?"

"I don't care," he said. "Davey's? Mexican? Pizza?"

Heath and Hayden were walking through to their room. "Pizza?" Heath asked.

"Pizza it is," Polly said. "Do you have homework tonight?"

"Just some reading. I can do that later."

"Do it now," she said with a smile. "We won't go out until later anyway."

"Really?" he asked. "I've been working all day."

She put her head down, shook it and laughed.

"Now," Henry said. He put his arm around Polly's waist and led her into their bedroom. "What was that laugh about?" he asked once the door was closed.

"I'm a parent," she said. "A full-blown parent of teenagers. I swear to you I never saw this coming, but here we are."

"Are you overwhelmed yet?"

"I'm still laughing about it most of the time."

"That's good." He walked into the bathroom, stripping off his shirt. "I'm taking a shower."

Polly locked their bedroom door and followed him. "What do you mean, that's good? Do you know something?"

Henry turned to face her, surprise on his face. "No!"

"You scared me, asking questions like that."

He turned the water on in the shower and pulled his socks off. "You're doing pretty well at the whole thing and we're moving into that big house one of these days. We haven't rescued anyone in months. Somehow I think that break is nearly over."

Polly flipped the toilet lid down and sat on it, then took her own shoes and socks off. "Don't say things like that. I don't need those words hanging over my head. I have enough to worry about with those two dead bodies and no killer." She pulled her shirt over her head, then unclasped the charm bracelet and placed it in a basket on the counter.

"You're worrying about only one killer?" Henry asked.

"It has to be the same person," Polly said. "And since they don't know who it is yet, I'm worried there might be more bodies on the way."

"You shouldn't worry. That's Aaron's job." Henry watched as she undressed. "And what are you doing?"

"I'm rescuing you from a lonely shower. Unless you want me to leave."

He laughed and pulled her in for a kiss. "I love you so much, Polly Giller. You are never boring."

"What kind of life would that be?"

"Not ours. What do you think is next?"

"Change," she replied. "Lots and lots of change." Polly kissed him again. "And that's just the way I like it."

THANK YOU FOR READING!

I'm so glad you enjoy these stories about Polly Giller and her friends. There are many ways to stay in touch with Diane and the Bellingwood community.

You can find more details about Sycamore House and Bellingwood at the website: http://nammynools.com/

Join the Bellingwood Facebook page:
https://www.facebook.com/pollygiller
for news about upcoming books, conversations while I'm writing and you're reading, and a continued look at life in a small town.

Diane Greenwood Muir's Amazon Author Page is a great place to watch for new releases.

Follow Diane on Twitter at twitter.com/nammynools for regular updates and notifications.

Recipes and decorating ideas found in the books can often be found on Pinterest at: http://pinterest.com/nammynools/

And, if you are looking for Sycamore House swag, check out Polly's CafePress store: http://www.cafepress.com/sycamorehouse

Made in the USA
Lexington, KY
18 July 2018